IN THE
BLUE

A SIERRA SPRINGS NOVEL

AVA BLAIR

For Alexis—my biggest cheerleader,
unwavering supporter,
and the kind of friend everyone deserves.

***

In loving memory of Leif, the bestest boy,
whose likeness and goofy spirit
is forever captured in these pages.

Content/Trigger Warning

This novel contains themes and content that may be sensitive for some readers. Please take care while reading.

Sexual Content:
This is an open-door romance with consensual sexual acts and descriptive intimacy on the page.

Discussion of Trauma:
Both main characters have experienced trauma in different forms, which are referenced and explored throughout the story as part of their emotional growth and relationship journey.

Sensitive Topics Addressed Include:
- Death of a sibling during childhood
- References to two separate incidents involving the death of a child by drowning (both occur off-page but may be triggering)
- Parental neglect and abandonment
- Financial abuse by a parent
- Death of a parent
- Past betrayals (including infidelity, not between the main characters)

These events are not depicted graphically, but are recounted and processed on the page through memories, reflections, and dialogue.

Your mental and emotional well-being is important—please step away or skip sections as needed.

"When you get a place where you understand that love and belonging, your worthiness, is a birthright and not something that you have to earn, anything is possible."

— Brené Brown

1

ARIA

"I swear every time a guest starts the Limbo using one of their ties, they act like they are a genius for thinking of it."

Pausing in the doorway that another server is holding open for me, I shift the heavy tray of dirty glassware so I can turn my head. I peer through the darkened ballroom space towards the dance floor to see that the wedding party has, in fact, started the trend once again.

"Wouldn't be a wedding without it." I have to raise my voice so she can hear me over the pumping bass of the DJ's speaker, which sits annoyingly close to both entrances to the resort's kitchen, and round the corner.

Balancing the massive tray—which earlier held stacks of plated dinner under polished domed lids but is now loaded with smudged highball and lipstick-stained wine glasses—I move through the servers galley to the dishwashing area. Muscle memory takes over as I ease the heavy tray onto the line. And despite having carried similar trays working here for the past six years, I offer a brief prayer of thanks for not wobbling or breaking anything, just like I always do.

The clink of the glasses blends with the kitchen soundscape—the hum of conversations, static from the radio, and shouted instructions I ignore unless they concern me. Sorting the glasses into the correct racks, I slid a full one into one of the empty commercial dishwashers.

I tug at the napkin looped over the apron strings at my waist to dry my hands, the white linen hopelessly stained and wet from endless wiping as I make my way back to the galley. Grabbing my water, I lean up against the counter to check the time.

Only 9:15pm.

This night is dragging on.

Rubbing at the dull ache that is gradually building above my shoulder blade, my body feels like it is more than just 6 hours into my shift. I've already had to dodge two old drunk handsy guys, and cleaned up a spill on the dance floor while the guests continued dancing around me (and made my cleaning motions into a new dance move). Then I caught a bridesmaid and her date in a compromising position in the bridal room when it should have been empty.

It's a typical Friday night wedding at the Alpine Club, the luxury resort that takes up most of the small town of Sierra Springs on the shores of Lake Tahoe, where I've lived almost my entire life. It's the type of town with a close-knit community of hardworking people who live here year round to support the hordes of tourists that flock to the Tahoe basin for the sun and the snow.

"Hey Aria..." Glancing up, I see one of our dishwashers—a grandfatherly short man named Manny—walking through our prep space. "Thanks for the muffins; she loved them."

"I'm glad." I give him a quick smile as he passes, arms loaded with clean pots before he disappears into the kitchen.

His wife has been in a long battle with cancer, and I try to make her little treats or snacks every so often just to let her know I'm thinking of her.

The kitchen at any Tahoe resort is a mix of locals and seasonal workers, but over the years, I've found a rhythm with the team here. It's a chaotic camaraderie—different from what I grew up with, but comfortable all the same. People come and go, many leave for good for other opportunities, but a few stick around long term.

If that isn't a mirror of my life, I don't know what is. My dad was in and out of my life as a child before passing away early on, and my mom left for good when I was 16.

Come and go. Leave for good.

Then there's my best friend Evie, who became my sister when her grandmother, who she lived with, took me in when my mom split.

The ones who stick around, the family that chose me, instead of the ones that didn't.

I majored in hospitality and tourism management, knowing it would lead to an easy job path because of living in a place where the economy centers on tourism. I needed a consistent paycheck and a steady career to avoid being a further burden on Mimi—Evie's grandmother. She swore multiple times that I wasn't and could live there as long as I wanted, but I needed to be independent.

I made sure I applied to schools with strong financial aid programs, and was lucky enough to get a full scholarship to Colorado. That was the biggest blessing, as it allowed me, along with working while going to school, to live on my own and not have to rely on anyone else in the future.

Once I graduated, finding jobs in the nearby resorts was easy enough, but eventually I found banquets provided a higher income than more administrative events jobs, and settled into that role waiting for something bigger to open up.

Though nothing did, and now I've spent the past four years growing increasingly aware of how easily I can spot authentically nice guests, and instantly distinguish the people who build themselves up only when making others feel small.

The past six months, I've noticed I have less and less of a desire to come into work, and less patience to deal with the unique issues that come from working in hospitality. I'm not even sure I want to be an event manager anymore.

To be honest, I'm burned out. I'm finding myself having to put on a mask more often, a friendly face that smiles despite rude or ostentatious patrons.

It's easy to do as a people pleaser. But it's grinding on the soul.

...

It's almost 1am by the time I unlock my front door and toss my bag down. It'll be another hour at least before I can fall asleep though—it's hard to wind down after a late night event and selfishly I just want a few minutes of downtime before giving in to sleep.

Banquet serving may be less mentally taxing than working in a restaurant, but it's far more physically demanding. It's more than just carrying trays full of enough steaming plates for an entire table at a time—though those can weigh around 40 pounds.

My shoulders and back ache from lugging stacks of chairs plus multiple tables up and down stairs today for setup—only to have to do it all again for the reset at the end of the night.

That's why most nights I just crash on my couch when I come home and have a drink just to relax, even though it's after midnight.

I kick off my ugly, yet required, black non-skid sneakers and pull my socks off, my toes flexing with freedom. The deep plush of the floral motif carpet I used to warm up the A-frame cabin's wood floors is a soothing oasis for my aching feet. Freeing my hair from it's bun, I shake the strands down past my shoulders as I attempt to make room for my 5'7" frame on the couch.

A large dark shadow takes up the majority, and I need both hands to lift the back end of my 160 pound Newfoundland dog, Brady, to make space for me on the last cushion. He hardly gives a huff in response, before stretching out and taking up even more of my lap and the couch.

"Well, hi to you, too. So sorry to disturb your beauty sleep." I run my fingers through his thick black coat, twisting the long fur in my fingers. Goodness knows if there was ever an intruder here past 10 pm, Brady would likely raise an eyebrow and then roll over and fall back asleep. All bark and no bite.

But I love him for that too. He is everything to me, and when I'm not working we are basically inseparable, whether it be just out for a hike, or on the water training. As much as I love spending all my time with him, I wish I had someone human to come home to and share stories with. Tonight would be how sweet it was when the groom was singing to his bride during their first dance.

Maybe even bitch about the more annoying guests a bit.

I mentally tally up tonight's estimated tips, and add it to my savings balance, grinning when I realize I'm getting close. Only a few more weeks and I will have saved up enough for the advanced water rescue program out on the East Coast this fall.

It's been a dream of mine to introduce the idea of a K9 water rescue component to the area. Training opportunities are rare, however, so it's taken me a few years to make progress and earn certifications. Once I heard about the one in Massachusetts, I could finally present my idea to the local rescue unit, and got permission to volunteer with them after completing the training.

It has taken me almost 8 months of saving tips to cover the cost of the registration fees and travel. I'll have to road trip out there and back since Brady can't exactly fit like a small dog on a plane.

Once Brady and I can attend, however, we can take our efforts further out into the lake and help families avoid the type of pain that aches deep in my chest.

2

IAN

Saturday, June 17th

"Ughhh."

The sound of my groans and both knees cracking echo in the half empty closet as I stand and stretch. The hockey season has been over for almost a week now and yet my body still feels like it was put through the wringer. Even the simple task of unpacking is painful, the grunts and jabs of pain in stark contrast to the opulent carpet and linen wallpaper in the closet-slash-dressing room in my new home for the summer.

There's no question that it's taking me longer to recover from this season than in years past.

Going to keep that little fact to myself. Even though I'm sure my coaches and my agent somehow already know.

I'm slowly accepting the fact that I'm getting old—especially in a sport where anything after 35 is considered a normal retirement age. Even just maintaining the status quo this past season meant more of everything: PT, massages, ice baths.

More dodging questions about my future, thoughts on retirement, and the likelihood of a one year contract instead of multi-year.

The thought must be like a bat signal, as my phone buzzes on top of the dresser. It's my agent, but seeing how I don't have the energy to discuss his recent emails or anything else, I let him go to voicemail. It might be a dick move, but answering all of his calls won't magically help me make my next big life decision.

Plus, I feel I deserve a bit of a break from the business side of things. I've earned it.

I finish hanging up my suits, close the paneled walnut closet door and walk out of the primary bedroom into my rental. The open concept living/dining and kitchen is spacious, with exposed beams, natural stone fireplace and vaulted ceilings. Drenched in a warm white paint with leather, navy and burnt sienna furniture and decor, it gives the entire place a luxury ski chalet feel. Crossing to the wall of windows and glass doors that lead to the back patio, I take in my new view for the summer. My 6'3" reflection stares back as I exhale, the alpine surroundings bringing a quiet peace, just like I had hoped it would.

After a grueling (yet successful) season playing defense for the Grizzlies, I needed some place to retreat to for the off season.

Somewhere I could decompress, and maybe even hide out for a while away from the press and the puck bunnies. Here I'll have the time and space to put some serious thought into the direction I want my life and career to go in the next few years and post retirement.

Retiring soon might seem crazy to people outside the hockey world seeing as I'm only 34. But I know my body likely only has another season or two in it before I decide on the path for the next half of my life.

Problem is, I just haven't figured out what would make me happy. Going the usual route of broadcasting or coaching, maybe color commentary or special events are all options, but nothing has piqued my interest yet.

Hockey will always be a part of my life, that I know. I'm just not sure what the other part is supposed to be. With the Stanley Cup this year to prove it, I've achieved literally everything I've set out to, and yet I still feel like I'm starting back at square one.

I thought once I clinched the Stanley Cup I would finally feel complete. My entire life, since I first got on skates when I was three, my goal has been to be the best. To win a collegiate championship, to be the best damn rookie and a solid team player as I went through trades, to finding my place and securing my spot on the Grizzlies for the past 5 years. This year, we finally came together as a team and went all the way, getting to experience the ultimate dream of any hockey player.

But something is still tugging at me, like this hole in my chest that I keep shoving more accomplishments in, more stats, more sponsorships, even the damn cup, and yet I still feel hollow.

Don't get me wrong, I am so fucking happy that we won. That was the craziest moment of my life and I've been riding the high of it for the past week. But after the parade and press events died down, I started itching for the next thing- what that is, I just don't know.

This house is the perfect crash pad for the summer, having a primary suite with a huge shower and soaking tub, 3 extra bedrooms, and a home gym. There's also a big patio decked out with cozy outdoor furniture, a fire pit, and hot tub. But the best part is the sloping lawn that leads right to the lake, with a dock and private beach area. It's the perfect seclusive spot that will provide plenty of adventure for when I want it and privacy for when I need it.

Needing to update the guys and using that as an excuse to stop unpacking, I pull out our text thread, snap a photo of the lake as it sparkles in the early afternoon sun and press send.

> *Group: Puck Bitches*
>
> ME: My new backyard
> HUGHES: Is that the rental? Fuck yes!
> WHITTY: KNEW IT, said he'd do the one with the boat included. You fuckers owe me.
> JONESY: obvi he would doucheface.
> ME: There's plenty of time to test it out this week.
> HOLDEN: I call the king bed.
> ME: You'll be lucky if I let you sleep on a deck chair.

The guys are heading to Coach's party at his country club in Sierra Springs tonight, and I wouldn't be surprised if they crashed here even though they've already booked hotel rooms. They might as well as I'd imagine they'll be here most of the trip anyway, and honestly, nothing makes me happier. We are a tight group and being around each other energizes me.

Coach Johnson is the reason I chose the Lake Tahoe area for the summer, and the small town of Sierra Springs specifically. He's constantly talking about how he can't wait to head to his house here, whether it's in the summer or during the holidays. Coach described it as being the perfect escape from the city, a small-town feel with all the amenities needed nearby thanks to the whole area being a place for tourists in summer and winter.

When I needed a place to escape the chaos of the past year—which included a broken relationship, a conniving ex-girlfriend, and far too much face-time in the media—he said it would feel like it did for me growing on the lake in Michigan. Trusting him and my gut instinct, I rented this place sight unseen until training camp in the fall.

Blake Whitlock, or Whitty as we call him, who is both the best fucking forward in the league and my best friend, had offered for me to spend a few weeks with him back home on his family's sprawling ranch property, where he has a house and a pretty cool training set up.

As much as I love going with him to visit, I didn't feel in the right headspace to do a long trip there this year, knowing I'd have to interact with everyone on the ranch and steer topics of conversation away about my future from his family.

Coach's suggestion to come here instead gave me the quiet escape I needed. Plus, it works out great that now I'm already here for the party, too.

As I watch the sun climb high over the lake, its vibrant blue color so deep it's mesmerizing. I know that I've chosen well, and am looking forward to a summer on my own terms.

Whatever this summer brings, or doesn't—which would be more than fine with me—I can do it peacefully in my little fortress, away from everyone and everything that tries to threaten the security and stability I've painstakingly built over the years.

Maybe I'll even be able to figure out what's next on the horizon for me too.

Glancing in the hallway mirror, I drag a hand through my hair, trying to smooth it down. It never listened—just flopped right back into that half-wild state like it had a mind of its own. Made me look more undone than I felt, which was saying something.

I give up on the hair, grab my keys, and head out.

My hair is a mess, and my head is buzzing. I didn't know what the night would hold, but for once, I wasn't overthinking it. Just me, the guys, and the party we earned.

3
ARIA

"Get away from the hot box!" A loud, grumpy voice calls out the next day over the blaring radio.

I jump back, practically burning my hand on the rack as the cloth napkin slips from my grip.

"Jesus Christ, Jose, I was just checking on the Beef Wellingtons for tonight." Turning towards the head chef, I give him my most sincere smile, knowing he caught sneaking a bite.

Even though technically I'm not supposed to eat anything in there until after we've served it all, since the radio is blasting oldies today and not death metal, I know he is in a good mood. Shaking his head with a smirk, I know he doesn't mind.

"You're lucky you're my favorite Aria, or else I would have thrown you out of my kitchen the first time you got in my way."

He puts the hotel pan of broccoli rabe in the box and then flips the kitchen towel over his shoulder. "But seriously, get a move on; the guys are all going to be here soon and I need to get the food out of the ovens and into the pans."

Like he needed to remind me about the guys coming. Everyone knows what tonight's event is, and we are all pretty excited about it.

It's not every day a resort gets to play host to the newest Stanley Cup Champions, The San Jose Grizzlies. However, their head coach is a member here at The Alpine Club—its pristine location overlooking the lake helps it cater to the elite and wealthy members of society. He invited the team here to celebrate and it's all anyone has talked about since the win. We are excited to celebrate with them, even if it is just in the two degrees of separation type of way. Coach Johnson may be a member, but no one I work with knows him all that well.

Just the reminder of the team that is about to grace our halls has me checking my bubble braid ponytail in the oven door's reflection. Unsatisfied, I move to the servers' space, pull my phone out of the short black apron at my waist, and use the camera to get a better view. I tame the frizzies in my dark blonde hair and make sure I don't have any remnants of my mid-shift snacking left in my teeth.

There's not much I can do with the requirement to have my hair fully pulled back. My black and gold statement earrings add a little flair to the otherwise dull catering uniform of black pants and black polo. At least it's our more casual look tonight compared to the black tie events requiring button ups and vests—those are both hideous and incredibly uncomfortable.

"Not like it matters; these guys are way out of your league," I mumble to myself. I've worked here long enough to know that it doesn't matter what the serving staff looks like during events.

I used to think that being able to be around rich and influential people would help me make connections in the community. And sure, as a lover girl the romantic in me has dreamt of being swept away by a handsome guest.

But I quickly learned that unless I am holding a plate of something delicious right in front of someone (and sometimes not even then) I all but fade into the background and go largely unnoticed.

It's pretty much on target for how I have felt all my life. Typically, I'd rather blend in than stand out so it's not a big deal. But I'm not going to pretend that it wouldn't be nice to be noticed, to be the object of someone's affection, or heck, just feel a strong connection with a male other than my dog.

My dating life has been a string of red flags and unfulfilling first dates and one college boyfriend who decided I wasn't enough for him.

A girl can dream, right?

I shake the thought away, knowing that the buzz of the athletes will eventually turn into another long night with no one except my dog to debrief the shift with. And depending on when this gets over, he might just ignore me and go back to sleep too.

Twenty minutes later we are at our standard pre-event meeting, known as pre-meal, where Betsy, our team captain, is finishing going over the logistics of the night.

"Alright, they are going to be arriving any minute now. Half of you water the room during cocktail hour, the rest of you guys are on butler trays and passing, and we will clear." She points to herself and the server next to her and places the assignment list on the table. "Got it?"

Betsey always assigns jobs based on our skills, which places me, being friendly and a people pleaser—I mean, people person—with passing the hors d'oeuvres pretty much every time.

"Dammit, usually I prefer watering, but tonight I'm ready to ogle some hockey butts," Adam, the server next to me mutters, eyeing the list like it betrayed him. He's stuck inside filling up water goblets while the rest of us get cocktail hour out on the massive deck overlooking the lake—with the team and their guests.

"I'll send some your way," I offer, biting back a laugh.

"Oh honey, if you find one that takes direction, send them straight to your bed," Adam says, flinging an arm over my shoulder. "Lord knows you need something new around here to shake things up a bit."

I snort and jab him in the ribs. "Yeah, ok big guy, I'll get right on that."

I'm good at playing the part—smiling, schmoozing, working a room full of wealthy guests without breaking a sweat. But tonight is different. Knowing NHL all-stars are here, and seeing the actual Stanley Cup gleaming on the round table in the center of it all... it sends a ripple of excitement through me. And something else too—something tighter in my chest. A little more self-consciousness than I'm used to.

•••

"Is it hot in here or is it just them?" A coworker fans herself with a cocktail napkin and lets out a low whistle as we take in the sea of men in front of us. Having just exited the kitchen with a round of passed apps, we are getting our first look at our guests for the evening, and it is certainly not disappointing.

"Thank you, Hockey Gods," I agree, my eyes taking in the people filling the space.

Though a small party compared some of the 300+ person weddings we've catered to in the past, the 75 people occupying the Upper Deck are anything but a sight for sore eyes.

We pass out the appetizers, carefully balancing the need to ensure guests sample everything with the need to avoid interrupting conversations or drawing too much attention to ourselves.

My stomach clenched tightly, and I can already feel the back of my shirt clinging to my skin, despite the cool early-summer breeze.

Something about being around all these big and successful men makes me feel small. But not in a bad way. More like a damsel in distress waiting for the big hulking knight that comes to pull her to safety. Which is ridiculous, of course. I've saved myself plenty of times. But still...

My eyes settle on a gorgeous specimen of a man, with light brown hair, and a smile that rivals the deck lights in brightness. He is tall, having to bend slightly over a short blonde woman that he is standing to hear her over the sounds of the party. I can't help but stare at his broad shoulders and strong jawline. Something about the way he carries himself makes it hard to look away.

His hair is just long enough on top to look unruly in the best way—thick, tousled, and begging for fingers to run through it. No matter how many times he tried to smooth it down, it rebelled with a cocky sort of charm, like it knew it looked damn good that way.

Damn good. Real. Damn good.

Obviously, I can't let anyone catch me staring at a player and what I'm sure is his girlfriend, I'd seem like a freak. But my eyes don't want to listen and I find it hard to convince them otherwise.

Until he abruptly looks up, gaze moving in my direction.

I quickly turn to the right and head towards a mixed group of what looks like more players.

"Would you care for some Scallops Wrapped in Bacon or Yellowfin Tuna?" I ask the group of guys who are leaning against the railing and taking in the sunset.

"Oh, hell yeah!" A cute blonde guy with a lopsided grin shouts out, and grabs a handful of both.

"You just want the entire tray here and I'll go get another?" I tease with a smile.

"Can you do that?" He looks so excited I have to stifle a laugh as I shake my head.

"No you idiot," a deep voice belonging to a tattooed hunk of man next to him responds. A loud burst of laughter comes out as the rest of the group joins in on mocking the poor guy.

"Tell you what, I'll finish passing these around and then see what else I can scrounge up for you to try next." I offer with a sweet smile, using one of my many practiced responses for when guests ask for the entire tray to be left with them, which happens more than one would think.

"Deal, thanks, uh," blondie glances down at my nametag, "Aria. Appreciate it."

"No problem, enjoy the view." I quickly move away, feeling flushed. I should just serve the food and move on, and keep my dang mouth shut.

God, I probably sounded like an overly flirty puck bunny. Classy, Aria. Real smooth.

I'm pretty sarcastic by nature; it's one way I can connect to people so easily as I never do it maliciously. But I have learnt the hard way that not everyone finds that type of humor endearing.

I turn to head back to the kitchen for another tray, dodging around guests who are standing about, passing off the remaining apps to hungry patrons. I escape through the swinging door and rest against the stainless counter near the coffeemaker.

My cheeks are still hot, my fingers slick from the bottom of the tray. I grip the edge of the counter like it might steady me.

They are just people, Aria. Stop acting like an idiot and just do your damn job.

After congratulating the coach and his wife while serving up crab cakes and then grabbing a picture with the Cup before they opened the doors, the dinner service passes rather uneventfully.

"These guys are actually pretty nice," I mumble, mouth half-full of roll as the others take a breather around me.

The shitty part about working a shift during meal time is we never get a dinner break until after everything is served and cleared, if we get one at all.

"Yeah, nice to look at," a voice that can only belong to my best friend in the entire world declares as Evie rounds the corner carrying a crate of wine and sets it on a cart across from me.

I nod in agreement as she winks, pushing the long copper brown layers that frame her face back. She readjusts her claw clip as she continues, "Sexy as hell and good tippers too."

As one of two bartenders on staff tonight, and with the amount of glasses and bottles I've cleared tonight from the tables, she is clearly seeing them plenty.

We smirked at each other, mentally transmitting that we 100% need to grab a drink together to discuss *everything* we had seen here tonight, as any single girl would do in our situation.

"Can everyone do a quick sweep and clear any remaining dinner plates?" Betsy pushed through the doorway, "We want to get dessert out asap before people leave."

"Stop by when you can so we can compare notes," Evie said as she headed towards the beverage walk-in, crate back in her arms, as the rest of the group dispersed.

"Will do!" I call over my shoulder and head back out to the event room.

Scanning the room, I see most of the tables are clear, but the one on the far left needs some attention. I approach the table, which is full of players, including ones I was joking with earlier, plus Jack Holden, whom I learn tonight is their star goalie. And sitting directly across from him, the gorgeous tall one I couldn't help staring at out on the deck. I can't help noticing the girl I thought he was with is absent from the full table.

They are engaged in a heavy debate about player stats, jumping in on each other before they can form complete thoughts. They rag on each other in a way that makes them seem like a close group of friends and not just teammates. It's a cute dynamic.

I slip around the table, silently collecting plates and trying not to interrupt their lively discussion. Clearing tables tonight has been a bit more challenging than most nights, some of these guys are way bigger than average. All the guests have been kind and most try to be helpful, just like this table is currently doing.

Trying to be helpful is key though, because it technically makes my job a lot harder.

There is a method to the madness of picking up and arranging the silverware and plates. When they lift their plates up to me, however, it makes it harder to stack more and overwhelming to carry.

It's hard to deny a plate from someone after they have generously stacked silverware and napkins on it and offered it to you.

After balancing the fifth plate with utensils haphazardly strewn on top in my left hand, I feel the tremble start in my elbow and work its way up to my wrist.

Shit, shit, shit.

I fight to keep that outburst purely mental as I feel the plates start to give way, adjusting with my opposite hand to move the plates to the crook of my arm, and watch in horror as a knife starts sliding.

It's the catering wobble of death.

The one where you know it's going to go over the edge and drop somewhere dramatically. Time slows as I watch the polished silver teeter on the rim of the plate before tumbling off the side.

Tumbling off the side and down, hitting Jack Holden's shoulder.

Oh, fuck.

"Oh my God, I am so sorry" I exclaim, reaching over to pick up the knife which rebounded on the table and turning to face him. "Are you ok?"

He grabs his shoulder with a huge grimace, making a groaning noise, and I know I'm done.

I've injured the star player.

I'm dead inside and so mortified I'm frozen to the spot.

There goes my job. My savings, my plan.

"Can I get you—" I start, tripping over my words, needing to make it right. The entire table seems to burst out laughing. I feel my cheeks burn bright as I fight the sudden burn in my eyes.

"Don't worry," I hear a smooth voice that cuts to my core and warms me all at the same time.

I lift my eyes across the table to the source of the comforting voice, and meet the most incredible blue eyes of that tall brown-haired drink of water I was admiring earlier. I'm lost in them for what must be only a split second, but feels like an eternity. Like there's an endless depth I want to dive into—like the shadowy stillness of the lake I know so well.

I'm almost positive he is holding his breath too, eyes holding steady with mine, spreading a calm across my body.

An amused quirk of his lips sets me at ease. "He's perfectly fine," he says, winking at me, and I snap out of it.

Looking back to the victim of my stainless steel assault, it is clear he was playing around without even a speck of food on him from the knife.

"It's fine, hun, no big deal." Jack gives a warm smile and I apologize again, and then turn and head back into the kitchen as fast as I can without dropping yet another thing out of sheer mortification.

Entirely embarrassed, I drop the dishes on the line, and hurry to sort them into the right piles and throw the silverware into the bin with a little more force than necessary.

Dammit, I can't believe I dropped a fucking KNIFE on the team goalie.

My vision blurs as shame tightens my chest. They seemed ok with what happened, but even if my job isn't at risk, I still embarrassed myself.

"I'm such an idiot."

"Who are ya talking about? Can't be you, not my girl." Rico lifts his head from his sous chef station and gives me a warning look.

"Definitely me. I just about killed the star player of the hockey team that's here tonight."

"Ah, you'll have to try harder if you failed!" Chuckling, he slides a finished plate across the top of the expo line for the restaurant side.

That gets me laughing, but I'm still way too embarrassed to show my face out in the room for a while.

I load a rack of glasses into the small dishwasher, and then head straight for the back exit that leads to the deck.

Closing speeches had started when I was in the ballroom, so the deck is bound to be empty. I can look busy cleaning up leftover glassware while I die from personal mortification alone.

4

IAN

I saw it happening two plates ago. I knew she was struggling with everything being handed to her because I couldn't take my eyes off of her as she approached the table.

Fucking mesmerizing.

Even in the standard server uniform, I could see that she had a curvy athletic build that made me want to grab her by the hips and throw her legs around my waist.

I realized she was the one I had glimpsed earlier out on the deck, when Hughes' obnoxious laugh made me look over. The guys laughed about something as the server made a beeline for the exit. I prayed those fuckers weren't giving the staff a hard time.

Coach was nice to invite all the guys and the team staff, but he told us to not embarrass him since he's a member of the club. I'm not familiar with the place, but the drive in and the place itself screamed fancy as hell, and he obviously wants to keep his membership. Yeah, fair enough, we've had our share of asshole behavior, usually after a night of partying like any team—but it's all in good fun and rarely illegal.

But now seeing her up close made my knuckles flex, thinking the guys might've said something to upset her.

Her dark blonde hair is pulled into a ponytail, giving me an open view of the slender line of her neck. I couldn't help but notice the way her soft green eyes stayed focused on the task at hand, how she nimbly moved around the guys and collected plates, trying hard not to interrupt, or—frustratingly—not even make eye contact.

But it's the bright red tint of her cheeks that makes me finally find my voice. While all the other jackasses at the table were getting a good laugh in after the knife fell off the stack of plates she was balancing.

"Don't worry," I say, "He's perfectly fine." I want her to look up at me, needing her attention. Craving it.

She lifts her face as I finish speaking and I instantly get lost in the depth of those green eyes, unable to break contact and having no desire to.

My body reacts immediately to her, my skin crawling like it needs to touch her. I shoot her a wink to help her breathe a little easier, which I assume does a little as she diverts her eyes back to Jack and apologizes again for dropping the knife.

"It's fine, hun, no big deal." Jack waves off the situation, and the girl—no, woman—heads back to the door they've been coming in and out of all night. My eyes follow her until it swings shut, unable to look away.

I've never cared about what happens in a commercial kitchen before, but right now, I just need to know what she's doing.

A napkin hits me in the face. I glance back across the table at Jack, who has a smirk on his face. "What the hell, man?"

"For the drool." I pick it up and throw it back at him as the rest of the guys join in and give me shit, too.

...

"I'll look at it and send it back to you in the next couple of days." I hold the phone in one hand and let my agent drone on as I take in the view outside.

Right after locking eyes with the most beautiful green eyes I've ever seen, I saw my phone light up and headed out to take this call. I knew I couldn't ignore him anymore, but man, I didn't feel like dealing with this shit tonight when we are supposed to be relaxing and celebrating the season.

"Look Jerry, we literally just finished the season. Take some time off, take a vacation, play with your dog or something."

A laugh comes from the other end of the line. "The money comes from work, not play. You'll be thanking me for working while you are out celebrating when you sign a contract."

"Alright, alright, but I'm going to go back in now. Just send it all over." Hanging up, I head back inside, quickly cutting around the corner, and instantly regret it as I collide with someone.

"Oh shit," a sweet voice exclaims. Looking down, I see it came from the same angel from the table as she fell right into my arms.

Or bumped into them. Tomato, Tomahto.

I reach out my hands to steady her, gripping her arms until she is stable on her feet.

"Hi there," I say, a grin unhurriedly taking over my entire face. The feel of her body pressed against mine as I try to keep her steady feels like a match made in heaven.

"Hi," she barely squeaks out and takes a step back. "I am so sorry for running into you; I didn't think anyone was out here and I wasn't looking where I was going."

"I think I survived that crash better than you. Built for hockey and all that." I try to get her to relax by joking a little.

She laughs gently and looks back up at me. "Speaking of which, congratulations on the big win."

"Thank you; it is a big win. You should see all the things that can fit inside it."

Confusion crosses her face. I burst out laughing.

"It's tradition to do random things with the Cup after winning it, like eating a giant ice cream sundae, or drinking out of it, or seeing how many babies can fit in it."

"Really? How many?" She tilts her head expectantly.

"Babies? 2 newborns for sure—our winger tested out the theory right there on the ice after the game."

That fact has her eyes lighting up as she smiles, her face like sunshine lighting up the deck, and I know I can't just let her walk away and go back to her shift.

"I'm Ian." I say, sticking out my hand.

"Aria. Nice to meet you." She places her hand in mind and it's like a shock goes through my system. She must feel it too, because she glances down and then nervously withdraws her hand.

My phone buzzes in my pocket, and I pull it out, seeing a text from Marcus Jones, one of our wingers and a close friend.

> JONESY: Can see you through the window dipshit.
>
> JONESY: Invite her out with us. Coach said a place called the Lift is a good spot. Heading out in 10.

"I hope you have a great night celebrating; sorry again for running into you."

Aria turns like she can't get away from me fast enough and without thinking, I'm reaching out my arm and grabbing her elbow.

She gasps in shock, then spins around to glance at where we're connected before meeting my gaze with those beautiful green eyes.

"Wait," I say. "What are you doing after this?"

I watch her forehead scrunch in confusion. Oh, sweet Aria. Now that I know her name, it fits like the angel she is.

"Heard of a place called Lift before?"

5
ARIA

"We're going, 100%," Evie says, pulling the water dispenser off the bar and wiping it down.

"You think we should? What if we get there and it's totally obvious that he was just joking or something?" I lift my head from my arms. I'd collapsed at the end of her bar after telling her about the knife incident and the awkward deck encounter, including the invite to join the team at the Lift, a local bar. Over an hour has passed, but this is the first chance I've had to talk to her during the event breakdown.

"Aria, that's not gonna happen. He wouldn't have invited you out with them if he didn't mean it; guys like that could pick up chicks wherever they go. He told you to be there, that means he's into you!"

Scoffing audibly at the idea, I grab a small round tray and start collecting glasses and half-empty beer bottles at the bar area's cocktail tables.

"I'm sure he was just being friendly; there's no way a guy like that is hitting on a server." Forget even being a pro athlete, he was so good looking that I could barely speak when he talked to me. I literally lost the ability to form sentences all while staring at his chiseled face.

"Well, that may be true, but you are one hell of a cute server—even in this ugly ass uniform." She gestures to her matching set. "But Mimi has Gracie tonight and I haven't been out in what feels like forever, so please? For me? Just a few drinks?" She gives me puppy dog eyes, the kind I can never resist.

I pause, knowing I'm going to give in. She deserves a night out more than anyone I know, and hardly gets the chance, working all the time as a single mom to the cutest 18-month old whom I consider my niece.

Plus, I have no doubt the entire female population of Sierra Springs will be in attendance once the word spreads that they are at Lift. They'll be all over the hockey guys, so it's not like they are going to recognize me as the knife wielding server anyway.

"I guess when else are we going to get to say we hung out in the same bar as a bunch of champions?" I shrug with a half smile.

"So that's a yes? YES! This is going to be so much fun!" she shrieks in delight and throws her rag back behind the counter before engulfing me in a hug.

Twenty minutes later cleanup is done. After punching out, I head home for a quick wardrobe change and a quick touch-up on my makeup. Thankfully, it wasn't a long night, and my makeup only needed a quick lip gloss refresh. The outfit, however, took a few attempts before I finally settled on something I liked.

Evie and I reconvene in the parking lot of Lift, a favorite spot for both locals and in-the-know tourists.

The place looks packed, so word has absolutely gotten around about our A-list visitors.

Taking a deep breath, I push open the door, eager—and slightly nervous—to see what's waiting for us inside.

6

IAN

I've been sitting here nursing the same beer for the last 30 minutes, scoping out the place but not finding anything more tantalizing than the girl I met earlier tonight.

"Hey handsome." A sultry voice calls out while hands stroke my arm. Glancing over, I frown when rather than seeing Aria, I see a bottle blonde with far too much work done fighting for my attention, much like the rest of the girls have been doing all night.

I nod in greeting but pull my arm away, acting casual enough not to be rude but clearly stating I'm not interested.

I've had plenty of girls her type before, but tonight she is not doing it for me. Not when there is another girl on my mind and has been since we took up residence at the high top in this mountain bar over an hour ago.

"Wanna dance?" She points to the dance floor, where half the team is grinding and moving to the country beat.

"No thanks, I'm fine right here." I shrug off her attempt to pull me out of the chair and turn back to the table where Whitty, Hughes, and Jones are currently sitting.

"Damn Sanderson," Jones follows her walk to the dance floor with his eyes, "Not sure why you're saying no, but that would have been an easy one."

"Not feeling it tonight," I admit. "Waiting on something better."

Holden shows up with a fresh round just as the door to the bar opens. My eyes scan over to see two ladies walking in, one a cute-looking girl with reddish brown hair, and as I see the second one is Aria, excitement spreads across my face..

"And that something just walked in the door."

Holy fuck. I knew under that plain Jane uniform was a body just waiting to be seen. But seeing Aria, toned and tan in a pair of shorts and some sort of off shoulder top, makes my mouth water like a damn dog.

She scans the room, and it's apparent she is looking for someone. When her eyes meet mine, I swear to God, time stands still again. I can't help the goofy expression that forms, but my heart feels suddenly lighter when she gives me a shy smile in return.

"Dude, what the—," Hughes starts, tracking my line of sight until he lands on the new bar patrons. "Oh, fuck yeah! Dibs on the redhead!"

"Go for it," I state, not taking my eyes off Aria as she gives a little wave. "The other is all mine."

I watch as she greets some of the other people in the bar, smiling at everyone and giving a few people hugs. She bends down to hug someone sitting and I get the perfect view of her heart-shaped ass right in front of me. Fuck, the things I'd like to do to her.

I notice she looks over this direction a few times, avoiding eye contact but definitely checking me out, yet never comes over. Not sure if she is playing hard to get or is just shy.

Either way, I've had enough waiting around. I shrug off the girls crowding around our table and walk over.

"Look who's here but hasn't come over yet to say hello," I say, giving her a playful smile.

"Hello," Aria's voice has a little laugh to it, a little uncertainty, but knowing she came made me at least feel like there's a chance tonight could end well.

"Hi yourself. Glad you finally made it, wasn't sure if you were coming or not."

She raises her eyes at me. "You realize someone had to clean up after you guys left, right?"

Duh shithead, way to insult her.

"Hope it wasn't too bad." She shakes her head a little and points to the girl beside her.

"This is Evie."

"Hey, ... Ian," I introduce myself, "It's nice to meet you. Weren't you at the thing tonight?" I shake her hand while she gives me a look up and down, seeming to nod her approval at what she sees.

"Sure was, big guy; nice to meet you too." Even though she says that, she gives a little eyebrow raise to Aria and I can tell she isn't hitting on me the same way the other girls here have been.

No, this is a girl's girl, and she is Aria's wingman.

"You guys want to join us over at the table?" I watch as they give each other a look, with Aria slightly more reserved than her very excited friend.

"Absolutely," Evie says, "Lead the way."

We walk over to the table and I introduce Hughes, Jones, and Whitty to the girls. I'm about to say Holden's name, but he beats me to the punch.

"Hi, I'm Jack, the guy you dropped a knife on earlier." Holden sticks his hand across the table and takes Aria's hand while giving a teasing grin. I shoot him a glare, ready to tell him to knock it off and stop being a dick, but before I can say anything Aria responds, giving a little bow-like hand flourish.

"That's me." The guys laugh as she shakes the embarrassment away. "Looks like you recovered thankfully, wouldn't want you going on the injured list from eating dinner."

The table cracks up, and I raise my eyebrows. Love a girl with some sarcasm in her bones. Holden holds both hands up. "Touché. Sorry we gave you a hard time back there."

"Do that again and you'll have to answer to me." Evie chimes in as she drapes her arm across Aria's shoulder, and I feel a pang of jealousy like I wish it was my arm.

Jealousy? Really? Dude, what the fuck is wrong with me?

Holden eyes her up and down. "Now that I look forward to."

Hughes saddles up next to Evie. "Are you from around here? I need some directions."

Evie nods, "Yup, born and raised."

"Good, cuz I need directions on how to get from here to our first date." The table bursts out laughing at his corny line, including the girls who shake their heads. They have no idea how many lines we hear from him. He's a playboy for sure, but an all-around good time.

Holden extends his hand to Evie, pushing Chase out of the way. "Wanna dance?"

Evie checks with Aria to make sure she is all set, and grabs Holden's hand, who tosses back a wink to Hughes, mouthing "That's how a real man does it," as he leads her out to the packed dance floor.

I admire Aria's side profile as she watches her friend go, and then bend down, pretending it's loud, but in reality just trying to get close to her.

"Can I get you a drink?"

"Uh, sure, that would be great, thanks." Her lips lift in a small smile, so I slip my hand to the small of her back to lead her to the bar, and give a nod to Jones. He grins and shakes his head, knowing I've found what I'm looking for tonight.

I stay close to her side as I order two local brews she recommended, inhaling her sweet scent of vanilla and cinnamon. Carrying our drinks back to the table, I ignore the guys and give all my attention to the girl at my side.

I suddenly want to know everything about her and feel certain my night will end with her coming back to my place. I've kept hookups to a minimum this season, focusing on getting over my ex and channeling that frustration into playing. But tonight, I'm in the mood for a little action, and she seems like the perfect person to christen my new house.

"They look like they are having fun," Aria says, motioning to Evie and Jack.

"We can join them later if you want, but first I want to get to know more about you." I lean in, voice dripping down to her ear like honey. Using all the moves tonight.

"Well, what do you want to know?" She pulls out a high top chair and gets comfortable, motioning for me to do the same.

"How long have you lived here?"

"My whole life practically. I left for college, but was born and raised in the area. What about you? Where are you from?"

"Michigan. Upper Peninsula area, where we also have some pretty amazing lakes."

"Ok, but are they as pretty and blue as here?" She's teasing, but I think she also genuinely wants to know.

"Well, seeing as this is my first time in Tahoe, I haven't explored it all, but it looks nice, though not sure it's better than our lakes back home." I lean back, stretching my arm over the back of the empty chair next to me, neither knowing nor caring where the rest of the guys are.

She laughs out loud, and I'm surprised at how easy it feels talking to her. Almost like we have been friends for a while and are catching up.

"You just haven't found the right spots here then." She takes a sip of her beer.

"Hmm, maybe so. Maybe I just need a tour guide." I matched her drink with one of my own, lifting my eyebrow at her over the pint glass.

"So Mr. Hockey, tell me about you, something outside of the team."

"Hmm, well let's see," I tick off items one by one on my fingers, "Only child, favorite candy is Sour Patch Kids, and I'm pretty mean with a paint sprayer." The last comment has her choking on her drink.

"A paint sprayer? Ok, was not expecting that; obviously there is a story there?" She reaches out and touches my arm briefly in a playful and flirty way. I love the feel of her fingers on my arm. I'm about to return the gesture when she does a quick recoil as I make eye contact.

"Helped my buddy Lucas with some home renovations last season. Just call me the King of Paint."

"Ok, your highness." Her chair squeaks against the wood floor as she slips off it and makes a half-assed curtsey before leaning against the table.

She is so fucking cute.

Determined to make my move, I stand as well. "Oh, sweetheart, you don't need to bow to me. If anything, I should be bowing before your beauty." I slide my arm around her waist, pulling her closer.

Still being playful, Aria tries swatting my smoothness away and I bring my other arm up, my hand stopping her attempt and I pin her wrist against my chest. Staring at her light pink lips, I'm debating kissing her right here, right now, or waiting til I get her alone.

"Well, looks like you guys hit it off." A deep chuckle breaks us apart as we both turn to look at the table, and see 5 sets of eyes staring back at us, including Evie, who is wearing the biggest grin as she looks between Aria and I.

Aria dips her chin in embarrassment and goes to look away, but I grab it between my finger and thumb and give it a little pressure, forcing her to look back at me.

"Ignore those fuckers." I give her a relaxed smile that does the job, as she grins and we turn back to the table.

The next hour flies by with laughter and casual conversation, the girls integrate seamlessly and add their own charm and banter. Aria sits on the extra stool we brought over, the one I pulled a little closer after she sat down—right next to me.

I've been finding excuses to touch her all night.

It's like she has this magnetic energy swirling around her that just calls to me, and without thinking, I'm reaching for her arm, or trying to catch her eyes as she listens to the guys chatter around the table.

"Are you guys playing the Celebrity Golf Tournament next weekend?" Evie asks. "Word is Coach Johnson is planning on playing again this year."

I glance over at the other guys. We had talked about it briefly. Last year's social media recap made it seem like a fun charity event with some pretty big names from not just the NHL but other pro leagues, plus movie stars and musicians.

"I'm playing." Holden nods, then adds, "but he still hasn't decided," pointing to me.

Aria's eyes find mine and I can see the hope in there, hope that I'll be back, that maybe she will get to see me again and tonight doesn't just have to be a one time thing. I can see the excitement in the same way I can feel it in my chest; the thought of getting to spend more time with her, maybe take her out after the tournament.

Ok hold on there, remember we are looking for a hookup, not wanting to get into relationship territory.

"Yah, I'm all in." I smile and can feel her relief and happiness radiating. Damn, I would play a million tournaments to see her smile like that again.

After another round, the night takes a turn when Evie announces it's time for her to go home, and Aria agrees. This isn't how I expected the night to end. We all try to convince them to stay, but it's no use.

"It's been fun, boys, but I've got to get home. 6am with a toddler comes early after a night out." A stunned silence comes over the group as we all raise our eyebrows at Evie, taking in this new information. Well, all except Aria, who just smiles at Evie and nods. Hughes, of course, is dumb enough to let his mouth fall open.

She's a mom, huh? That's cool.

"Sure you can't stick around for longer? I could give you a ride." I play with a loose lock of Aria's wavy hair and tuck it behind her ear. She looks shocked at my offer for a minute, and I can see her debating it before shaking her head.

"Yah, no, Brady is probably wondering where I am. He doesn't like to go to bed unless I'm home. But thanks." She gives me a smile and starts hugging the guys around the table and saying goodnight while I remain frozen to the spot.

What. The. Fuck?

Did I miss something here? Does Aria have a fucking boyfriend and spent the entire evening acting interested in me?

My entire body tenses up and I shoot a glare at the guys, my jaw tight. They know my background and cheaters are not something I take lightly.

I'm about ready to make that known too, but just can't get past the fact that Aria really doesn't seem like she would be the type of girl to do that. At least I didn't think she was. But my track record of being able to pick out manipulative women is historically poor.

"Whoa there, down boy." Evie laughs, eyes sparkling as she pats my arm. "Dial it back a notch. She is talking about her dog—Brady—not a man." I let out a breath.

She leans in to whisper, "Aria is as single as it comes and would never do that."

The tension in my shoulders immediately deflates as I look over at Evie, who gives me a knowing smile.

"Interesting reaction, though, I must say." She gives me a hug and makes her way to thank the guys for the "drinks and entertainment."

"So I'll see you next weekend, then?" Aria pauses briefly before giving me a little side hug around the waist.

Still recovering from shock, I give her a quick squeeze but don't make any further effort. "Yeah, see you then."

Something flashes over her eyes, sadness or disappointment maybe, but I don't realize why that might be until after the door closes behind them and it hits me.

I completely forgot to get her number.

7

ARIA

Tuesday, June 20th

"God, I just wish I knew what it felt like to kiss him—just once. Maybe I shouldn't have left so early." I tie my sweatshirt around my waist now that the temperature's warmed up.

"You've been saying that for the past three days. Maybe you'll get your chance when he comes back this weekend." Evie wiggles her eyebrows at me in between pushing her daughter Gracie on the swing.

We are at the park like we are most Tuesday mornings as a chance for Gracie to play and for me to let Brady run free for a while, chasing the ball and interacting with other people and dogs.

"I can't help it—did you see the man? Holy Smokes," I grasp my chest with my palm. "And every time he grazed my leg, or touched me, I thought my body was going to collapse."

Before walking into Lift, I honestly wasn't sure Ian would remember inviting me- after all, he likely invited any girls he met while in town just to ensure some fun for the guys.

But once I made eye contact with him across the bar, and I saw a huge smile grow across his face, I started thinking that maybe, just maybe, he was hoping I would show up. Seeing him standing there in his dark jeans, a black long sleeve tee that fit snugly over his muscled arms and chest, and backwards hat, I'm glad that I did.

My body can still feel how his hand molded to the small of my back after introducing me to the guys, and he never let go. Not when he led me to the bar to order, not while waiting and not on the way back, my skin tingling with desire the entire time.

Of course, every other girl had their eyes on him in the place. The bartender put the girls on display while taking our order, and the rest of the Sierra Springs female population looked just as eager to capture his attention. On the way back to the table, no less than 5 girls touched his arm or congratulated him or tried to get him to join them.

"Hell yes, I saw him. I saw all of them. Plenty of yummy meat to go around." Gracie laughs at the face Evie makes.

"Plus, if he was interested he would've asked for my number or something." I kick at the sand. "Which he didn't, so I'm sure he found one of the many willing tributes at the bar and took someone else back to his hotel after we left."

"I mean, it's possible, but you didn't see his reaction when he thought you had a boyfriend, so—." She lifts Gracie from the baby swing, and I instantly make grabby hands for my niece.

"Was that a fun ride, sweet girl?" I snuggle her little body against my chest and give her head a kiss right between her little reddish blonde pigtails. She squeals with delight and almost throws herself out of my arms as she sees Brady approaching with his ball.

"Baydee Bear! Fetch!" Her little voice is the best sound in the world.

My Newfie wanders over like the cheerful guy he is, giant tail wagging and tongue hanging out to the side of his enormous jowls.

Many children and even adults might be afraid to see 160 pounds of a black bear of a dog running towards them. But Gracie has known Brady or "Bear"—as we also call him—since birth and snuggling Bear is her favorite thing.

The two of them are the cutest pair I've ever seen.

"Wuv you, baby bear," Gracie leans over and I lower her so she can place a big kiss on his snout before indicating she wants down.

Brady nudges his oversized tennis ball at my feet and gives her a big lick, sending her collapsing into a fit of giggles.

Picking up his ball, I launch it across the grassy area next to the playground and turn back to Evie and Gracie.

"I guess we'll just wait and see if we run into them again this weekend."

I'm crossing my fingers, hoping we do. I find myself unable to stop thinking about staring into his vibrant blue eyes. It was like looking out on the lake, the colors and shadows blending together right before you dive in, and it made me want to dive straight into him.

...

"We need a bigger parking lot," Adam grumbles, tossing his keys on the shelf and stashing his water bottle. "Not sure how they expect to fit 200 more people when the parking lots are already full from morning golfers."

"Mm-hmm," I agree, recalling the trouble I had finding a spot before my 8 a.m. shift the following Saturday. I scan the event paperwork.for the setup instructions.

Today's the Charity Celebrity Golf Tournament, an annual fundraiser hosted by The Alpine Club for local and national charities. While it's always fun for people watching, it's a lot of work with many moving pieces.

Lucky for me, I got the best assignment—lunch bag prep and distribution—avoiding the grunt work of moving tables and chairs across the property. I've had enough of those shifts the past few months.

"I hear Coach Johnson got a few last-minute players," Adam says, fanning himself dreamily. "More eye candy."

I chew my lip, thinking about one player in particular. Only Evie knows about the night at the bar, and I don't share my personal life with coworkers, but my heart races, and my stomach's in knots at the thought of seeing him again.

"Yup, should be a good day!" I grab the stack of lunch bags and start arranging them to load the prepared lunches.

We make small talk as servers move in and out, each with their own task. Packing lunches isn't rocket science, so while distributing sandwiches, chips, apples, and pre-packaged desserts, my mind drifts back to the night at the bar. I get lost in a daydream of those brief touches turning into lingering ones, leading to a panty-melting kiss or an invitation back to his place.

Shaking myself back to reality, I hope my flushed cheeks don't betray my less-than-work-appropriate thoughts. With a quick breath, I load the lunches onto the portable cart, gathering the other supplies I need for my station by the golf carts.

Twenty minutes later, I scan my setup, my eye for detail aligning everything perfectly. I can't help it—I love when things look pretty, even if it's just sack lunches and coolers of drinks.

It's still early, only 9am, but everything's ready for the golfers to grab lunch to eat during their round.

Gradually, the grounds fill with all kinds of people. Retired golf pros, athletes from pretty much every sport, musicians. Some wealthy business guys with assistants glued to their sides are there, and of course, a sea of fans clutching Sharpies and phones, hoping to snag a signature or a selfie before security shuffles them along.

"Gorgeous day today!" I hear, and glance over to see Coach Johnson approaching my tent with a few older gentlemen.

"Absolutely!" I reply with a smile. "You'll have a great day on the course; it's perfect weather." It's beautiful out, low 70s and blue skies. "Please help yourself to a bagged lunch to take on the course, and can I get you drinks as well?"

"We'll just take some waters for now and then buy something off the cart where they have the good stuff."

He smiles at me and then grabs the water I hold out in my hand and the others do the same.

Coach adjusts his ball cap. "I got a few more of my guys to join—make sure you take care of them well." He pats the shoulder of his golfing buddy next to him and promises to introduce them to his players after the round.

"Will do, sir. Have a great round." I smile and wave them off.

If only he knew how much I'd like to take care of one of his players in particular.

After refilling the lunch table more times than I can count,I glance at my watch—only 10 minutes left before they tee off—and I still haven't seen Ian, Jack, or the other guys who promised to be here.

My heart sinks as I wonder if they were just being polite and, in fact, aren't coming. I've made it through the week hoping to see Ian again, but never considered how it would feel if he didn't show.

And I have to say, that feeling sucks—like a lead weight pulling my shoulders down or a zap to my aura turning it into a black cloud. Of course, it is stupid to get my hopes up. To him, I'm just another fan, enamored with his good looks and charm.

I'm debating packing up when suddenly I hear, "Ooh, is that food for us?"

I look up to see Jack Holden, Chase Hughes, and Blake Whitlock smiling as they approach the table and peek into the bags.

"Yes, it is—please help yourself to a lunch and a drink for the carts."

Blake double-takes back to me and his smile grows into something genuine and mischievous. "Well, hello there, Aria."

Before I can respond or ask if Ian's coming, he turns and calls, "Hey SandMan, your girl's over here!"

8

IAN

"So you're playing in a celebrity tournament today? Ooh, do you think Jade Taylor will be there? You know how much I love the look of that man. If you see him, give him my number."

My mama lets out a girlish giggle. I roll my eyes, but my heart tightens. She's so kind and sweet. I just wish she had a partner who loved her the way she deserves, unlike my father, who cheated after I left for college.

"Yes Mama, I'll pass along your obsession." I open the car door and step out to grab my golf bag from the back. "Maybe he will make you the inspiration for his next big album."

"A girl can dream, honey. Where is this one at this time?"

"The Alpine Club, the place here in town. I think you'll really love it here."

I think about the past few days getting settled in my new home for the summer, and last weekend at the bar, which, of course, makes me think about Aria.

The way her smile felt genuine when we were comparing who has the better home lake and how my fingers teased her bare skin when they slipped around to give her a hug. I can't help the little smile that escapes along with the last half of that sentence.

"Hmm, sounds lovely. I can't wait to visit. Was it a hard drive?" My mom moved to a little suburb outside of San Jose when I got a place on the team, so she could always be near me. The two of us have always been a pair, and having her at games makes me skate even harder.

Plus, I enjoy having her close, knowing I can look out for her, keep her safe, and make sure she has everything she needs. It's my job, my mission, and I take it seriously.

"Not at all, about 3.5 hours, across the valley and then up through the foothills, but I can fly you into Reno too." Part of why I picked a house here was it would be easy enough for her to come visit whenever she wanted to this summer.

"That sounds wonderful. A perfect place to escape the city. Not that I don't love being here, but you can take the girl out of Michigan, but that need for nature doesn't get filled the same way visiting the botanical gardens."

"Maybe you can drive up here after you get back from your trip?" My mother is visiting friends for a few weeks back home, as she travels more in the off season as well.

"I'd love that, honey—we can talk more about it later. I have to run to my hair appointment. Can't be looking like a mess the first day I roll back into town!"

We say goodbye and I hang up, tucking my phone in my back pocket and opening the rear passenger door to double check that my gift for Aria is back there for later. Since Aria has a dog (and not a boyfriend) I'm thinking a little present is a way to win myself some time with her after I find her at the club. And this time, I'm not leaving without her number.

After signing in at the check-in table, I followed the signs to meet the guys by the carts as planned.

I know it is Aria before Whitty yells out. The moment I turn the corner to the back lawn and see the guys head to the food table, I recognize the shape of her firm body and the slender line of her jaw that would feel great under my hand.

Seeing her under the tent appeased my protective side. I am glad it shielded her from the sun, but I worry about how hot she must be in the black pants on such a warm day.

Just friendly concern, that's all.

She turns, following Whitty's voice, her entire body tracking the sound as if she can't wait to see if it is me. A brief flush crept up her neck when she processed what he'd called her. And damn, I liked the sound of it.

Her being mine.

Yeah, that had a nice ring to it. At least for the night, so I can catch up on what I missed at the bar.

"Hi Aria," I flash what I know is my most endearing smile (thanks to fan votes of course) as I approach, sticking one hand in my pocket and leaning against the metal pole of the pop up tent.

"Ian. Hi. I wasn't sure if you, I mean you guys, were coming or not." She bit her lip in a way that definitely told me she had been hoping, and possibly even praying, that we would be.

"Told you, I'm all in." I grab the bag she offers and gesture to the rest of the guys, "We wouldn't miss another chance to come back here." I let my eyes roam over her, feeling happier than I have all week to be standing here with her again.

"Always a fan of a foursome, I like to say," Hughes lifts his chin with a smirk that has me rolling my eyes and everyone, including Aria, laughing. At 25, he is the baby of the group, and man does he act like it sometimes.

"Well, what you guys do on the course is no business of mine, but just remember today you'll have people watching, so maybe keep it PG." Aria surprises me with a clever response and I chuckle.

Wit is such a fucking turn on. This girl is good.

"No promises." With that, Holden turns and gives me a wink and then the guys head over to where the carts are being staged and the other participants are milling around.

But I can't leave. Not yet, at least. There's something I still have to do before I let this girl out of my sight.

"Aria, I have to tell you, I made a mistake the other night." Before I can tell her that mistake was not asking for her number, I see her face fall. A look of pure dejection comes across her face for the briefest moment before she gives the slightest shake of her head.

"Oh, I understand. Honestly, I'm surprised you even remembered my name." She tucks a piece of hair behind her ear. "I'm sure you had fun with all the girls; I didn't think it was anything, no worries," she rambles, both cute and disheartening at the same time. How could she actually think spending time with her was a mistake?

"What? No, I don't mean spending time with you. I had a lot of fun with you, and I haven't been able to get you out of mind since." My arm reaches out to touch hers, right below where her club polo sleeve ends. She looks up with a confused look.

"What I meant was, I'm sorry for letting you leave without getting your number. I've been kicking myself all week for not having a way of contacting you." I gently run my fingers on the curve of her bicep and then lift my hand to move that wayward piece of hair that has again fallen into her eyes.

"Really?" she asks in the most hopeful tone, her eyes sparkling and searching mine for reassurance. "I figured you just moved on to any of the willing girls in the bar."

Chuckling, I rest my hand on her shoulder, needing to touch her but not wanting to be too forward, and hold her gaze.

"Really. The guys and I called it a night as soon as you left." She gives a small smirk, liking that answer, and I match it with one of my own.

9
ARIA

OMG. I have to tell Evie.

That's the first thing to cross my mind as I watch Ian walk away and join the rest of the group, though not before turning back with a grin, lifting his phone in silent confirmation.

After he told me he left the bar alone and, to my surprise, had wanted my number, my heart practically soared out of my chest.

It was like unwrapping a surprise present and it being full of all the best hopes and dreams that magically come floating out.

Of course, I gave him my number, and teased him asking if he would actually use it. He gave me the cutest little smirk while nodding his head, and said "Challenge accepted."

I pack up the rest of the lunch stuff, store the coolers in the golf garage, and head back inside more than a little giddy. I enter the kitchen to do side work and get ready for the post golf mini buffet that consists mostly of finger foods, a cheese and antipasto station, and desserts.

A lot of the big celebs that attend don't want to stay around for long dinners or be forced to mingle through a packed cocktail hour. Over the years we realized having a filling but simple spread gives those who want to hang out the option, but those who are just hungry from playing the chance to grab a quick snack and head out.

• • •

Two hours later, as I exit the locker room (home to a rotating display of candy and snacks for the ladies of the club we love to raid) my phone suddenly vibrates in my apron pocket. I pull it out to see a photo of Gracie covered in what looks like yogurt, sitting in her highchair. I heart the picture and start to type out a response but then am interrupted by an incoming text from an unknown number.

Opening it to read, I see a photo of the lake view, mountains in the background, in a shot that was obviously taken from the course. My heart races as I read it.

Unknown Number: Hi, It's Ian. This view is nice but I liked the one at the start of the course better.

I can't believe it, Ian texted me.
I quickly save his number in my contacts. I'm a little stumped on what view he means though as we have a lot of gorgeous spots on the course.

ME: Do you mean from the tee box on the first hole? It is quite charming.
IAN: Maybe, but the view under the lunch tent was by far the best. Hottest. Lunch Lady. Ever.
ME: LOL guess the competition isn't too hard when most lunch ladies are like what, 70?
IAN: IDK as a kid don't all grown ups seem the same age?

I laugh out loud at that as I make my way back into the kitchen, swiping a cookie off the sheet pan Jose has sitting on the central table getting ready to be plated.

ME: Right? They do! It's crazy, and now I can't tell how old people are in general anyway, so I guess it never gets easier. How's golf going?
IAN: It's fun. My golf game sucks but it's fun hanging out with the guys, we don't get to go golfing much together.
ME: I'm glad you are having a good time! Any crazy fans?
IAN: Not for me, but Hughes had someone ask him to sign her chest.

I practically choke on a piece of cookie at that.

ME: People do that for real? That's insane. I hope they don't bother you. I'm sure overzealous fans get annoying.

Ian: Naw, they're cool for the most part. It's nice to be appreciated. And I might turn into a crazy fan myself if I see Jade Taylor. My mom is obsessed.

ME: Who isn't? He is amazing!

I grab a stack of cups and head out to the deck to continue setting up for the after golf event.

IAN: Amazing huh? Not sure I like you calling him that.

My eyes grow big. I can't believe I'm texting with Ian Sanderson, but it's even harder to believe that it almost sounds like he is jealous.

I squeal a little out loud at the idea of him being jealous of me and my attention before I come back to reality. Yah right, a pro hockey player being jealous over me? Impossible. I think about how to respond while still trying to be a little flirty, hit send then arrange the cups on the table.

ME: Yah? And why's that?

"Because I'd rather you call me amazing instead."

I spin around at the familiar voice behind me, and see Ian standing on the deck, looking downright edible in his white golf polo, navy shorts and, holy mother of god, a backwards hat. I'm a sucker for those.

"What are you doing here? You aren't supposed to be done for a while!"

"Just taking a, uh, a break to use the bathroom in between holes." He looks away slightly, grabbing at the back of his neck with one hand.

"Oh, ok, well, the closest ones to the course are down those stairs, in fact, you must have passed it on the way up here..." I leave the last part like a question.

"Fine, maybe I just didn't want to go 18 holes without seeing you. I had Holden stop the cart when we were passing by after the 9th," He looks a bit sheepish at his admission, but it sends tingles through my body.

I'd almost think he was just joking—just messing around—but finding him up on the Upper Deck meant he'd gone out of his way to look for me.

I stare up at his rugged face, admiring the bone structure of his nose and jawline, the desire to pepper it with soft kisses washing over me before I tamper it back down.

"Um, that's sweet of you." I admit, playing with the chain of my necklace like I often do when I'm not sure what to do with my hands.

I mean, I know what I'd like to do with my hands.

I'd like to rub them all over his body and dig my fingers in his hair.

Jump up and wrap my legs around his waist while letting my hands roam over all of those muscles peeking out from his shirt.

I blink to refocus. *Whoa there, down girl.* All that from just proximity?

"What are you doing after this?" Ian steps closer, closing the distance between us.

His smoldering look sears into my skin, making me bite my bottom lip. His cologne is deep and woodsy, and my senses are in overload from the smell. My brain remembers the feel of his hand touching the bare skin at the bar where my shirt had lifted, the feel of my hand against his chest. I don't know what type of dream this is, but I do not want to wake up from it.

I swallow languidly. "After work?"

He nods.

"No plans, I guess, why?"

"Want to show me that lake you say is better than my Michigan ones? I have the afternoon free before another obligation tonight."

Is he actually asking to have me play tour guide like he joked about? Holy cow! I try not to look overly excited, and pause a minute for my voice to be calm.

"I'd love to, on one condition."

"Name it." Pretty sure with the look he is giving me I could ask for just about anything.

"I get to bring my dog along. He loves the outdoors."

"Deal, in fact that's perfect, I happen to have a little present for him."

. . .

"Alright buddy, be nice to Ian and try not to get too much slobber on him, okay?" I glance back at Brady to where he is tethered in, taking up the entirety of the back seat.

He gives me a dopey smile, and cocks his head as if to say "Seriously Mom?"

"Yah, I know, what am I thinking asking that of you, Mr. Drool King." I give him scratches on the top of his head. "Plus, if he wants me to show him around, he needs to accept you, excessive drool and all."

Newfoundlands are famous for their constant drooling, the loose and floppy jowls that help make them incredible in the water also mean carrying a drool rag around or plopping on a stylish bib or bandana to catch the drool.

Despite being a tricky dog to keep clean and groomed, Brady is the sweetest dog alive. He is my giant love bug and my partner in crime in the great outdoors. Together we have tackled almost every trail and every cove in the county. I am glad Ian agreed to let Brady come along, because I needed to get him outside for a walk to stretch his legs after staying indoors most of the day during the event. After finishing up my shift I ran home and had to shower after being outside all day, as I was a sticky and sweaty mess, so I would have felt bad leaving him again.

And I'm praying that Ian loves him just as much as I do. Given the general reaction of the public to his giant breed, I'm fairly confident he will.

Pulling into the parking lot at the trailhead at Hidden Cove, my most favorite beach, I turn the engine off to wait for Ian. Since Brady tends to get hot easily thanks to his thick water repellent double coat, I do a half key turn to keep the AC running.

A black Range Rover pulls into the lot and parks a few empty spaces away.

I turn the ignition off, reach back and release Brady's tether but tell him to stay put for just a minute. Jumping out of the Jeep with excitement, only to realize I need to dial my excitement back a notch.

This is not a date, it's just me showing him around. Maybe we can be friends after all this. That alone would be cool as he seems like a really nice guy.

A really sexy, nice guy, that is.

My pulse kicks up a notch when I see him step out of his car, his tall frame silhouetted by sunlight, casual but confident in a way that makes it hard to look away.

This isn't a date.

I repeat the words like a mantra.

A small part of me wishes it was, and maybe even hopes it can turn into one.

Hope is dangerous, though, and I've learned it's best to just not let myself fall into that trap.

10

IAN

The guys gave me shit for stopping halfway through the round to go see Aria, but look how it turned out. She gave me directions to meet up at a trailhead just a bit out of Sierra Springs, though still on the west side of the lake—some place she said is the perfect introduction to Lake Tahoe.

I spot Aria as soon as I get into the parking lot, and I suddenly feel lighter. Even though it's been a great day so far, I'm more excited now than I was for any of it earlier. After running into her I finished the back nine (with more lost balls than I can count), the guys and I grabbed food and some beers and chatted with some of the other participants on the deck while I kept tabs on Aria.

That little social hour kept her busy, without a doubt. From carrying endless platters of food to somehow balancing massive trays full of dirty dishes, perched on a single shoulder as she maneuvered through the crowd. Most of the servers, including Aria, quietly snuck in and out of the event without drawing attention to themselves, almost like undercover ops. Well, other than the one or two servers that were a little more annoying and star-struck with various guests that is.

I liked that she didn't seem phased by all the celebrities around. Having to deal with paparazzi and attending events and such is a pretty big part of my life, and I haven't had the best experience when it comes to someone thriving off that second hand fame.

But then again,it's her job to be professional around guests, and anything can happen once someone gets a taste of fame.

Not like I need another reminder of that.

It took me a long time to get over how quickly things went sour with my ex. Amber went from the one person I trusted everything with to being the person who makes it impossible for me to trust anyone now. And even though she was the unfaithful one, she tried her best to stain my reputation on the way out.

It's the main reason I haven't dated anyone in the year since it happened—I don't want to get all vulnerable with someone else, only for them to not be dependable and break my trust.

But even if I try to deny it, something is pulling me towards Aria. It's more than just thinking she is gorgeous, which she is, but I also like how she interacts with people and how kind she is to everyone.

What I like even more is how every time she looked at me, a sweet smile appeared on her face when she made eye contact, just like I can see through the windshield that she is doing now.

I reach over to the passenger seat to grab the dog toy I found, a Chuckit! Ultra Rubber Ball—it's smaller than a tennis ball but the packaging sold me on the extra bounce for fetch—and then opened my door to go meet Aria.

Sunlight catches the highlights in her hair as she crosses toward my car, looking relaxed in pink shorts and a light yellow tank top.

"Find the place okay?" She does a little half-wave, making me smile at her cute mannerisms.

"Yeah, it was no problem." I look around in fake indifference, gesturing to the parking lot gravel as she comes to a stop next to me. "So this is where you chose as the best place to introduce me to your little blue lake?"

"Yes it is, but this is JUST the parking lot—thank you very much." She elbows me in the ribs playfully.

I want to sweep her up in my arms at just the feel of her making contact. She barely nudged me in the ribs with her elbow and all I want is to feel her touch on me again.

My stare must burn as her cheeks go pink, and she diverts her attention, breaking eye contact.

"It's got a great little hike and it's one of my favorite coves for seeing why it's called Big Blue."

"Perfect. Did you bring your dog? I brought him a little something." I pull out the ball from my back pocket and watch her eyes go wide as she tries to stifle a smile.

"Oh wow, um thank you, that is so kind of you!" She looks like she is choking back a laugh now.

"What am I missing here, is this too forward of me? It's just a little gift for your pup." I am genuinely confused at her reaction. The cashier assured me that her dog loved this toy when I was buying it.

"It is a very sweet gift," she chuckles, and walks over to open the back door of her jeep.

Suddenly a giant black thing leaps from the open door and begins bouncing around excitedly before Aria grabs onto his collar. It's the biggest dog I've ever seen, and I'm not even sure it is a dog. In fact it looks a lot like a black version of the Grizzly we wear on our jerseys.

"Ian, meet Brady. Brady, this is Ian. Do you want to say hi to him?" After a pause I look up and see that she is, in fact, asking me, the human, the question.

"Of course! C'mere Brady." I stretch out my hand for him to sniff expecting a cautious sniff. Instead he does a little half hop and gallops like a horse over to me and starts wiggling in circles as I lean down to pet him.

"Oomph." I let out a groan as he pushes his full weight into my knee, almost taking me out right here in the parking lot.

Holding up the ball next to his massive face I see it is comically too small for him, and unquestionably, a choking hazard.

"So I'm guessing you were laughing at my "little" gift for such a big dog, am I right?" I use air quotes to highlight where I clearly went wrong on the assumption that she would have a normal sized dog.

Aria's shoulders shake as she gives up trying to contain her laughter.

"Yup. Sorry, it's fun seeing people's reactions to him anyways but this was just the perfect lead up." She moves the few steps closer and pats Brady's butt, giving it hard thumps he seems to enjoy.

"But seriously, thank you for thinking of him and getting him something. Honestly, I can't believe you even remembered I had a dog." She reaches over and gives me a quick hug around the waist, releasing way too early for my liking.

"Looks like I need to find a pet store to get a proper sized gift." I scratch Brady's muzzle and when I pull my hand back, it's covered in drool. I glance over to Aria, a bit horrified, and hold my hand up with my eyes wide to find her folded in half laughing.

Apparently it happens enough that she was expecting it as she hands me something to clean the drool off. We each grab the backpacks we brought and head for the trail, Brady leading us like he knows the way well. Aria goes in front, leaving me staring at the way her body moves down the path in her little tank and shorts.

"Has anyone ever mistaken him for a bear out here?"

She turns her head with a small laugh, "Happens all the time. We do have black bears around here often, plus some of the tourists have never seen a bear in real life so they are even more confused. But he is the friendliest bear you'll ever meet."

"Isn't that Winnie the Pooh?" I counter.

"Nope, Brady Bear has him beat."

She gives me another of those dazzling smiles before cutting off the trail to follow Brady down a small path leading to a grouping of boulders. Beyond the smooth sand, a crystal clear cove, dotted with deep shadows that hang in the blue-green water, reveals itself.

"Wow, this is incredible." I turn my head to take in the full 360 view. The water is such an alarming color of blue it's hard to name it correctly, like aqua and sapphire colliding, vibrant and entirely calm. Throughout the water are enormous boulders, some thoroughly submerged, signaling that the water is much deeper than it appears at first glance. A light breeze rustles through the tall pine trees that surround the cove and across the lake, mountains shooting up from towns along the shore.

I hear a splash to the side and look to see Brady pacing the sand at the waterline, staring at Aria. "Can he swim ok?"

"Oh, he's a great swimmer. He's just waiting for permission." And with that Aria gives Brady the ok to go and he leaps into the water, popping his head up and starts swimming around the rocks.

We sit on the sand and Aria tells me about some of the best places around the lake, both on the California and the Nevada side. As she talks she seems like a natural extension of the landscape, her love for the alpine area coming through authentically that is fully adorable. I can tell she is an outdoorsy girl who maybe does a lot of the stuff I grew up doing, but also isn't too crunchy for my taste.

The conversation flows easily, like we've been friends forever. And it sort of feels that way, she just feels, familiar I guess is how I would describe it.

I can't remember the last time I met someone and just hung out with a girl as a friend, without hockey being a central subject. She asked me a few questions but they felt more like she is just trying to get to know me, rather than just trying to get a glimpse into my life as someone famous.

Maybe it's the idea of having someone take an interest in me as opposed to me as the hockey player, but I know I want to see her again, and not just for a hookup. I've had a hard rule as of late where I don't see the same girl more than once or twice for fear of them getting either too close or too attached. Something about Aria is making me want to bend those boundaries.

Letting my guard down and inviting another girl into my world seems like the scariest thing possible right now, and something I wholeheartedly swore off more than a year ago.

But now I feel like maybe just letting her in a little would be ok. It would be nice to have a friend in the area for the summer, someone to hang out with that knows the place well to make the most of my time here.

As she gets up and walks to the water to throw a bumper for Brady, my brain starts questioning whether hooking up with her right away would ruin this unexpected friendship. Plus, if I tried to shoot my shot, and she doesn't do casual dating, then I'd spend all summer feeling awkward as fuck.

I watch her play with Brady and wage an internal war. I'm so attracted to her though, it would be hard to not give in to that.

By the time she sits back down, the angel on my shoulder has won, despite my intense desire to know what it feels like to be inside her. I'll treat this as a budding friendship.

Sacrifices for the greater good and all.

I'm inducting her into my circle of trust—which only my boys are in—but testing the waters to see what she is like on a casual level might not be such a bad thing.

11

ARIA

This is such a perfect day.

I can't help but smile to myself as I watch Brady bounce across the water to fetch the ball. At least my back is turned to Ian so he can't see it. From the warmth in my cheeks I can feel a smile isn't the only thing staining my face. The last thing I expected this morning was to be out on the lake, my sacred place, with the hockey hunk I was just hoping to at least see today.

But now we've spent the past hour talking and laughing, and it's turned into the best day ever.

Brady finally seems to wear out just as my arm starts to as well, so I turn back. Ian sits perched on the sand, the powerful muscles of his legs peeking out under his shorts and he sits, forearms propped on his knees.

"Do you like working at the club?" His question is open and curious, and not at all shameful.

"Most days, yes. It's an okay job—I like being a part of the fun celebrations and events. It's not glamorous work by any means, but as far as work goes, it's fine." I sit next to him, and Brady comes and lies down in front of our legs, the long wet topcoat making me tuck my legs in while Ian reaches out to pat him on the head. "If you didn't play hockey, like if you never started in the NHL, what type of job would you do?"

Ian tilts his head, and looks past me reflectively as if the sun held the answer. "Hmm, good question. Maybe like a chef?"

"Are you a good cook?"

"No, not at all," he laughs, "but maybe that would have helped me learn." I shake my head, reveling in how easily he makes me laugh. It's refreshing how open and honest he is about himself, rather than trying to play up his skills.

"Hey, I should be heading back. Do you mind if we get going soon?" Ian says, looking at his phone while we sit side by side on the granite boulder overlooking the clear water about an hour later.

"Oh yeah, of course I'm sorry, I didn't realize I kept you here for so long. I hope that doesn't make you late." I start grabbing my stuff in a hurry and call for Brady.

I easily lost track of time talking to him. Everything he said was so funny or interesting, and I felt like a sponge and wanted to soak it all in. It was surprising how comfortable it felt, how natural just sitting there soaking up the view and sharing stories felt. Just like chatting over coffee with an old friend, or like listening to the stories Old Man Stan tells as he sits on the bench out front of the library, keeping an eye on the town.

It made me forget he is famous. That he wasn't a part of the landscape.

"No not at all, I had a great time seeing this place." His smile seems genuine enough that I relax a bit. He hands me my Nalgene and I turn to put it in my backpack as he says "I can see why you think it's so beautiful, the view is pretty spectacular."

I agree, zip up my backpack, and then call again for Brady to come out of the water, which of course leads to him shaking off his enormous coat covering us in droplets of water. Ian is a good sport and just laughs it off.

We head back to the trail and made quick work of getting to the parking lot. While hiking back up I think about how I didn't want our time to come to an end, but obviously Ian being who he is, I'm sure he has lots of things to do. It is clear that our time has run out. Now I'm totally kicking myself for leaving the bar early last weekend.

To spend part of an afternoon with a pro hockey player who ended up being so down to earth was a dream. He is genuinely so nice and I would love to spend more time with him and get to know him. Of course, I'm also insanely attracted to him, but I could even see him being a good friend, someone that Evie would get along with, someone who would fit in great with the bigger friend group.

But knowing we come from vastly different worlds makes me believe this was definitely a once in a lifetime experience. Plus, he doesn't even live here, so I doubt he would want to continue texting or anything, much less build and maintain a friendship.

I am glad I got to show him one of my favorite spots on the lake though, and every time I come here I'll be able to look back on today. This past week has been so unexpected—between the event, the night at the bar and today—and makes for a great story.

Sometimes that's all we get out of life. Just a brief encounter with something remarkable and then a story to tell.

When we reach our cars, Ian says he has to make a quick call once he gets service while I try to get Brady somewhat dried off, and he moves out of ear shot over towards his car.

After he walks back, I turn to him, fidgeting with my hands because I'm uncertain where to go from here or how to extend an invite for a friendship or even maybe just keep in touch.

"If you ever find yourself back here I'd be happy to show you more of the lake or other stuff around, if you want." I give him what I hope is a friendly smile without looking too desperate.

"You would?" He cocks his head at me and smiles back.

"Yah, of course." I laugh and open the door to let Brody in. "This was fun. I don't know how long you are here or what else you have planned, but I am going to do a bit of a longer hike and a swim with Brady tomorrow to another one of my favorite spots. If you happen to still be here and want to join, that is."

I feel a little foolish asking, but I truly loved spending time with Ian, and knew he would love all the top spots as much as I do.

"That would be great, I'd love to." My heart leaps at learning I get one more day with him. "Just send me the details." He smiles and reaches through the open window to give Brady a few last pets.

Not knowing how to end this conversation—Would a hug be appropriate? A high five? *What no Aria you idiot you aren't five*—I awkwardly climb into the driver's seat and give him a little wave. "See you tomorrow then!" He pats his hand on the window frame twice and then steps back with a wave as he heads back to his car.

As soon as I pull away, I dial Evie and put her on speakerphone.

"Oh my god girl you won't believe it..."

12

IAN

Sunday, June 25th

"Wanna join him?" I nod towards Brady who is already swimming around in the water, which he jumped into not 30 seconds after the hike the next day led us to another stunning beach.

I take off my shirt and throw it on top of the bag I put down in a dry area, leaving me in just my swim trunks. I turn back to Aria to find her staring at me, mouth hanging open, eyes taking in everything I just uncovered. I stand still for a second, proud of the work I've put in to make her look at me like that.

Like she is hungry.

Like she wants to put her mouth over each part.

I can feel the blood pooling below the belt. My thoughts take a detour and I have to force myself to remember the promise I made to keep things friendly. "AHEM," I try clearing my throat in an effort to clear other symptoms. Her eyes darting up to mine, looking guilty and cute as fuck when she realizes I caught her staring.

To be fair, I stared at her ass the entire hike down to get to this little secluded spot she wanted to show me today.

I decide to let her off easily and climb over a boulder that is jetting out in the water to a deeper area.

"Ready for a swim?" I can see her swimsuit straps under her tank top, and want more than anything for her to strip down and let me see what's been hiding under her clothes.

"Wait...-" without letting her finish or object, I dive headfirst into the smooth water.

ICE. It is fucking ICE! "Holy shit cream of wheat that is fucking cold!"

Aria stands with her hands on her hips laughing, body shaking with laughter. " Cream of wheat? Seriously? And you didn't let me finish, the lake is still freezing this time of year." She throws a stick out in the water and Brady turns to retrieve it. "Actually, it's cold year round. You need time to adjust to it."

"Seems like one of us is too chicken to get a little cold." I challenge her, hoping she will give in, strip down and come out and join me in this icicle of a lake.

"Challenge accepted." She gives me a look like she is used to the temperature and reaches down, grabbing the hem of her tank top and then pulling it over her head.

Thank God the water is shielding me because there is no stopping my dick from reacting to seeing her in her yellow bikini top.

Tanned and toned, her athletic figure is in full view, leading up to the perfect set of round breasts begging to be released from the two triangle cups.

Aria slips off her shorts, using a nearby boulder to help balance as she slips them off her foot and drops them on top of her other belongings.

My eyes take in her entire image now, my cock straining in my shorts as her slightly curvy hips emerge, giving her the perfect hourglass figure.

So many of the girls I've hooked up with are super thin, which is fine to look at, but honestly,I prefer someone with more of a natural figure, like Aria's. She is stunning.

And off limits for now. I tighten my fist under water and exhale at the reminder.

She wades out deeper, taking a sharp breath in when the water hits her flat stomach.

"Cold?" I bite back a laugh.

"Um yah, of course! But you'll get used to it soon." She reaches up and pulls her soft dark blonde waves to the top of her head, securing it with a band from her wrist.

"Oh, I'm used to it, and let it be shown, I'm also the only one to complete the challenge." I gesture to her messy updo, which, while cute, is still totally dry.

"Ugh, no, not fair; I already got in all the way!"

"Not all the way." And I reach my leg out, hooking hers, and dragging us underwater.

13
ARIA

Oh no, he didn't!

I push up to the surface and immediately chase him down as he escapes further out, to where neither of us can touch the bottom, leaving both of us treading water.

"Ugh you jerk, that was so mean, I wasn't ready!"

"Well now you're all wet so we're even." He shrugs, swimming around me in a close, taunting way.

"Hmm, not sure about that," I say, and with the close proximity I reach out and push down on his shoulders and try to dunk him to extract my revenge. He goes along with it playfully, which is good because he outweighs me by at least 75 pounds, and when he comes up pretends to be struggling to stay afloat.

"Oh no, the strong lady has dunked me, I'm going to drown, help me!"

I laugh just as a loud splash sounds and I turn to see Brady swimming straight towards us.

Perfect.

"Oh are you? Do you need help?" I ask Ian in a conspiring tone.

"Yes, desperately so. Help, I can't swim!" He laughs, continuing the charade by splashing his arms and bobbing his head.

Suddenly Brady is there with us, circling around Ian before taking his outstretched hand in his mouth, his hold soft yet firm, and he maneuvers them so Ian is facing away from shore while Brady starts swimming back.

"Brady! What the—What is he doing?" Ian looks at me half in shock and half amused, like doesn't know what to think about what is happening.

"He's rescuing you." I shrug.

"He's what? How, wait, what?"

"Brady is a water rescue dog. He has been training to assist swimmers in danger who need help. And it looks like he's identified you as someone who needs to be saved." The sounds of our laughter combine as Ian goes along with it, floating on his back and letting Brady gently yet persistently pull him back to the shoreline.

After giving Brady lots of praise for his valiant rescue efforts, we settle down on the boulders, drying off with towels and pulling out water bottles, and take a few drinks.

"That was pretty incredible. How did he know how to do that?"

"We've been training for a couple of years." I look over to see Brady flipped over on his back, his double coat packed down with sand. We will, without a doubt, need another swim to rinse him off before heading home.

"He's been K9 Lifeguard certified and is working towards his full Water Rescue certification."

Ian looks amazed at that information.

"I didn't even know that was a thing. Are there a lot of dogs that do it?"

Shaking my head, I smile, "No, not many, at least not here in the states. But he's built for it. How much do you know about Newfoundlands?"

"Just that they are giant and look like bears, that's the extent of it." He laughs, giving Brady a few hard pats on the rump.

"Newfies are a very unique breed, they are the perfect water and rescue dog. Their body is pure strength, but it was made for the water." Grabbing one of Brady's big paws, I spread his toes. "They have webbing between their toes to help them swim, and they are the only dog breed that swims a modified breaststroke, rather than a dog paddle. Kind of like a polar bear."

Ian lets a laugh break free. "Once a bear, always a bear."

"Something like that," I laugh and move to pet my own bear's sandy coat. "Anyways, they have this innate instinct to rescue people and were used in history on fishing vessels. They are able to handle way more than just a single lifeguard could, they can pull a daisy chain of up to like 10 people back to shore, or even pull boats with people aboard."

"The Italians figured all this out a while ago and have an entire branch of water rescue dogs, mostly Newfies. Some even ride jet skis, and the most elite can even jump out of helicopters. They've trained a few dogs in the States, but not many."

Ian's jaw drops, and he glances between me and Brady. "Are you for real? That is insane! So cool." He climbs back up from where we are crouched next to Brady on the sand and settles back onto the rocks, picking up our water bottles and handing me mine . "Is that something you want to do with him one day?"

If only Ian knew how much I long to have Brady get to experience those things, the types of volunteer and rescue programs I'd love to implement here after I take the final course.

But all that is pretty silly sounding, so I downplay it.

"Maybe someday, that would be pretty cool." I shiver and reach for my bag to grab a sweatshirt. "We should probably be heading back soon. This trail doesn't have many lights and I didn't bring anything for us to be out here after dark."

Ian takes Brady for one last dip to rinse out his coat, and then one more for himself after he was too close to the splash zone when Brady shook his coat out after exiting the water.

We grab our stuff and head back to the trail that leads to the cars. At one point Ian reaches out and grabs my hand to help me over a fallen log, like the perfect gentleman. The feel of my hand in his, his hands big and encompassing, slightly calloused and strong, sends a ripple effect to my core.

It would be so easy to fall for Ian, I know that in my heart. I can tell he is a good guy. The way he watches out for me on the trail, making sure I don't trip even though this is my home turf, offers to carry my bag and never once complaining about Brady's antics.

I can't let that happen though. In all likelihood, he's just an undeniably upstanding guy that looks out for all his friends. Plus, he's just here for a few days. And while I think we might be able to maintain a friendship now that we have spent more time together, dating me isn't something he'd ever consider, not with everything he has available to him back in the city. Talk about a lowly, small town girl.

Even though I'm pretty sure he was checking me out and he has been a little flirty at times, I'd bet it's just how he is with everyone. It feels lucky, however surreal, to have formed this little friendship at all.

I feel the ghost of his fingertips in my hand long after he let go. Upon reaching the parking lot, he places his backpack in his car and walks back over—there was no way I was going to let Brady ride in, and ruin, his Range Rover when he offered to pick me up.

As silly as it sounds, I'm trying to figure out how to ask if he wants to be friends or stay in touch—despite feeling like I've known him forever these past few days—when he comes around the car.

"What is that look on your face? You seem like you are trying to figure out what to say."

I laugh and nod, a little embarrassed at how well he reads me, seeing how hard it can be for me to express my feelings sometimes.

"That's exactly it, to be honest." I fidget with my hair, feeling nervous. "I had a lot of fun hanging out with you, and I know you are like this big famous guy and leaving, but I was wondering if maybe you wanted to keep in touch. You know, in case you ever come back for some more top secret spots, or I don't know, maybe...be friends?" I blush and divert my gaze at how elementary that sounds.

Ian cocks his head and grins. "First of all, we are friends. Second, I'll tell you what's next. First, we are going to go get some ice cream because you have to have ice cream after a day at the beach. Then we are going to brainstorm every possible thing you want to show me of your world, because I'm going to be here all summer."

My jaw drops open causing me to look like a gaping fish from the bottom of the lake, but I can't care at that moment.

"You are? What do you mean?" I look deeply into his eyes, begging him for more information.

"I rented a place on the lake for the summer. Consider me a full-time summer tourist." Ian waits to see my reaction, looking almost on edge to see how I'll respond.

"For real? That's amazing! When did you do that?" My body alights with the news and I rock up onto my toes and back and do a little cheer.

I can't believe he will be here the entire summer. Just a few minutes ago I was thinking he was headed back to San Jose and now suddenly the summer is ripe with possibilities, of opportunities to spend time with him and hopefully get to know him better.

"Believe it or not, but back before the party. I need a place to decompress this summer after last season and it seemed like a great spot that was a little like home." He looks out towards the lake through the trees and then back to me, smiling. "And now as a bonus, I met a beautiful, funny, and sweet girl who said she wants to show me all the best spots."

I simultaneously blush at his words, and laugh at how he just inserted himself into my summer plans. I'm secretly thrilled I get to spend way more time with him, and don't mind that in the least.

"Well lucky for you, Brady loves ice cream so your plan is a good one."

"Good because that would have been incredibly awkward if you said no."

...

The air is cool the next morning as I get in my car at 7:30 for work, The sky a light blue with remnants of purple lingering after daybreak. Joggers and people walking their dogs on the paths along the road to the club, nothing except the call of birds and the soft lapping of the water on the lake shore as I head inside for this morning's event.

It's a quiet shift, just requiring me and Betsy to be there to set up for a breakfast and fashion show for the local women's club. After exchanging casual greetings and discussion about the setup needs, we each do our own thing as we prepare the room and stations, leaving me to my own thoughts.

As I cover the tables with linen, I think of how Ian's sunglasses reflected the sun and the water as he told me about growing up in Michigan, giving me insight into his life as a little boy.

Putting down a fork and knife at each seat, I recount laughing over and over at his stories and funny comments about his life and friends.

With coffee cups and saucers, it's how his fingers felt against my skin as he touched my arm, my hand, the small of my back as he spoke.

By the time I get to placing water glasses, I'm reliving the final look in his eyes. For the briefest moment, I thought he was going to kiss me goodbye, and realizing now—after he didn't—it was probably more of just me secretly wanting it.

I replay it over and over in my head, and conclude that the longing in his eyes I thought I saw must not have been there.

After grabbing ice cream at Treats & Trout, the half ice cream, half tackle shop owned by two formerly feuding shop owners who fell in love and combined their businesses in matrimony, and me sharing all of the best places he has to visit now that he will be here for longer, we headed to our cars parked side by side in front of the shop.

I toyed with my keys, not ready to part ways. And for the briefest of moments I almost thought he was going to kiss me goodbye. I was being open enough that if he wanted to make a move, I'm sure he would have known I would be more than willing to oblige.

His eyes stayed locked with mine and then I could have sworn he looked at my lips briefly, but then he ran a hand through his hair and told me to drive safe.

Ian is such a nice and outgoing guy, and if he had any romantic interest I'm sure he would have no problem showing it. So even though he says he wants to hang out this summer, I'm pretty sure he means as friends. Not to mention, he is so clearly in a league all his own, and not just the NHL, which makes it all the more unlikely that he would reciprocate any type of little crush I might have.

It's a bitter disappointment, but I force myself to feel grateful for a special new friend who will be around all summer long, and the excitement that comes with getting to know someone while sharing my favorite spots with. Dating or not, I steel my shoulders and get excited for the weeks ahead.

14
IAN

ME: You land ok?

    WHITTY: Yah, uneventful flight. Apart from the babe across the aisle. Fire emoji

    HOLDEN: Damn get it boy. Looks like I need to get on a plane.

    WHITTY: Update on Aria?

    ME: Smirk emoji. We went swimming.

    HOLDEN: This I gotta see, I'll be there next weekend. Fire emoji

    ME: I take that back. I revoke your standing invitation.

    HUGHES: You finally jumped back in the dating pool?

    ME: Just hanging out for the summer, she's going to show me around and stuff.

    WHITTY: Famous last words...

    ME: Nah man, that's the last thing I need. Finally moving on, don't need someone to screw everything up again.

I groan as I hit accept on the incoming call from Whitty. "What?"

    He chuckles. "You know it's ok to try again right?"

I sigh, and collapse into the couch. "I don't think that's the right move. Everything finally feels stable again. I didn't spend all last year working my ass off to win the Cup and get to where I am just to give it all up again for some girl to mess it all up."

"You know not every girl is going to do what Amber did."

God I hate even hearing her name. Just the sound of it brings me back to watching her pack her stuff as she carelessly throws away 3 years of my life after imploding it all.

"Yeah well, you don't know that. They might."

"Gotta learn to trust at some point to see if that's true."

"I'd rather stab myself in the eye then trust a girl again and have her manipulate me like that." I run my hand through my hair, tugging on it out of aggravation.

"Ok so is Aria just a friend then?" He asks as if he can feel the way my chest is aching when I think about her.

"Yeah, I think so. I like hanging out with her, she's cool, and it will be nice having someone to hang out with here when I want some company you know?" I plan on staying fairly secluded and focused this summer, but it will be nice to have someone to do some hiking with or go on some adventures.

"Ok man, whatever you say. But just remember that if you decide to take it further, you should. You deserve to find someone who will treat you right after that bitch and what she did to you, and Aria seems pretty fucking awesome."

"Thanks buddy." And with that we hang up, and I pull up the map of the lake and try to find some of the fun spots Aria mentioned at the ice cream place.

...

Over the next week I get out and explore a few of the beaches, bike paths and places in town Aria recommended, sometimes alone and twice I convince Aria to join me, once for a hike and another for a bike ride to explore the town. Each time she does, it feels even more comfortable to be around her, and soon I'm thinking about what we can do together next rather than just trying to fill my time. She is like the sun, and I am in her orbit, and can't help gravitating closer and closer to her, unable to resist the pull of her charm and genuine personality.

I do daily workouts in my home gym, and connect with someone at the local rink to get some skate time in.

While there one day, I see a local youth league and stay to watch, offering a few pointers to a couple of kids and making small talk with the coaches. That leads them to ask me to come on board, which I agree to do in an unofficial capacity.

I find myself enjoying falling into a routine of alternating spending mornings or afternoons working out or at the rink, and exploring the area. My favorite times have been spent with Aria, whenever she isn't busy with work, since her schedule is based on whatever events are planned at the club.

On our bike ride yesterday, Aria invited me to join her for one of her rescue training sessions with Brady, and I eagerly accepted, wanting to see for myself everything Aria talked about so passionately.

Which is why I'm standing here, looking out the window, waiting for her to pick me up.

I couldn't wait to see what all the training sessions for Brady consists of. While I was totally thrown for a loop when he grabbed my hand in his mouth while "rescuing" me, once I realized what was happening it was such a cool thing to see/be a part of. Plus I get to spend more time with Aria, so that in itself is a plus.

Aria insisted on picking me up instead of us both driving and refused my offer to get her. She said it makes sense as she has Brady's stuff and all the training gear loaded up on her Jeep for regular use. I think she is more worried about what Brady might do to my car, not that I would care, but either way here I am waiting for a girl to pick me up for the first time in my life.

I'm watching out the front window when I see her white jeep pull up, complete with roof rack built for adventure. Brady hanging his enormous head out the backseat window, creates the perfect picture—an outdoorsy girl and her giant dog—something that has me laughing and shaking my head at. I take a mental photograph of the image and grab my backpack, then open the front door so she doesn't have to get out. Brady gives a big 'WOOF' when he sees me. Petting his head, I rest a hand on her door where her window is open.

"Hi." I smile up at her, feeling tens pounds lighter just looking at her. Just being in her presence calms me.

"Hi," she smiles while putting her sunglasses on top of her head, resting on top of two braids that follow the slope of her neck. "You ready to go?"

I give a tap on her door, "Yup, let's do this!" Jogging around to the other side, I let myself in. Turning to talk to her, a giant fluff ball sticks his head between the seats and gives me a big wet lick.

"Brady! Sit down you big lug." Aria nudges him back but can't help laughing. I rub the drool off my face, grinning. "Sorry about that," she says, dragging her thumb across part of my jaw to get some I missed.

I swallow, the skin where she touched on fire. "No worries, he's just happy to see me." And based on the lightness in my chest and the smile on my face, I'm happy to see her.

I turn back towards the dash and my eye catches on a line of at least 10 colorful rubber ducks, most of which are decorated or in costumes.

"What are all those for?"

"Oh it's a Jeep thing. Ducking." I do a double take and she laughs. "Ducking, with a D."

Not the other thing my mind is bringing up. I shift in my seat to keep the image of that from traveling downward as she tells me about finding and leaving ducks for other jeep owners, filling the car with her smile and infectious energy.

We finish dropping the gear and get settled down the beach from the tourists, just past a small dock, as Brady runs around sniffing everything in sight.

This part of the beach has a small grassy area and some sand, and a few of the boulders I've come to expect given the mountainous terrain.

"What are you working with him on today?" I ask as she grabs what looks like a life jacket from her gear bag.

"I thought I'd run him through some of the basics as a refresher for him and to show you what he can do. Then do some jumps and maybe if it stays calm, we can do some work off the paddle board. My eyebrows lifted at that, and the image that came to mind of her and the black bear dog on the paddle board together.

"Is that safe, won't he tip you over?" I ask, concerned for her safety.

"Well that does happen, but we are getting better at balancing together aren't we boy?"

Aria grabs his muzzle between both palms, scrunching them together to make him look like a smushy face before kissing him on top of his head.

I'm honestly a little jealous of the affection he's getting, and would sort of like her to smush my face and kiss me. Even though I know we are just hanging out as friends, of course.

She buckles the lifejacket onto Brady, with clips under his chest. It has a military look to it, with straps and a big handle right on the middle of the back—it looks well made and expensive. Not the same as the ones I've seen some of the guys use for their dogs at times when we've been out on boats.

Aria pulls out another life jacket and my forehead creases as I wonder why she is wearing one too since I know she can swim. She must have noticed my confusion.

"This makes it a lot easier for me, since we do drills in deep water and oftentimes repeatedly. I have one for you too if you want, or you are welcome to stay on the shore, I know it's cold." She is being considerate, giving me an out.

I grab the jacket, "I'd love to be in with you or help, just tell me what to do."

We start with some basic fetch using a plastic bumper, taking turns throwing it out in the water and having Brady retrieve it. Then Aria adds a life vest in the water and has Brady do a double retrieve, grabbing the life vest first and the bumper second, with Brady following verbal commands on which to go after first. He is incredibly attentive, eagerly waiting for her commands and jumping into action as soon as he is allowed. It's fascinating.

After that Aria has me wade out into the water fairly far, while keeping Brady on the beach with her. She gives him a knotted rope (a floating line, she called it) to hold in his mouth, and then has him swim the line out to me.

"Don't take it if he drops it, he has to offer it to you while he still has it in his mouth." She calls out before he reaches me.

Brady swims to me, treading water as he waits for me to take the rope. "Good Boy Brady!" I give him some love and then she recalls him to her.

"Ready to start some more rescue-like scenarios?"

"I've been waiting for it, hell yes." This is like the first day of hockey season for me, and I'm excited to see what is going to happen.

Aria and Brady wade/swim out to where I am, with Brady sticking close to her side but never trying to climb on her or disrupt her swimming. Even just that is impressive compared to my experiences with dogs in pools and whatnot.

She tells me to grab onto the handle on his life jacket and then directs Brady to take me to shore. I grab it and then feel a small tug and I'm being pulled through the water, allowing this dog who easily weighs 60 pounds less than me to propel me towards the beach.

"This is amazing." I watch as Aria grabs on to Brady's rescue vest as well, and then he is pulling both our weights without missing a beat.

"Such a good boy!" Jumping around in Aria's praise once we are on the beach, Brady looks eagerly at the water like he can't wait to do that again. And he does.

In situation after situation, Brady keeps powering through from the shore and jumping from the dock. Aria shows me how he can decipher which person in the water is in need of rescue by having me splash around normally while she feigns drowning. Without even a cue, he bypasses me to go straight to her and pulls her to shore.

We bring out the paddle board, and I get to watch Brady jump into action from there too.

He is swimming around during a break and I pull myself up to hang onto the paddle board, which Aria is straddling in the middle.

"This is truly incredible, Aria. You must be so proud."

"I am, Brady has worked really hard. I couldn't be prouder of him." She gazes lovingly as she watches him swimming about.

Touching her shoulder, I waited until she looked down at me before reiterating, "I'm sure you are, but I meant you must be proud of yourself for everything you have accomplished with him, everything you have taught him."

She snorts a little, brushing off the compliment. "I'm not the one who can do all the special rescues, that's all him." It pains me to realize she doesn't see how incredible she is that she is patient and smart enough to teach him all of that.

I hoist myself up on the board, mimicking her position. Reaching a hand out, I play with the braid coming over her shoulder. "All of which wouldn't be possible without you. Sometimes it's the people who are invested in us that make our skills be able to come to light."

That gives her something to think about, and the faint tilt of her lips hints at a shy smile she is trying to keep from breaking free.

"What are your plans with him, you must have something you want to do if you are putting in all this effort." I don't actually know if K9 lifeguard is a job or what that would entail, but I can't see going through all this constant training for just her and Brady to be out on the water together. There's something bigger, I just don't know what.

"Well there are actual water rescue K9 and handler teams, a bunch of programs exist internationally and some in the states, but nothing like that around here." Shrugging her shoulders, she stares out over the open water. "That would be awesome if we had something like that, but I'm mostly just doing it as a community awareness type thing. I want people to understand how dangerous the water can be and take steps to prevent tragedies."

It's clear she has some sort of dream in mind, a way for her to work with Brady in a more official capacity, and I can't help but dig.

"Ok, so if you could do anything you wanted with it, what would that look like?"

"Some of the bigger state parks plus search and rescue orgs have k9 teams that patrol on the water and on beaches, assisting lifeguards in rescues and teaching water safety, especially to kids. Brady would be so great at that, but I'm not sure something like that is possible." Adjusting her legs up to criss cross them, she fails to mention that she too would be amazing at that.

"So for now, I'm just getting his certifications as I can, and volunteering in schools and local camps to do water safety training. It's important that kids are aware of how dangerous the water can be." Her eyes seem to cloud over and go downcast at that last remark. Something dark seems to have come to mind.

I wait patiently to see if she says anything else. But it's either too painful or she's not ready to go there, because she shakes her head as if to clear it away and forces a smile. "Ready to see him tow us in?"

Aria pops up onto her knees, grabs the line, and throws the knotted end to Brady, which has him grabbing for it and turning us towards the shore straight away. I pull my legs up onto the board to reduce the drag, but honestly I probably didn't need to. Like the beast he is, Brady pulls us all the way to the beach.

Later that night I can't help but think of Aria and how much of herself she gives to those around her. She didn't seem to understand how her dedication to training Brady was such an incredible thing, and she put all of the recognition on Brady rather than herself.

Based on what I've seen in the little time I've known her, it seems like she is always giving or helping others. The little glimpses of her kind heart I've seen while together, from helping strangers in the store figure out a destination on a map to holding the door for people and picking up things they dropped, or babysitting, she is always helping those around her. The more she helps others, the more it seems to energize her, and bring her happiness.

I think that is part of what keeps drawing me to her. She is one of the most authentic people I've ever met. She doesn't seem caught up in money and prestige and gossip, she just has her life set up in a way that suits her and she enjoys it. It's refreshing to be honest, to be out of the city and with someone like that.

And that's a big reason I've been trying to ignore this growing urge to kiss her, because I haven't felt a level of friendship like this with a female in a long time. I don't want to ruin that.

I'm attracted to her, that I know, but I'm also finding myself opening up to her more than I have to anyone except the guys, giving her little tidbits about my life both in and outside my career.

I want to spend all my time with her, which is why I've planned a fun day for the two of us tomorrow. It's not a date, but I did put some extra thought into it. She has a full day off from work, and it seems like she is always doing so much for other people. I want to show her a fun time where she can just sit back and enjoy it.

And as dangerous as it feels to be getting close to her, I keep doing it, just lowkey hoping it doesn't come back to bite me in the ass.

Speaking of being comfortable, I opened our text thread to give her a heads up.

ME: Be sure to wear sneakers tomorrow.

Less than a minute passed before I got a response.

ARIA: Good to know, thanks. Any other clues? :)
ME: Nope. Have to wait and see.
ARIA: I'm looking forward to it.
ME: Me too.

I've always enjoyed activity type dates, and while this isn't a date per se, I know Aria likes this type of stuff too.

She hearted my message and left it at that, so as much as I wanted to continue the conversation I didn't, knowing how it might come across if I do.

I can go a day without texting her. It's just like texting with the guys. Sometimes there's a lot to say, sometimes we don't hear from each other for a while.

I just keep telling myself that as I press the side button to light up my screen every 30 minutes the rest of the night, just in case she has something else to say.

15
ARIA

Monday, June 26th

The next day Evie declares it a perfect beach morning for Gracie so we pack up and meet up at one of the local dog friendly beaches. Gracie would be sad if Brady wasn't there to dig in the sand with her.

Giggles explode next to me so I pop my eyes up over my book to see Gracie sharing her sunhat with Brady, who looks quite amused to be wearing shocking pink with purple daisies.

I snap a pic of the two of them and show it to Evie who is trying not to fall asleep on the blanket next to me after a long night with Gracie.

"Swim!" Gracie climbs to stand in the way toddlers do that looks like it takes all the effort in the world. She begins to toddle towards the water. Fear instantly overtakes me, my mouth opening as my stomach falls and I jump to my feet.

"NO! Gracie!"

She turns around just as I am scooping her up, and I nuzzle her little neck rolls. Returning to the blanket, Evie is there giving me a puzzled look and asks, "You ok?"

"She doesn't have her floaties on." Putting Gracie down I grab her arm bands, slipping her little arms through the holes and snapping the chest part around her back.

"She wasn't going in without them." Evie gives me a sad smile as she tries to reassure me.

"You don't know that. She could have." My voice trembles as tears fill my eyes. I try to wipe them away without being obvious, but it's no use, they just keep coming.

Evie takes my hand in hers. "She's safe Ari, I won't let her go in without them, I promise."

"I know you won't, I'm just extra worked up today." I have been since yesterday's conversation made me go back in time.

"Want to talk about it?" Evie settles Gracie in her lap with a little snack cup of goldfish crackers.

"I took Ian out with me for training with B-man, and something triggered me. Just been thinking about Peter a lot since then."

"Did you tell Ian about him?" Evie curiously asked. She knows I don't talk about him much.

"No, not yet." Or maybe never. It's not exactly a fun conversation.

"I think he would be supportive if he knew."

"Hmmm." I bet he would be; after all he is such a nice guy. But family trauma doesn't always have to transfer to friend circles. Not everyone gets it.

"Ari sad?" Gracie's sweet voice carries as she pats my hand with her small pudgy one.

"I'm ok baby girl. Want to go for a swim?" I stand, brushing sand off my ass, and reach out my hands to grab her. I lift her up and plant a big kiss on her cheek.

"Bay-dee swim too!" She does a little gimme hand motion to Brady to get him to follow us as we head to the water. Which of course he does, and while we swim Brady takes extra care not to stray too far from Gracie—just like he does every time.

She is his baby too after all.

We leave before lunch, which gives me plenty of time to dry Brady off and shower before Ian picks me up for our afternoon plans.

Dropping my keys and phone on the console table, I cross the living room to my reading chair next to the fireplace, falling into it.

My eyes find the frame with the picture, taken over 20 years ago. Tears fill my eyes as I lift it up, cradling it against my chest, my head falling against the back of the couch.

"I miss you, little bro."

16
IAN

July 3rd

I pull up to the address Aria had sent me, and take in the small but quaint A frame cabin she calls home. Even though we had been spending time together, we usually just met up, so this is the first time I am seeing where Aria lived.

There are pots of colorful flowers outside, and the entire thing looks like a little storybook plopped down in the middle of an enchanted forest. It's adorable, just like her.

I cross the flagstone walkway and pause to listen to the sounds of a wind chime swaying in the wind. My mom loves wind chimes, and has quite the collection on her back porch. It's a sound I've always associated with being home.

I knock on the door and laugh as the sound is immediately greeted by an impressively deep bark, one that will easily let Aria know I am here if she didn't hear the knock.

The door opens, and rays of sunshine perfectly frame an angel in the doorway. She has on a white tight tank top that even though it had a high neck, still showed off her figure in a beautiful and feminine way, and a pair of light green linen shorts, along with tan sneakers. Her wavy hair is down, soft layers framing her face, and her skin appeared to shimmer from an innate summer glow.

Stunning.

"Hi" She smiles sweetly while holding on to the door with one hand.

"Hi. You look beautiful." I lean down and place my hand on her hip and can't help myself, give her a kiss on the cheek. Her sweet smell of vanilla traveled up to my nose when I leaned in close. I notice her cheek flushes with pink at the touch.

"Thank you, is this ok for whatever we are doing today?" I hadn't told her where we were going, just that it was a mystery and I had it all taken care of.

"It's perfect." I chose shorts and sneakers as well.

Just then Brady noses his way past Aria and plops himself straight on my foot. "Well, hello to you too, Brady." I scratch him on the head and he turns it into my palm, tongue lagging out the side of his enormous mouth.

"He'd let you do that all day." Aria gestures to where my hand is cradling and rubbing his head.

"I'm going to need a raincheck on that then boy, because I need to take your mama out for some fun."

Aria tells Brady to go inside and then grabs a sweater and her purse from the console table in the hall. I can't help but admire her ass in those shorts when she turns around.

"Ready?" I clear my throat, mentally clearing the need to adjust myself in front of her.

"Ready!"

I lead her out to my car and open the door for her, holding it while she climbs in.

"Thank you." It is obvious she appreciates the gesture. Good, I don't like when women try to do everything themselves. I love good old-fashioned manners like my mama raised me on.

"My pleasure." I give her a wink and circle the front of my car before climbing in.

"Where to?"

"You'll see."

As we pull up to Heavenly Village, I park the car and look over at Aria. "I assume you've been here a bunch, but I thought we'd start the day off having some fun."

She smiles and unbuckles, and I make my way out of the car to open her door. Before I know what I'm doing, I offer her my hand, which she takes, and we head over the Gondola line.

17
ARIA

OMG. We're holding hands? What is this?

I don't know what made him do it, but as soon as he grabbed my hand it just felt right, even though it made my heart race a little.

Friends can hold hands, right?

I'm sure he just doesn't want me to get lost in the crowd, since it's so busy and all.

I'm still internally reeling from the feeling of Ian holding my hand—something he has never done—before when I realize we are going to take the Gondola up the mountain.

There is a range of activities to do up on the mountain, from hiking, and summer tubing, to zip-lining and the mountain coaster. I love all of them and haven't been up here in a while, so I'm excited for whatever the day brings.

Letting go of my hand, Ian scans tickets on his phone and we step into our car, sitting on the bench side by side. The doors close and we lurch forward, and begin our ascent up the mountain.

"You are going to love the view from the top." I say, glancing out at the steep incline below.

"It looks beautiful from here." I turn my gaze to see what he is looking at, and find his eyes focused on me. I feel my face flush from his stare and the fact that he called me beautiful twice today. He does a quick blink like he is in a trance and maybe didn't mean to say that out loud and we both shift our focus out the window, ignoring his statement.

As the car climbs higher, I point out a few things, and we talk about what Tahoe is like in the winter (So. Much. Snow.).

"Do you do any winter sports besides hockey?" I want to know everything about him, my curiosity insatiable.

"Honestly, it's been a long time. I love skiing and snowmobiling, but I don't get to do them much because I can't risk getting hurt during the hockey season. Coach would kill me if I got injured doing something off the ice." He doesn't appear sad about it, just absolute in his commitment to hockey.

"How long does the season run? I know general stuff about it, but nothing that specific."

"Training camp starts at the end of September, and the season runs to the end of April, or longer, depending on if you make the playoffs. June if you make it to the Cup." He runs his hand through her hair and stares off, almost like he is seeing the schedule play out before his eyes.

"That's a long time. Barely a break." I reach over and squeeze his hand. He squeezes mine back and holds it in place as our gondola arrives at the top of the mountain, gestures for me to stand and exit first.

His palm finds the small of my back and I crave more connection. My body is on fire from the proximity in a way it hasn't been the past few days hanging out with him, though I'm not sure why it is doing that now.

The view at the top is an incredible 360 degree glimpse of Lake Tahoe and the Sierra Nevada Mountains. We make our way over to the mountain coaster, and I clap my hands in excitement. "Oh, you are going to love this!"

"I'm glad you approve. I wasn't sure how you felt about rock climbing or ziplining and I saw we could go together on this one. Looked like fun." He seems relieved that I am happy with his pick.

There's a long line of people waiting, but somehow we bypass that and are led to the front by a staff member who greets Ian excitedly, like they were expecting him.

"How did you get us to jump the line?"

"Perks of the job, baby." I know he is just saying it jokingly, but hearing him call me baby gets me all worked up and I bite my lip to keep the sparks I'm feeling inside from showing.

After the staff member double checks our weight combined is under the limit, he leads us to the coaster cars, which are like long sleds with a straight back seat. There are two spots to sit, with the driver sitting the furthest back and the rider sitting inside their outstretched legs.

It's definitely cozy and the closest to each other we have ever been.

"Are you sure you don't want one of your own?" I ask, standing looking down, uncertain if I'll even fit there with his muscular legs.

Ian moves behind me, puts his hands on top of my shoulders and gives a little squeeze. "I'm sure." Then he moves around me to climb in and buckles up. He spreads his legs, creating an opening for me to climb into.

Right. In between. His legs.

I climb in and settle as far up as I can to give him room, saying, "Pretty sure this front seat is meant for kids."

"Sit all the way down, princess." He reaches around my waist and pulls me back flush against his chest, my ass and legs molding to the inside of his body. Our bodies have never touched like this, and my entire body tingles with the connection.

I buckle and wiggle around, trying to get comfortable when I feel a tight squeeze on my arm.

"Going to need you to stop doing that." He says in a low growl.

I turn my head to look up at him over my shoulder. "Sorry, just trying to give you space."

"I don't need, or want space from you." His voice is low and right at my ear, for only me to hear. "But what I don't need is for your firm little ass to keep rubbing against my cock making me hard before we take off."

I gasp at how direct his words are, and how they are turning me on, and suddenly am aware of what exactly I'm rubbing up against. I can feel the outline of his cock through his shorts, and try to keep myself as still as possible.

"Better?"

"Much."

We take off on the coaster, and the force of the ride presses me even more into him. His arms wrap around me protectively, my arms filling with goosebumps at this touch.

His large hands caressing my skin, "Cold?" I shake my head, unable to say it's his touch making it happen.

The thick cords of his forearms wrap around me as we speed up and soar down, around, and through the forest.

"This is great!" Ian yells over the wind, and I squeeze his forearm in response. We both shriek at a tight turn and laugh at ourselves. Soon we are whooping and hollering, cheering like kids as we cover the rock and tree dotted terrain.

The coaster slows and comes to a stop back at the loading area. Ian's breath is warm on my neck, "That was fun. Thanks for going with me." I glance back and tilt my head up to look at him, locking eyes with his deep blue ones.

Ian stares without breaking the connection, his eyes searching mine. Unable to control myself, I glance down at his lips, and back up, biting down on my bottom lip expectantly. He slowly lowers his face, like he wants to close the distance as much as I want him to.

"How was it?" We jump apart, as much as we can while still strapped in, and look up to the worker standing next to the coaster car.

"Uh, great thanks." I hurry to unbuckle and hop out of the car, with Ian following, both of us looking anywhere but the other and completely ignoring the moment we just shared.

Once we were back down the mountain, Ian had plans to take us to a Tapas bar and then an Apres Ski lounge for a drink. It was the perfect thing to cool my body after the fire that broke inside my core on the coaster.

We talk about his family, and I learn that his mom raised him and now lives close to him in San Jose. We compare which actors would play us in a movie about our lives, and our favorite playlists, and other random questions to figure each other out on a deeper level.

It feels so natural and easy being there with him, just like it has the past few outings we did together. He is open and generous with his words and compliments, and has an infectious energy that just lights up the table and the entire room. He asks thoughtful open-ended questions about me, and didn't once try to brag about himself or his accomplishments.

Walking out the door of the lounge, I want nothing more than for this night to go on forever, but tomorrow I have an early shift. As it starts to get late, we head back towards his car where he, like the gentleman I'm learning he is more every time we hang out, opens my door for me, just like every other door this evening. My inner cheerleader is waving a green flag all over the place and I'm having to remind myself that he doesn't see me like that, despite the close call we had on the coaster. The heart racing was almost certainly due to the high speed of the coaster more than anything else.

"Today was...kind of perfect, thank you for all of that., Ian" He grabs my hand across the console and rubs his thumb over the back of my hand.

"My pleasure." He gives me a smile and glances over. My smile brightens—and I bit my lip, thinking about how much I'd loved to just lean across the console and kiss him. I quickly shake the thought out of my head and face the front, buckling myself just to keep my hands busy.

The ride home goes by far too fast, and before I know it we are pulling up to my little rental cabin that I've called home the past few years.

I unbuckle my seatbelt and fidget with my sweater, feeling out of sorts.

He opens my door and offers me his hand, which I take. He pulls me quicker than I expected, causing my body to land flush against his and he grabs my biceps to steady me. I look up to see him staring down at me, eyes alit with desire, his fingers grazing down my arms.

I tentatively slide one hand to his hard chest, cautiously testing if he will pull away, and gently feel the lines of his muscle through his shirt.

He lets out a little groan, and I watch his eyes burn with an internal struggle. His chest pounds under my fingertips and he inhales deeply, lowering his face to mine, which he has cupped in one hand and bringing his lips so near I can feel his breath dancing against mine.

"Fuck it."

My heart surges and I rise up as he gives in, closing the gap and bringing his mouth to mine, in a kiss I've been secretly desiring for all evening.

It's like fire, all-consuming, leaving me parched for more. His lips are soft and tender, and then he is teasing my lip with his tongue and I open willingly for him.

He snakes his other arm around my waist and presses me against his hard body and the car, kissing me hard as our tongues play. Every sound around me is blocked out as I fall deeper into the most amazing first kiss I've ever experienced.

My arms find the back of his neck, and then his hair, and I run my fingers through it dragging him closer to me like I need to breathe him in just to survive.

All too soon he slows the kiss, giving soft kisses on my lips and the forehead, pausing as if trying to collect himself, before pulling himself back and whispering "Goodnight Aria."

After he watches me get inside and drives away, I throw myself on the couch on top of Brady, using his fluffy body as a pillow.

Wow. What. a. Fucking. Kiss.

...

"Eek, gimme gimme" I make grabby motions to Evie and pull my favorite little girl from her arms. Evie follows me through the open door carrying Gracie's diaper bag.

"Thanks again for agreeing to watch her so last minute. I knew having the 4th off was too good to be true." I wave her off.

I love taking care of Gracie and being able to be there for Evie. So when the bartender who was supposed to cover the Alpine Club's Celebratory Boozy Brunch called in "sick" (on a holiday of course) I was more than happy to step in and spend time with my favorite girl on my day off.

"Do you have some time before you have to leave? I feel like I haven't seen you in forever!" I say.

Evie gives me a look. "I wonder why that is, Miss hockey player's best friend," grabbing Gracie's toes as she says it in a taunting tone.

"I know I know..." Part of me doesn't want to tell her what happened, my brain still believes that even though I've been spending a lot of time with him—even though he kissed me—that I'm just helping him find his way around as a friend and eventually he will grow bored. "I'm sure he will find plenty of people to keep him busy once he knows literally anyone else in the area."

The thought of that brings major depressive vibes as I don't want anyone else playing the role of tour guide for him.

"He doesn't seem to be putting in the effort to get to know anyone apart from you." She smirks, obviously insinuating.

I fidget with my fingers, needing to fess up. "Well, um, he did, kinda, kiss me last night..." I glance up to see Evie gaping at me.

"WHAT THE HELL! You're just telling me? Details, now, all of them!" She pulls me and Gracie down to the couch and crosses her legs, waiting for me to spill.

And so I do. I recount every minute of our day together. How, even though it wasn't a date, it seemed so much like one. The way our connection seems to intensify the more we get to know each other, and how toe-curling the kiss was.

Evie takes all of it in, squealing at all the right moments, and fanning herself when I describe being pressed up against his body and then his car. She wiggles her eyebrows. "One hockey boyfriend, coming right up."

I chuff at that. "Yeah, okay, don't get ahead of yourself."

"Yeah, okay is right. You're funny, gorgeous and outdoorsy." Evie ticks each characteristic off on one of her fingers. "He'd be an idiot not to lock that down"

It's not that I don't think he likes me—obviously he wouldn't have kissed me if he didn't want to, but I don't want to set myself up for false expectations. I couldn't even hold on to a normal college boy. Ian's a famous athlete whose type—according to past Instagram posts which I have, of course, stalked—seems much more like the special guests I cater to, and not the server taking care of them. Gorgeous models draped his arms at event photos, dating back as far as I could scroll.

"You know just because he is famous that doesn't make him better than you right? You are a catch, the most caring, kind hearted and generous person I've ever known, and any guy would be the luckiest man on earth to be with you." I pull her into a hug, letting her words soak into me, even though she is saying that as my best friend and is delusional.

"And this is why I love you, a daily dose of mood booster." I then change the subject, asking Gracie about her day.

"Om baby, nom nom nom" She pushes her baby doll up to me with a block.

"Oh, is the baby hungry? Let's feed her." Together with the block as a baby bottle, we feed her doll until Gracie is satisfied and squirms to get down to go give Brady some love. Evie and I watch as she toddles over to where he is laying in the sun as it streams through the window, waiting patiently for her to approach. He is gentle as she gives him little pats, rewarding her with a kiss.

Evie grabs my arm, making me turn to face her.

"But for real, I need you to fast-forward to the action stage, because I'm dying to know what kind of power a hockey player has in bed." Evie raises her eyebrows suggestively a few times and I laugh.

"Why don't you just call Jack or one of the other players for a hookup then?" I link arms with her as she heads towards the front door to leave.

"Hmm, think Ian would invite them up for the weekend for a booty call for me?" Laughing, she heads out to her car and I go inside to spend the morning with my mini bestie.

ME: *cute picture of Gracie laying on Brady like a pillow*

IAN: World's furriest pillow. Is that the famous Gracie?

ME: Isn't she precious?

IAN: She's cute, you at Evie's today?

ME: Yup, watching Gracie for her. Getting my cuddle time in.

ME: *Photo of me snuggling a sleepy Gracie*

Ian hearts the photo. Realizing we never discussed if he had any plans for the 4th, I invite him to join Evie and I for our annual picnic dinner on the beach to watch the fireworks. He responds that Coach Johnson invited him to join his family, and is heading over there for a BBQ and fireworks at his lakeside home.

A flutter of disappointment washes over me, and I feel my mouth turn down. The past week I've spent much more time than I would have anticipated, between the bike ride through town, hiking and training. But my soul wants more. I feel the pull to see him again, just to be in his orbit.

I go out on a limb and invite him to go swimming with me and Brady after my morning shift tomorrow, and almost wake Gracie who has fallen asleep curled up against me, when he accepts.

And cross my fingers the kiss wasn't just a one-time fluke.

18

IAN

Wednesday, July 5th

ME: I kissed her.
    WHITTY: About time.
    ME: *flip off emoji*
    WHITTY: And....
    ME: holy fuck. Kind of want to do it again.
    WHITTY: So do it man. If she makes you happy, then this can only make it better right?

I just hope he's right, and I didn't just screw everything up.

Waiting on her little porch area, my brain is rehashing how the feeling of her mouth on mine and her body heat seeping through my clothes ignited a flame that left me finishing with my hand in the shower when I got home.

I want to make sure she is ok after we crossed the line and kissed. I don't know what this might turn into, but I do know the feeling I got the other night was the best I've felt in a long time and I need to experience it again, and again.

As much as I wanted to spend the 4th with her, I had already promised Coach I'd go over there. The guy's lucky I like him so much or I probably would have ditched him for Aria instead. When she suggested heading to the lake today, I couldn't pass up the chance to spend time with her and see her in that itty bitty bathing suit once more.

I glance up as I hear gravel crunch beneath tires, and see her smiling as she puts the Jeep in park and jumps out. I make my way to meet her halfway.

"Hi! I hope you haven't been waiting too long." Her smile is bright as she nervously adjusts her hair. Little does she know with the way I'm feeling looking at her I'd wait forever just to see her.

"Not at all." I don't know what to do with my hands but I feel like scooping her up and kissing her senselessly. Probably not the best way to go about getting another chance.

Aria grabs her bag with both hands, motioning with it towards the house. "Just let me get changed and we can go."

I follow her into her cabin, and give Brady pets as he runs up to greet us. Aria lets Brady out before bringing him back in to hang with me while she changes.

I take the opportunity to look around the place. It is clean and cozy, not at all sparse like the rental I am in. There are plants and candles, blankets and dog toys, everything neatly organized but on display as if they are a part of daily life. Her fridge has messy artwork I am assuming Gracie must have made, based on the little handprint I see on one.

This place feels like her. It is comfortable—it feels like home.

"Ok, that is much better, I despise that uniform so it feels great to take it off." I turn to see Aria exit her bedroom, and I take in her long tan legs, and her wavy hair that she has let free from her work bun to hang loosely down around her shoulders.

She looks beautiful. Natural. Comfortable in just a long sleeve sun shirt and athletic shorts. Stunning.

"Want me to pack something to eat?" She walks towards the kitchen.

"I've got that taken care of actually." I lift the bag I brought with me, complete with a picnic and a blanket.

Her mouth parts, stunned. "Are you for real? That's so nice of you. Let me just grab a few things then." Aria sets her water bottle on the little island and reaches into a cabinet, grabbing something and turns around with a smile.

"Sour Patch Kids? Those are my favorite!"

She grins. "I know. You mentioned them at the bar. I figured I would buy some in case you came over at some point." Now I'm the one who goes quiet from stunned disbelief. I can't help but stare at this girl who just shrugs away her kind gesture.

Not only did she remember my favorite candy from a random comment at the bar the first night we met, but she bought them for me as well? That's one of the nicest things someone has done for me.

"You're so thoughtful, thank you." I grab her hand and pull her in for a hug, inhaling her sweet scent, taking longer than necessary to release her.

Back at Hidden Cove, which is now in my top 3 beaches, I glance up to see her notice my slow perusal of her body as she strips out of her clothes.

"Why are you looking at me like that?"

If she only knew the thoughts going on in my head. "Just seeing how long it will take you to get in before I have to come out and carry you in."

She laughs as she takes her time wading out to me.

"Oh my god it feels colder today somehow!" She checks on Brady who is happily swimming around as she makes her way over to where I am treading water.

I move to where I can stand and reach out a hand to help pull her the final foot and once she grabs on, pull her into my arms.

Holding her around her waist with one arm, I tuck a section of hair behind her ear, my eyes locked on the intense expression of want and desire I see in hers.

"I didn't say hello the way I wanted to." I should have kissed her as soon as I saw her but the vision of her bathed in sunlight took the movement from my body and the opportunity passed. I waited the entire time in her cabin and the car, the whole hike down from the parking lot.

She peers up under long soft eyelashes. "And what way was that?" Her fingers toy softly with the hair at the base of my neck.

Unable to hold back another second, I slowly lower my face to hers, giving her plenty of time to pull back, in case for some reason she's changed her mind since last night. Instead she tightens her grip around my neck, and pushes up, our mouths collide like magnets drawn to each other.

Heaven. If someone told me that Lake Tahoe was Heaven, I'd believe them.

Because right now everything I associate with the Gods is happening. My body is alive, thrumming with intensity as I take her mouth, gently at first and then plunging, desperate for a deeper connection. I lick the seams of her lips, begging for entrance, and when she grants it, I attack like a traveler desperate for water in the desert.

My hands grip the back of her head and push it even closer, as if my body could not be close enough unless it can climb inside and become one with her soul.

She runs her fingers through my hair and I groan, thrusting my hips and moving both arms down to her perky ass, gripping and lifting her up.

Aria wraps her legs around my waist and squirms, bringing my cock to life and I press her core to it, feeling the imprint with just swimwear between us.

Everything about this kiss is magical, and I never want it to end, but I know if I don't pull back I'll end up inside her right here in the open where anyone could see us.

And I don't want to share her with the world.

I slowly let the kiss taper off, kissing her softly on the lips, then on both eyes, and finally, her forehead, before letting my forehead fall to hers.

"Fuck, Aria. That was incredible."

"Yeah," she whispers, caressing my hair with her fingers. "It really was."

The intimacy of the moment is interrupted by Brady barking from the shore.

"He's a bit jealous, I'm giving you all my attention."

"I don't blame him one bit. I quite like having your attention." I squeeze her ass and slide my hands along the curve of her spine, and bring my mouth down for another kiss. Keeping this one short took all my willpower.

She slides down out of my grip to stand, and I take her cheek in my palm and make sure I have her attention, the sudden need to take her out and shower her with extravagance coming over me. "Go out with me."

"Like on a date?" She asks, like I couldn't possibly want it.

"Yes, like a date. I want to take you out. Say ok." I know she wants to.

"Ok." Her teeth bite her lip like it so often does when she is nervous, and I groan, and pull her in to place my mouth over hers instead.

"Good. Now, the last one back to the shore is a rotten egg!" I push off with maximum effort and start back to shore, only to hear her laughing and complaining about the unfair head start behind me.

19
ARIA

Thursday, July 6th

The next evening, I twirl in front of my full length mirror, quietly assessing and stressing over my choice of outfit for our date tonight.

I still can't believe Ian wants to take me out on a date. Or that we kissed. I'm nervous about how that might change things between us—I've grown to love having him as a friend but am excited things have progressed to this level.

Part of me is already dreading the end, which I know will come, but I try to stay in the present and be grateful for the opportunity to get close to him.

"How do I look?" I ask Brady who gives me a bit of a side eye from his position on the couch.

Without any indication either way, I convince myself I look cute enough in my thin strapped navy wrap dress and heels. I took extra time to do my hair and makeup today, and hope I didn't go overboard. After all Ian has seen me mostly casual, but I wanted to dress up for him tonight.

Ian told me he made reservations at the Wine Bar inside the Casino nearby, which makes me think we might hit some slots afterwards too. I love how everything we do has some sort of element of fun.

A knock at the door has me doing one last glance in the mirror, and then I'm opening it to a beautiful bouquet of flowers held by an even more beautiful man. He is wearing dark denim that hugs his hips, a button down that matches his eyes, and a sports coat.

"You look stunning." He leans down and softly kisses my cheek.

"Thank you. Are those for me?" I admire the gorgeous arrangement of roses, anemones, and sweet peas.

"Nope, they are for Brady." Ian laughs out loud and drapes his free arm around my waist, giving me a playful squeeze. "Of course they are for you, Aria."

"They are beautiful." I take the flowers and move into the kitchen to put them in water. "I appreciate you getting them for me. Thank you."

After saying goodbye to Brady, Ian takes my hand and leads me to his car, but before he opens the door he takes my face in his hands, and presses a sweet, lingering kiss to my lips.

"I've been waiting all day to kiss you again."

Though I had been nervous leading up to the date about how things might differ from the other times we hung out, everything is just as easy as it was before.

I ask Ian tons of questions about his team, wanting to know all about his position and his love for the game. Hearing how grueling of a career it is and how much focus and dedication he puts into being a leader for his team makes me admire him that much more.

When he reaches out and grabs my hand across the table, it feels like a dream, as it does when he kisses me in the elevator on the way up to the casino, a kiss so hot that my panties are instantly wet and makes me wish there were more floors to slow this ride down.

Ian takes my hand and pulls me out to the casino floor. I take in the sight, the mix of bright flashy lights coming from the slots to the luxury coolness of the sleek wood surrounding the game tables. We make our way over to a bar in the center, positioning me in front of him while we order, and kissing the slope of my neck while we wait.

Two hours later we had lost, won back and lost again our winnings for the evening, and neither of us caring in the least. We spent the entire time laughing and challenging each other, with him finding my hidden competitive streak truly hilarious.

Walking hand in hand out of the casino, we make our way out to the courtyard area which has a great view of the lake. At this time of night, it is a black abyss lit by a bright full moon, with lights from houses and the surrounding towns dotting the shoreline. The stars shone above like diamonds, casting a mystical glow on the lake surface.

I pause at an especially pretty point and feet his muscular arms wrap around me from behind. Pressing back into his chest and taking in his warmth, it feels perfect here, and I never want to move from this spot.

"What are you thinking?" His jawline is scruffy as he rubs his cheek to mine.

"That this is a dream and I don't want to wake up." I snuggle into his embrace.

"Why do you think it's a dream?" His voice hums in my ear.

"I mean look at us, you are this amazing famous athlete and I'm just me. And yet here I am on a date with you." His right arm tightens on my hip and he pulls me around to face him.

"You are amazing. I'm the lucky one that you agreed to come out with me." He gives me a soft peck on the lips.

"Whoa it's Ian Sanderson!" We both turn to see a couple of college age guys grabbing at each other and pointing, with cameras out, begging for a photo.

And just like that, our intimate little moment turns into a fan meet and greet, which Ian handles with professional ease before leading us away and taking me home. He left me at my door with another toe curling kiss that made me want to invite him inside and into my bed, though much to Evie's dismay the next day, I did not.

• • •

A deep nutty and cinnamon aroma of freshly brewed coffee hits my nostrils as I put the lids on the two travel coffee mugs I've prepared for our morning adventure. It's only 5:15am Monday morning, but Ian should be here any time for our next date.

I had been busy with weddings all weekend, and haven't seen Ian since our casino date, though we've been texting and FaceTiming daily.

Today was my idea, and I can't wait to show him the best spot for a sunrise in all of Tahoe.

Gravel crunches as a car pulls up, and I give Brady a kiss on the head where he lays sprawled out on the couch. All I get is a huff in return—he's definitely not a morning dude. I slip on my sneakers and my quarter zip fleece, make sure my beanie and sunglasses are in my bag. As I open the door I see a handsome guy on my stoop getting ready to knock, his breath visible in the chilly morning air.

"Good morning!" I say, taking in his hair which is a little more roughed up than usual and the adorable sleepy look on his face.

"Mornin." He yawns, making me laugh.

"I know it's early, but I promise it's worth it." I lift one mug to him.

"Of course it's worth it, I get to spend time with you." He grabs both mugs from my hands and leans down, giving me a soft kiss on the lips, a featherweight pressure that lingers unhurriedly, before resting his forehead on mine.

"Did you sleep ok?" His voice is gravely and unused. I nod. "Good."

We walk to the car, and I reach over and take a mug. Gesturing with it in my hand to the other, I add "I thought you might want some caffeine."

Ian takes a drink of his while opening the car door for me. "I knew I liked you," giving me a wink. My heart leaps a little at the comment.

We drive to the lookout point, our conversation more subdued than usual due to the early hour, and pull in, the lake a glistening beacon as the sky begins to lighten in preparation for the sunrise. I slip on my beanie as Ian grabs his coat and a blanket from the backseat before getting out of the car.

Even though it can get around 80 during the day in the summer, the temperature drops to the 40s overnight and mornings are always brisk and cool. It's one of the things I love about living here, every day feels like the perfect camping trip, where you can curl up by a fire in cozy clothes and swim in the lake on the same day.

We walk to the rock wall, a waist high granite ledge that makes the perfect seat to capture the start of a new day. Swinging our legs over, we sit side by side, warm inside the blanket Ian wraps around us both, and sip our coffee, quiet and content just being in the moment.

The serene surroundings reflect the calmness I feel inside when I am around him. Even if my heart is racing from the chemistry, there is an innate calm whenever Ian is near.

Fingers latched and holding the blanket around us, Ian's pinky caresses my own in lazy circles.

Ever so slowly the sun rises, revealing the reason this spot is utter perfection. Right in the middle of the curve of Emerald Bay, we are looking out across the lake to the sun as it rises directly over Fannette Island. It's the only island in the lake, and this viewpoint frames it as the centerpiece.

We take it all in, moving only to take sips of our coffees, or to glance at the effect of daybreak from various angles.

The sky ignites into a symphony of vibrant oranges and pinks, before blending into deep purples as it stretches into the waning night sky. The lake is completely calm, allowing the voluminous clouds bursting with colors to be reflected across the water as if it were nature's mirror.

I sigh with happiness, and rest my head on Ian's shoulder. He wraps his arm around me, kissing the top of my head. "It's incredible," he whispers as if to not break the spell of the moment. "I've never seen anything like this." We stay snuggled together, my right hand intertwined with the fingers of his around my shoulder, as we watch the day continue to enter with extravagance.

"I can see why you love it here." Ian leans back, straddling the rock wall and faces me.

"It's one of my favorite spots."

"I mean the Tahoe area in general. It's like another planet compared to the city—the water, the trees, mountains, it's unreal. It's almost hard to imagine the traffic and the buildings when surrounded by everything here." He pauses, taking in the evergreens and the granite points of the island. "It's peaceful."

"Do you like living in San Jose?"

He laughs, "No, not really...not at all, actually. The people there are great but I'm not exactly a city guy. Definitely wouldn't be there if it weren't for hockey." He shrugs. "But it's not that bad, and there are lots of cool places to explore within a few hours driving distance. And during the season I'm hardly there, and if I am, it's basically for practices or games."

"It must be hard, growing up somewhere so full of nature and then going to a big city like that." I can't imagine not living among the towering pines and open water.

"It was at first, but having a reason for living there made it worth it."

"Do you think you'll stay there after you are done with hockey?" I ask, even though I don't know when that would be, how long he would keep playing.

He purses his lips like he is considering it. "It depends."

"On what?"

"On what I end up doing after. If I were to stay around and work with the team in some other capacity, or what I decide to do when I retire."

Curious, I inquire a little deeper. "What are some of your options, or I guess, what do you want to do after?"

He slaps his leg lightly. "That's the question."

I cock my head slightly, trying to get him to divulge further but not wanting to rush him.

After a minute, he continues. "I'm honestly not totally sure what I want to do when I'm done. A lot of guys go on to coaching, or sportscasting, or doing something related to the game. So I could go that route. Or I could do nothing, and just do whatever makes me happy in the moment." For some reason, I don't see him just sitting around and being content. He likes movement, adventure, going places and doing stuff.

"Would either of those things make you happy?" I take his hand, and play with his fingers in mine.

"That's the thing. I don't think so. I have always been so steady with having a goal, a mission that I put everything into. Lately it feels like once I meet it, then that whole next stage of my life is seriously lacking in that department." He stands and paces a little next to the wall. "I don't know what I want, or what would make me happy, and everybody keeps asking what's next, knowing

I'll probably only play another year or two, and I just don't have an answer." He finishes sounding utterly defeated, facing away from me.

I rise, and standing behind him, slowly wrap my arms around his waist and hug tightly. "I'm sorry for being yet another person for asking." I mumble into his jacket.

He pulls me around to his front and wraps me tightly in his arms before releasing just enough to put enough space to look into my eyes.

"I didn't mean you, I appreciate you asking me. I know you want to get to know me more and that is a big part of my life." I relaxed a little, knowing I didn't cross any imaginary lines.

"I'm just having a hard time figuring out what's next, and it scares me a little to not have it all worked out." His vulnerability is so, if I'm being honest, hot. It's nice knowing that even people who have achieved major success in life still feel lost from time to time, and being able to admit it makes me fall a little harder for this incredible man.

My heart expands and then tightens, knowing that by the time he has it all figured out, I'll just be a memory from a summer past, and won't be there to see him thrive in a new role.

The thought saddens me, and I struggle to keep it from showing.

"You don't need to have it all figured out. Just do what feels right when the time comes; whatever you choose will be perfect," I say, trying to offer encouragement.

"You know what feels right?" Ian lifts his other hand to cup the back of my head. "This." He brings our mouths together, and we kiss as the sun turns the sky a brilliant blue.

20

IAN

Thursday, July 20th

We fall into an easy groove after our sunrise date, with me spending time training in my home gym or helping the kids at the rink while Aria is at work, and spending time together when she isn't.

We went paddle boarding over to Bonsai Island, where I had to give one too many dudes an evil stare when I caught them checking out Aria's perfect body.

I get most of my cardio outdoors now taking hikes with Aria and Brady, both of whom are way more adept at that than I am.

And I fall more in love with Tahoe as we explore the numerous bike trails that circle the lake, giving break taking views that even I have to admit are more stunning in person than the ones back home.

Rather than feeling at peace secluded in my lakefront house as I had planned for the summer, I find myself waiting for her to get off work so I can see her again, eager to get out and rediscover my love for the outdoors.

Being around Aria is like second nature. There's no pressure to live up to some crazy expectation or to impress her with flashy gifts and dates. Don't get me wrong, I find myself wanting to shower her with gifts and plan extraordinary dates that she is definitely worthy of. But unlike when I dated Amber and the vibe I caught from more recent hookups, Aria isn't looking for those things.

Or at least I don't think she is.

She seems content with how things are right now, cozy and simple in this little bubble we've created for ourselves.

We've agreed to just take things slow and just let things progress naturally. We haven't made anything official, which makes it easier to pretend I'm not starting to get attached to her.

Not starting to think about how she might fit in with the guys, or how great it would be to see her wearing my jersey and sitting in the stands at a game.

All things I should avoid if I want things to stay stable.

I find myself opening up to her, giving her the genuine parts of me that not many people see. That day on the rock wall she listened as I rambled on about not knowing what I want to do after retirement, and unlike when I've talked about it with people before where everyone has an opinion, she just...offered support.

Encouraged me, told me I can't make a wrong decision.

It's times like that, she is so easy to like. Drives me crazy with how much I do in fact.

My phone buzzes on the dresser as I get dressed. I lift it to see it is Whitty.

"Hey what's up man?" I finish buttoning my jeans and head over to the closet to find a shirt.

"Not much just calling to see if you want to game tonight?"

"Can't tonight, heading out to a little music fest in a bit."

"Oh yeah? Anyone good?"

"Don't even know who's playing. Something they do weekly here I guess, but the stage is right on the water here, with a bunch of food trucks and a brewery, so it sounds like a good time." I grab a black henley from the hanger and pull it over my head.

"Nice man, taking Aria?" Whitty asks, knowing we've been seeing each other. Tonight will be the first actual public event I attend with Aria, apart from the casino night.

"Yeah, and we are meeting up with Evie and her brother, who I guess lives here too." I run my fingers through my hair to try to get it to do something halfway decent.

"Meeting the friends huh? Sounds like it is getting serious." I can hear him tapping at the video game controller in the background.

"Nah, just hanging out with them. Not a big deal."

"So it wouldn't bother you if she dated someone else?" I grind my teeth at the idea of that. Fuck yes that would bother me.

Whitty takes my non response as an answer. "That's what I thought. Figure it out man, I don't want to see you get hurt again."

The idea of Aria being with someone else completely pisses me off. Not that I think she would, but I don't want anyone else getting to have her. This may not be a long term thing, but I can at least make sure she isn't entertaining other guys while we are together.

I push the thought to the back of my mind as we catch up about life. He tells me about the ranch and fills me in on what's going on with his family. I replay the day I had at the rink, where the seasonal Learn to Skate/Play group had their first "game" of the season, leaving both of us reminiscing about the early days when we first got on skates, back before we were even in Mini Mites.

There is almost nothing funnier than seeing 4-year-olds trying to skate after a puck when the gear almost swallows them whole.

Eventually he hangs up and I toss my phone aside, needing to finish getting ready for our date.

···

"Aria! Over here!" Evie flags us down from where she is sitting with a guy I assume is the brother Aria mentioned, at a prime table in the Quaking Aspens's outdoor deck space, overlooking the music stage and the lake beyond. We walked here together from her cabin, Aria knowing that the traffic would be a nightmare since according to her it usually is on music nights.

At the sound of Evie's voice, Aria grabs my hand and pulls me towards the table, something that Evie clocks immediately with a smirk.

I feel Aria's fingers twitch almost uncertainly where they are intertwined with mine, so I squeeze them tighter, wanting her to feel safe in my grip. Aria glances up at the pressure, her face in a soft yet appreciative smile.

"Evie is probably thinking she can't remember the last time she saw me holding hands with a guy." I silently rub my thumb across the back of her hand in reassurance as we approach the table.

"Evie, you remember Ian," My hand instantly misses her connection as Aria lets go to bend to give her a hug hello.

"Of course, so glad you are here for the summer!" She smiles as she reaches out to greet me with a hug as well. "Aria has been telling me all about the fun you've been getting up to." Aria's cheeks go red at that and I place my hand on the small of her back.

I like that she was talking about me.

"And this is Hunter. Hunter, this is Ian, my ugh, friend." She motions to the guy at the table, stumbling over her words. I can feel my jaw set in a firm line as I take in Evie's brother, and the lack of clarity in Aria's voice.

In that instant, my determination to make sure she knows she is more than just my friend solidifies. Tonight I'm going to show her I plan on doing a whole lot more than just being friendly with her.

"Hey man, nice to meet you." I reach out as he stands and shake his hand firmly. I don't like not knowing what, if any, history is between him and Aria, but clearly if he is important to Evie then I want to make a good impression.

While also feeling out why he's been able to be around Aria without being into her, if, in fact, that is the case. Because that seems impossible to me.

"You too." I pull out Aria's stool and motion for her to sit, and then take my seat across from Hunter, taking in the large deck with weathered high tops and industrial stools. "This is a cool place."

"Thanks man." I turn, confusion written on my face.

"He owns the brewery," Aria clarifies. "It was pretty run down when he bought it, but he has turned it into something amazing." Her pride is clearly evident, and something tugs at my heart—I want to feel her pride for me like that too.

"Wow, I didn't realize. That's cool man, congrats." We settle in, with a server coming to take our order, which ends up being a round and a tasting of some of Hunter's most popular menu picks.

The first band comes on and as we eat, drink, we talk about Evie's daughter Gracie, summer people they've seen, and other random shit. The sun sets and the lights wrapped around the deck and stage come to life, creating the perfect ambiance for a night out.

I keep one hand planted on Aria's leg the entire time, slowly making lines up with a soft touch of my fingers, creeping higher and higher in a way that has her shifting her body towards me, granting me more access. But I'm playing the long game tonight, and only want to get her riled up so she is ready.

It's a perfectly normal, small town evening with friends. And one of the best nights I've had in a while. I love seeing how Evie and Aria are together, how they finish each other's sentences and can decipher what they are talking with looks and short exclamations. Hunter and Evie seem to have a good relationship too, and I'm glad Aria has people around her like this.

...

Walking back hand in hand to her cabin later that night, my thumb traces small circles on Aria's as my brain battles the absolute need to stay casual with the intensifying desire to know she isn't with anyone else. She opens the door, inviting me in, and Brady comes by, tail wagging sleepily for pets before going back to bed. After toeing off her shoes by the door, she comes and sits next to me on the couch, snuggling into my side.

"What's the deal with Hunter?" I ask, causing her to look up at me.

"What do you mean?"

"Like have you and him ever..." I trail off, not wanting to put words to it.

"Oh god no. I pretty much see him as a brother, and definitely not one I've ever been attracted to." I feel a sense of relief at that.

"That's good." I kiss the top of her head as it rests against my chest. "I don't like the idea of you being attracted to anyone else." She turns and I lift her and bring her on top of me, while she moves to straddle my hips, placing her legs on either side.

"You don't huh?" She asks coyly. I shake my head. "And why not?"

"Because I want you all to myself." I move a chunk of hair out of her face, brushing it back behind her ear and whispering in her ear. "The things I want to do to you, need to do to you."

"So do them." She leans down and kisses me, pressing her hands to my chest.

I grab her hips and thrust her down, so she can feel how hard my dick is under her. "Do you feel how much I want you?"

"Hmm." She circles herself on me, rubbing her center over my cock. "Maybe." She bites her lip, and then, fuck me, licks the spot.

I slide my hand down her throat, circling it softly, groaning as she presses forward into my hand. "I don't like to share though."

"There's no one else, Ian. Do what you want to me." She tightens her grip, tugging at my shirt. "Please."

Her begging causes me to groan. "Say you're mine."

"I'm yours." She leans down and kisses me. Pressing her hands to my chest she stares into my eyes with an edge of concern. "Are you mine?"

I grab her hips and thrust her down, so she can feel how hard my dick is under her. "What do you think?

"I don't know… I'd like for you to be." She circles herself on me, rubbing her center over my cock.

"I'm yours baby. No one else." I slide my hand down her throat, circling it softly, groaning as she presses forward into my hand. "Say it."

"No one else."

I pull her down, taking her mouth with a fury unleashed, knowing that she is all mine, and no one else gets to savor this sweet mouth. Her tongue dances and plays with mine, as she grinds on top of me seeking friction.

I slide my hands over her ass and down her thighs, before sliding them under her skirt and back up. As my fingers dance along her skin she tilts her head, my mouth falling to her neck as I suck and nibble my way down, feasting on her pulse.

Aria's hands tangle with my hair as she pushes my head farther down, and I lick the valley in between her breasts.

"More," she pants. "More." She grabs the hem of her shirt, and lifts it over her head, removing it completely before tossing it aside.

The sight of her breasts spilling out of a lacy pink bra has my cock straining to be released. I lean forward, using one of my hands to cup her creamy breasts and rub circles over the lace, her nipple immediately responding. I take my mouth to the other, kissing the exposed skin above the bra line while rubbing my thumb over the other. Freeing the other hand from her perky ass, I slide my fingers under the strap, letting her breast fall free from its cage, and take it into my mouth.

Aria gasps as the sensation as my tongue flicks her nipple, using her hands to direct my head further into her like she is trying to enmesh the two of us together. Reaching behind her, I undo the hook and let her bra fall off. I help it to the floor quickly with a flick of my wrist before bringing my mouth to her other breast and showering it with the same attention.

"Fuck, you are gorgeous." I can barely take a breath to say it before I dive back down for more.

"Oh God, Ian, that feels so good." Aria's voice is breathy and deep, full of desire. She pulls my face back to

IN THE BLUE **143**

hers and attacks, holding it place with both hands as she takes what she wants, and what I freely give of my mouth.

I move my right hand back under her skirt, my fingers finding its way to the damp center of the silky panties underneath.

"Are you wet for me baby?" My voice comes out husky and needy.

"Find out," she huffs a breath out as she rocks on my hand, urging it to where she needs it most. God this side of Aria is something I want more of.

I slip my fingers under the fabric, and fuck, she is absolutely drenched, slick and warm, my fingers sliding easily through to her clit.

She jerks back as I circle her nub, first with my thumb as I gently stroke her core, and then with my finger as I drag lazy figure eights, hitting her bundle of nerves from all directions.

I push a finger inside, her head falling back as she begs for more.

I slide a second finger in, and continue to circle her clit with the thumb, driving her higher and higher, feeling her clenching around me.

"That's it baby, come for me" I dive forward, taking her peaked nipple into my mouth, and she shatters, drenching my fingers as she bucks into my hand, finding her release as I drag out every last bit.

21

ARIA

The sensation flows from my body, leaving me utterly drained as I come down from the high, and I fall forward onto Ian's carved chest, my head hanging loosely as I work to regain my breath.

"Incredible," he mumbles into my hair, his fingers slowly moving in bigger and bigger circles out from my dripping core.

I lift my head to see him drag one finger up to his mouth, where he inserts it and licks off the taste of my release.

"Fucking Incredible." He kisses me, sharing the taste with my tongue, and my belly ignites with desire for more. I drag my hands down his chest to the bottom of his shirt, and tug, forcing him to sit forward and let me take it off. He kisses my neck. I pull it over his head and off, before I dip my head to kiss and lick the muscles I've drooled over every time we've been swimming.

I swirl my tongue over his nipple, causing him to groan and throw his head back on the back of the couch. I adjust to give me more clearance, and then make my way down to his belt.

Ian covers my hand with his, and using a finger, forces me to look at him. "You don't have to" His eyes dilate with desire but stays restrained; he wants me to know he means it.

"I want to." I move his hand and unbuckle the belt, kissing his lips as I pop the button to his jeans and slide down the zipper. He grabs my face with his hands, keeping us attached as I lift off to help shimmy off his jeans and briefs, down over the pure muscle of his legs to the floor.

I bite my lip as I take in his naked body, carved like the smoothest stone of the Greek Gods, and his thick, long cock, standing ready against his stomach.

His thumb finds my lip, pulling it from my teeth. "That's mine to bite, not yours."

He follows through with the promise, dragging his lips and then teeth over my bottom lip before I break free. I slide to the floor in between his legs, taking my time and kissing my way down his chest as my hands seek out his cock.

My fingers flutter over the head, my thumb circling the tip and dragging the precum off, which I pop into my mouth and suck.

"Fuck baby, that is so hot." Ian encourages me without touching, looking like he is using all his restraint to hold back and let me set the pace.

I moved my hands down, slowly stroking the length, following one hand after another before returning to the top. I dip my head, and lick from the base, my tongue flat and firm as I slowly drag it up. Repeating on the other side as Ian's strong hands caress my back and arms tenderly.

I swirl my tongue around the entirety of his cock before taking it fully into my mouth, the reverent sounds of Ian's pleasure urging me to take him deeper.

"You take my cock like such a good girl." Ian says as he drags his thumb across my cheek. His declaration spurs me on, a praise kink planting itself deep in my soul.

Sucking him into the back of my throat and out, I grip him with one hand, pumping his cock in time with my mouth, while slowly caressing his balls, rolling them between my fingers as he bucks his hips.

"Ari, fuck, I'm going to come baby," Ian pleads with me giving me a choice. I double down, taking him deeper and putting his hand on the back of my head, allowing him to take control.

His fingers lace in between the strands of my hair as he firmly but gently pushes me to take his cock, setting the speed that ramps up as his cock flexes with tension, before he finds his release, shooting hot salty cum down my throat, which I swallow before licking the tip.

He grabs my face with both hands and drags me up to kiss me, breathless and drained. I curl into his lap and snuggle his chest as he finds his breath again. I shiver, and Ian reaches across the couch and pulls a blanket over both of us, and we sit, just being together in the quiet and the calm. It's everything I didn't know I needed in that moment and I relish in the knowledge that he needed for me to be all his.

When we got to the brewery earlier with his fingers intertwined with mine it made me feel safe, and grounded. When I approached Evie holding hands with a man in her presence for the first time in a long time I could tell she was thinking the same thing as she squealed and pointed us out to Hunter.

When I introduced him to Hunter, Ian was cordial but I couldn't help but notice that he pulled me into his side, leaving me wondering if my hug with Hunter set him on edge.

I turn my head, gazing up at him. "Were you jealous of Hunter when I hugged him earlier?"

"Um, not exactly." He gives me a kiss on the forehead. "It was more because I didn't know much about your relationship with him and I didn't want any competition." His strong arms wrap around me, pulling my back to his chest and his head is heavy as it settles on mine.

"Which is basically the definition of jealousy." A soft poke in the side makes me squeal, and then he is full on tickling me.

"Stop, Stop, I can't take it anymore! Fine I take it back, you weren't jealous, ahhh Brady save me!" I begged my protective bear to come rescue me from the bedroom where he went to bed a long time ago after not getting enough attention, but it's to no avail.

Ian's fingers finally come to a rest, and instead begin softly stroking my hair as he leans down, his words dripping like honey in my ear.

"Fine. I was jealous. Because you are mine."

That night I went to bed the happiest I have ever been, his words and actions on repeat.

I'm his.

22

IAN

Friday, July 21st

A warm breath caresses my face, stirring my consciousness out of the most peaceful sleep I've felt in forever. I register a pressure on my shoulder, and soft silky hair tickling my jawline.

Visions of last night dance behind my shut eyes, of Aria on the couch, her words echoing in my head, "I'm yours."

A smile breaks free and my hand reaches up to caress her hair, enjoying the moment of waking up with her for the first time with her being all mine. I stroke her hair, and she shifts with a cute grunt.

"Good morning, beautiful."

"Good morning to you too." The sound came from farther away than expected, my brain fuzzy, trying to make sense of the direction.

I shift and peek an eye open, and am greeted with wet sandpaper dragging across my cheek.

Both eyes fly open to see a black furry head digging into my collarbone, causing me to shift and sit up.

"Ah-ahh, Brady!"

Giggles erupt across the room to the doorway, where Aria stands, two mugs in hand, using the doorframe to support her as she fills the room with laughter.

I take in the scene fully awake now, and see Brady standing next to the bed, his head resting on the mattress, tongue lagging.

"Guess he likes to cuddle in the mornings too?" I pat his head and he jumps up onto the bed, sitting firmly in my lap as if to answer.

Aria crosses the room and hands me a steaming cup of coffee. Thanking her, I grab her free hand before she can fully turn around, and pull her down for a slow kiss.

"Just in case it wasn't clear, I was calling you beautiful, not him."

Her response is sleepy and sweet. "Don't go hurting his feelings now."

She gives me a soft peck and then moves around the bed and climbs in next to me, both of us putting our coffees down on the opposing nightstands.

Brady moves to lay across the bottom of the bed and I lift my arm, feeling instantly at peace as she snuggles into my chest, this time for real.

"Do you have to work today?" I ask as I softly stroke her arm.

She sighs. "Yeah, I actually have a double today. A lunch event and then a wedding rehearsal dinner." She groans, hiding her face in my chest.

"Call in sick." My arms become a steel chain, designed to keep her anchored to me and the bed all day.

Swatting at my chest, she pushes off me. "Tell them I have, what, a summer cold?" Giggling she runs her fingers through her tousled waves, and then stretches her arms out. Brady copies her and sprawls out, his massive stretch taking up the entire width of the queen bed.

"Oh biiiig stretch." I say, causing Brady's tongue to lop out the side of his mouth in a canine smile, before he moves up the comforter and curls up between the two of us. I lay my head on his back using him as a pillow, and we spend the next hour talking and slowly waking up together.

It is a slow and simple morning, and one of the best I've ever had.

Keeping myself entertained while Aria is at work is harder than usual. I run through my daily workout with the same effort at usual, but find myself wandering aimlessly around the house afterwards. I'm tempted to go break Brady out of house jail just to have company that reminds me of her.

Can an addiction develop this quickly?

Because after getting a small taste of her last night, my body is craving more, it needs to taste her, to feel her, explore every inch of her and make squirm with ecstasy and scream in pleasure.

Not tonight, of course—she already set the boundary that she was going to be too tired after working a double. And then she has a wedding tomorrow.

But soon.

...

Sunday, July 23rd

6 holes into mini golf, I'm cursing myself for agreeing to a date where I have to wait 12 more holes to get us out of here and get my hands on her the way I'd like.

When Aria told me about this glow in the dark indoor mini golf with a punk rock vibe, I thought it sounded pretty cool. Now all I can think about is how her ass felt in my hands as we made out on the couch the other night, how her pussy drenched my fingers and her taking my cock deep in her throat. Her little skirt isn't helping either, as every time she makes it in the hole she bends down and the fabric slides a little higher up the back of her thigh, just like she is doing right now. I position myself behind her and run my hand up the back of her leg as she bends, causing her to do a little yelp and jump up.

"Ian! There are families here!" She bites her lip, clearly not mad but putting on a show.

I pull her towards me and position myself to block anyone from seeing her. I let my hand venture higher up, under the hem of her skirt.

"I think you wore this to tease me." I swipe my finger back and forth on the flesh just under her panty line.

"I promise I didn't, but I did try to look good for you. It's not my fault you are insisting on me getting the ball out every time rather than being a gentleman and doing it for me." She pushes playfully at my chest.

"Just putting that skirt to good use." I kiss the tip of her nose and then grab both of our putters and link hands with hers. Walking over to the next hole, I motion for her to go first. She takes her putter from my grasp and lines herself up in front of the lighthouse she intends to shoot through.

"Uh-huh. You aren't going to get it that way." I shake my head.

"What's wrong with this way?"

I saunter over, standing directly behind her. Looking around to make sure we are alone in the corner, I bend her forward slightly, and she pushes her ass back straight into my cock. It twitches in response and I groan.

"Like this?" Aria's voice is seductive.

"Just like that baby." She wiggles her ass a little, pressing into me more, and then takes a steady swing, clearing the obstacle with ease. She turns to face me and looks up into my eyes.

"You know I would have made it through just fine the first way."

"I know. I just needed an excuse to touch you." I drag her into me and attack her mouth, biting her lip and wanting nothing more than to pick her up and press her against the wall covered in glow in the dark icons. I regain my composure and release her lips, and press my forehead to hers.

"Let's get out of here."

"We will, in 11 more holes after I've won."

I groan loudly, accepting my defeat. "Fine, but I promise you we will both be winning once we get out of here." I slap her ass as she moves to the next hole, and start smacking the ball hurriedly, grabbing both balls from the cup before they've even stopped spinning around. I pull Aria from hole to hole to get us out of there quicker while she laughs and makes me more impatient with every stop.

Good thing we ate dinner before playing, because the only thing I want to eat is staring at me, as if she knows my exact thoughts and is more than happy to oblige.

I open her car door and offer my hand, and pull her out and up into my arms, throwing her legs around my waist as I cover her mouth with mine. I use my hip to slam the car door shut and make quick work of the front door lock. My house was closer to mini golf, and I wasn't wasting another minute. Based on the way Aria stroked my upper thigh on the ride over, fingers ever so slightly floating atop my cock and then pulling away, I knew she wanted the same.

I toss the keys on the couch. "Couch or bed?" I bit her earlobe, hands squeezing her round ass.

"Take me to bed." Aria barely takes a break from kissing me to reply.

I carry her down the hall to my room, hands fumbling while I try to touch her everywhere all at once. Tossing her onto the king size bed, I'm kissing her mouth before dragging mine over her clothes. Down over the center of her breasts, down her core, kissing her bare legs before reaching my hands down to remove her shoes, kicking mine off as well. I reach back and pull off my shirt, and watch as her body squirms with desire, hands clutching at the comforter. She sits up and reaches for my belt, but I take a palm and lightly press her back down so she is laying flat on her back.

"Oh no, you don't get that yet."

Aria pouts. "Why not?"

"Because you tempted me all night with that short little skirt, and now I'm ready for my prize for being so strong." I lift her skirt up slowly, bringing my face down to inhale her scent. Before diving in, I lift her shirt, kissing her stomach before removing the shirt completely. I place my lips on the hollow of her neck, moving them over the lace of her bra, and running my tongue along the soft contour of her ribs. Her breath is sharp, creating even more of a ridge for me to lick. She sits up, fingers grasping desperately for the back hooks of her bra, and flings it to the side.

Placing my palm on her sternum, I gently push her back down on the bed, fingers trailing down her breasts, over the soft curves of her stomach.

I put my hands on the waistband of her skirt and looked back up to her. "This ok?"

"Yes." Her breathy response is full of anticipation.

I pull her skirt and panties down together, and groan at the image of her laying completely bare before me.

"God you are stunning." I take time looking over all of her, letting my eyes roam freely over the perfect creature in front of me. She reaches for me, clearly ready for me to continue.

"Ok baby, enough looking for now." With that I dive down, and lick her once completely, before dragging my face across her wet center and flicking my tongue repeatedly.

"Oh God," Aria's hands instantly found my hair.

"Not God," I smirk, "But this is heaven."

Her legs kick out and she moves, like her body is fighting the pleasure while she intertwines her fingers in my hair and pushes my head down for more.

I lick her pussy while spreading her thighs, placing my hand flat on her stomach. She covers my hand with hers as she whimpers, her head falling back as her eyes close. My tongue dips and twirls, licking from back to front before dipping in, narrowing in on her sweet nub and sucking hard.

She cries out, and I grab her thighs tighter, feeling her juices flow and knowing she is getting closer. I attack with vigor, using my fingers to aid her in the quest. I slip two fingers inside her and pump, before bringing it back out to paint her nipple with her own wetness. I roll her nipple in my fingers and tug, and she explodes, and I'm there to suck up all of the evidence.

She has barely come out of her post-orgasm haze and she moves, pushing me back to sit and reaches over for my belt. "Off."

"Straight to the point." I grin as I undo my belt, and jeans, pull a condom out of my wallet, and slide both the jeans and my briefs down. She pulls me back to her so quickly I almost trip over the jeans still wrapped around my ankles.

"I need you, now." She pants, kissing my mouth, her arms looping around my back and neck to pull me into her. I lay her back against the pillows, wanting to make sure she is comfortable.

"We don't have to." I want to be sure this is what she wants.

She grabs the condom out of my hand and tears it open.

"Ian, I swear to God if you don't get inside me right now…" I laugh and take the condom out of the wrapper and slide it over my aching cock.

I hover over her, running one hand down the side of her face, smoothing the errant hairs out of her eyes.

"Tell me if it's too much." I say gently.

Aria locks eyes with me, understanding I need to hear she understands. "I will."

I kiss her as I place my cock at her entrance, and slowly slide in. We both let out a heavy breath as I pulse forward, pushing myself to the hilt.

"God you're huge, I feel so full." Aria's eyes are closed as she adjusts to feeling me inside her.

"It feels like you were made for me." It's a perfect fit, her walls so tight around me, hugging my cock as I begin to slowly retreat and slide back in. She pulls me in and wraps her legs around my waist as I increase the pace. We both watch as my cock slides in and out of her pussy, the look of desire flaring in her eyes as I stare back at her.

I alternate between fast and slow, driving her wild but not daring to make this be over too quickly, until her legs drop and she pushes me onto my back.

"My turn."

She straddles me, sliding down on my dick, taking it to the hilt. Her arms grab at my biceps as her breasts bounce above me. I kiss her throat, her neck, and wrap my arm around her waist, fingers search and find her clit, rubbing it to bring her even higher. "Ah that feels so good." She moans and leans back, hands resting on my thighs. My hands reached up to massage her breast before grabbing onto her waist and lifting her up and down, piercing her with each movement. I reach around her and pull her close, flipping us onto our sides.

Her leg lifts around my thigh, and I grab hold, shoving myself deeper inside of her. "Fuck baby you're so tight." I pull myself on top and bring her legs up, forcing them to spread out and down under my grip. I take her right nipple into my mouth, swirling my tongue over it and sucking the entire breast into my mouth while I pick up the pace. Her breathing picks up, her moans and gasps telling me she is getting close.

"Don't stop." Her nails dig into my back, begging me to go harder.

"I won't, take it sweetheart, come for me." She tightens around me and then explodes, and a few more pumps I follow her right over the cliff.

"I need to get home to let Brady out." Soft kisses flutter on my chest as she mumbles defeatedly.

"Want to just pick him up and bring him back here for the night?" There's no way I'm letting her sleep alone after our first time together.

"No that seems silly, I can just sleep at home." She pushes up to sit and tugs the comforter up over her tanned breasts, tucking it under her arms. She begins looking around for her clothes, then pauses.

"You don't mind him being over here though, for other times?"

"Mind it? Hell no. I actually considered kidnapping him the other day so we could have a boys day while you were working." That makes her light up, her expression surprised but happy as she stands and starts to get dressed.

"And selfishly I want you to stay over whenever you feel like it. I'd buy him a dog bed, but we both know he will just make himself comfortable on the couch or bed instead."

She leans down and kisses me, hands framing both sides of my face.

"Thank you. It means a lot to me that you love him so much."

Love him. It's easy to love a dog, their pure souls and loyalty make that happen almost instantly.

As I watch her finish getting ready, I can't help but feel like Brady isn't the only thing in the room I might be starting to feel that for.

"If you want to stay over you can." She makes eye contact with me in the mirror across from the bed.

"Baby I was going to, whether or not I got an invitation." My response has her just shaking her head with a smirk..

And I do. That night, and most nights in the following weeks after, we spent them together.

We alternate where we stay, neither of us having much of a preference. Or at least I don't, because as great as my house is being right on the water, I've never felt a more cozy home than Aria's, and as easy as breathing, our lives come into sync.

23
ARIA

"My mom is coming to stay for a few days." Ian throws a ball for Brady in the backyard of his house. It's a few days later after mini golf and the festivities (or should I say sextivities) that followed and we are spending some downtime at his gorgeous lake house.

"Oh yeah? That's great. I hope you guys have fun while she is here." I'm glad he gets to spend some time with her but selfishly I'm a little bummed to not get to spend it with him.

"We will, we can show her some of our new favorite spots, and she is going to love Brady, isn't that right you big fluffy bear?" Ian snatches the ball from Brady's mouth and gives his snout a big smush.

"You want me to meet your mom?" That seems like a big deal for just becoming exclusive.

"Of course I do, why wouldn't I. You're my girl." He gives me one of his swoony winks and throws the ball again.

"Your girl huh?" I blush at the sound of that, but if I'm honest, my heart grows three times as big at the idea of being his for the long term. We may have decided to be exclusive, but I know that isn't the likely long term outcome, so I try to veer us back to the topic at hand.

"Is she staying here?" I don't see why she wouldn't but I can't think of anything else to say with the thoughts swirling in my head."

"Yes of course, that's why I got so many spare rooms." He gives Brady a final throw and comes to sit down on the outdoor sofa next to me where I'm scrolling through recent videos that the US Water Rescue Dog Organization posted from their training with the Italians.

"Whoa wait play that one again" Ian throws his arm around my shoulders and pulls the phone in between us. His eyes light up as he watches the Newfie, decked out in his rescue vest and goggles, jump from a hovering helicopter into the water below.

"How do we get Brady to do that?" I can't help but laugh at how excited he sounds.

"I don't think we can, that's a training they did in Italy, where their dogs actually do it with the military."

"How do they get them back up?"

"They either swim to shore or their vest has a hook to be winched back up, like this." I show him a video where a dog is being lifted back in. "Or they can ride in the basket too."

"That is so cool. We should do that."

"I don't think Lake Tahoe necessarily needs helicopter rescues, but I have heard of helicopters being used to recreate rough weather conditions for training. It gets the dogs used to big waves if they are working out of boats or in a storm."

That would be such a cool thing to train with, getting to practice real life situations in rough water. Ian seems to agree as he gets a pensive look, mulling over the thought in his head.

"Anyways, tell me more about what you want to do when your mom is here." I am eager to see who played a role in making Ian the incredible man he is today. I don't think his Dad is in the picture, at least he hasn't mentioned him and I don't want to pry into something he isn't ready to share.

"I'm thinking about picking a pretty hike, and maybe show her sunrise at Emerald Bay." I smile at the flashback of our morning date last week. It was so dreamy, with just the two of us sitting, wrapped in a blanket, dangling our feet over the rock wall, drinking coffee and whispering as the world lit up over the lake. Definitely a core memory.

"Mmm, sounds perfect." I fidget a little, wanting to make an offer but not sure if it was enough. "I'd love to make her dinner while she is here if you want, I mean we could have it here if you don't want her to see my house, I know it's small and all."

"I appreciate you wanting to do that for her, and I think she would love it at your cabin. In fact, the first time I went there I thought about how much she would love the wind chime outside on your porch."

I breathe out, not even realizing I had been holding one in. "Ok, deal."

•••

"Well, Ian's mom is coming to visit, and he wants me to meet her." I say as I drop a rack of clean wine glasses on the bar for Evie.

"No joke? Wow! That is huge! Didn't realize you were at the whole 'meet the family' part yet..." She gives me the side eye.

But at least I know I'm not crazy thinking it might be early to meet the family with things being a little up in the air.

"I think it's just because she is coming to town? I offered to make dinner though, I need to figure out what to make!"

We throw out a few ideas, before finally settling on Chicken as the main course.

"Ari, have you told him about your family yet?" Evie pauses what she is doing behind the counter and comes to sit next to me at the bar.

I cast my eyes down. "No? It, um, hasn't really come up?" She gives me a look that tells me she isn't buying it.

"I don't want to get into it. It never feels like the right time to bring it up you know? Like we are having a great time and then what, I'm supposed to say oh by the way my brother died and my home life kinda sucked after that?"

I wipe an erratic tear angrily away, and try to get the stupid plastic sleeve off the cocktail napkins that I'm holding open. I can't and finally give up, throwing them on the table.

Evie moves her chair closer and puts her arm around me, pulling me into her. I close my eyes and lay my head in the crook of her shoulder, more tears breaking through.

"Sweetie, you have to tell him about it. It's a big part of your past and who you are today. You can't hide something like that, nor should you. Being in a relationship is about being vulnerable and sharing the things that hurt us, not hiding them."

Deep down I know she is probably right, but I don't want to bring any of my burdens to the surface. I don't want him to have to shoulder that pain for me, as I can tell he has enough of his own history to deal with too—with what, I'm just not sure.

"I don't know how to do that."

"That's because you are the one who always wants to save the day for people or to be there to comfort and help them. You don't let many people see that other side of you."

"Well they don't need to, people have enough to deal with than to hear some sob story."

"But think about how much closer we got after we finally opened up to each other about our own stories. It gave me a better understanding of the other person and then we were able to support each other in a more meaningful way." I nod, thinking back to how even though it hurt to recount what happened, it had brought us closer after the fact.

"Ok, I will. I don't know how or when, but you're right. At least once it's out there it's not some secret I'm holding onto."

But internally another thought crosses my mind—what if he finds out that I couldn't be or do enough to make the person who was supposed to love me the most, to love me enough to stay at all? Would he realize I wasn't worth sticking around for too?

24
ARIA

Tuesday, August 1st

Ian's mom arrived yesterday and plans to stay until Thursday morning, and despite his multiple requests, I insisted on giving them some time alone before hosting them both for dinner after she gets settled.

Ian wanted me to join them for dinner when she got in, but I knew he needed time with just her. This morning they took out his rental's boat on the lake before catching a few of the most scenic spots on a drive around it during the afternoon.

By the time the alpine air turns crisp, I have an apple crumble cooling on the counter and lemon garlic chicken roasting in the oven.

I do an extra sweep of Brady's fur, which is completely necessary because I had also brushed him, leaving me with a mound of his blown coat so large it looked like an entire other dog was on the floor.

My treasured, yet modest possessions are all tidy, every surface is clean, and ready for guests. Lighting a candle that smells like Sugar Cookies, I open the windows to get the evening breeze inside.

Gravel crunches as a car comes up the drive, and after peeking to see that it is Ian's, I opened the door, using my body to keep Brady inside the house.

Ian had assured me that his mom loved dogs, but I know loving dogs and being greeted by one the weight of a good sized human are two totally different things.

But of course, once Brady sees Ian's Range Rover there is nothing that will keep him away from his favorite guy (not that I can blame him). He pushes past my propped knee and bounds out the door towards Ian and his mom, whom he is helping out of the car. My heart does a little flutter seeing his manners in action before yelling, "Brady, no!" Despite the constant training and expert recall that Brady usually demonstrates, he fully ignores me and crashes into Ian, his massive tail whipping around like a broken rudder.

I hear a gasp, and then "OH MY WORD... I LOVE HIM!" Ian's mom yells out, and then throws her arms around Brady's neck. With someone new to get attention from, Brady plops firmly on Ian's foot and gets in his good boy sit to impress the newcomer, enormous tongue hanging out as he is all smiles.

"Aren't you just the biggest cutest boy there is, yes you are!" She gives his head pats and strokes under his chin, finding all his favorite spots. "He is just the sweetest thing, and I can see why you call him a bear!" Ian laughs and joins in on the petting, and Brady just sits there, soaking it all in.

Ian breaks away and comes to meet me as I walk to greet them and kisses me right on the mouth, right in front of his mom. I blush at the outward sign of affection, but his mom just beams.

"I missed you." His mouth is near my ear, a whisper for just me to hear.

My heart leaps, "I just saw you yesterday," I counter.

"But then I was doing all the things I love to do with you, and yet you weren't there. And so I missed you." He takes my hand and turns towards his mom.

"Mom, this is Aria, and that's Brady. Aria, I'd like you to meet my lovely mother."

"It's so nice to meet you, Mrs. Sanderson." I reach out to shake her hand, but she gives a little *tsk* and playfully swats my hand away before pulling me into a hug. Momentarily shocked, it takes a few seconds from my body to catch up and hug her back. "Please call me Jenny," she says. "It is so wonderful to meet you, Aria. Ian talks about you constantly."

I laugh, "hopefully all good things." She chuckles in agreement.

I motion towards the cabin. "Please come in, can I get you something to drink?"

"Oh in a minute dear, I want to look at your plants. I just love gardening, don't you?" I nod. "These are beautiful!" She inspects all of my pots, not with a critical eye but with enthusiasm.

A soft breeze floats through, setting my hummingbird wind chime off, and she puts a hand over her heart. "My goodness, isn't that just the prettiest sound. I just love wind chimes. I have 5 on my back porch!" She looks closely as Ian wraps an arm around my waist and gives me a reassuring squeeze.

"If the outside is this cute, I can't wait to see inside. Show me the rest of your adorable home, Aria."

A few hours and a few bottles of wine later, Jenny is my new best friend. From my armchair, which she declared the coziest reading spot she'd ever seen, Jenny tells me stories of Ian's childhood, with Brady curled at her feet, while Ian and I sit together on the couch.

Jenny recounts Ian trying to hide bullfrogs in his pockets coming back from the lake. I almost cried from laughing so hard when she made a loud *Riiibbet* sound to show how he got caught, and then tried to cover up as if it were a cough.

I pat his leg in commiseration, and he drapes his arm around me, softly stroking my arm as if it were the most natural thing in the world to show affection in front of his mom.

The night grows late and Ian offers to take Brady outside so I don't have to be in the dark. Jenny crosses over to where I'm standing, watching them out the sliding glass door and touches me on both arms. "I am just so glad Ian has finally allowed himself to find someone to love again."

"Oh, we've only been seeing each other for about a month." I try to play off her comment, not wanting to embarrass her if she didn't know we hadn't been together all that long.

"Hmm, well, it may be too early for it to be said, but it's certainly not too early to tell that you are the perfect girl for his heart to follow to find it." She says, my eyes tear up at the sweetest compliment I think I have ever heard.

"Oh, I don't know about that, but I love spending time with him. He is such an amazing man, you must be so proud of him." She gives me a kind smile, gracefully allowing me to bow out of that earlier conversation.

"I am very proud of him. He has worked tirelessly to make sure he has created a life of security for me and for himself. And now I just want him to learn to enjoy his life and to love it with everything he has." She gives me a big hug, making me promise to join them for some adventures while she is here.

Later that night, I stare out at the star-filled night, and try to reconcile the mother I had, and lost, to the mother who is so proud of her son who has reached the pinnacle of his career, and yet the thing she wanted the most for him to be happy.

If everyone had a mom like that, how amazing would this world be.

25
ARIA

Thursday, August 3rd

It may be the middle of summer, but as soon as that icy air hits my cheeks I wish I had thought to wear my beanie. I'd come watch Ian coach/help out with the youth hockey team. He's been busy skating and training the kids, but since I have the day off today I wanted to surprise him and come watch, rather than just meet him here afterwards like we had planned.

The ice rink is in the middle of town, and is busy year round. There's both an indoor sports rink and my favorite, the outdoor rink that tourists and locals flock to for a fun activity when friends come to town. It is absolutely perfect in winter thanks to the hot toddies that you can buy at the little snack stand once fall comes around.

As I make my way past families spread out on benches all throughout the interior, I can't imagine having to figure out how to get a kid dressed in all that hockey gear.

But they sure do look cute! I think as I silently laugh, watching the littlest ones try to skate, and imagine what it was like for Ian's mom when he was little.

Though at the same time it's hard to ignore the little tinge my heart feels looking at them too.

Peter never got to do that. He would've loved learning to play.

The memory of the one and only time I got him on skates, washes over me as I stare out at the kids weighed down in oversized hockey pads.

"Hi Aria!" I look up and Janet from down the street waves as I turn to climb onto the raised bleacher seats above the ice. Her son is 8 and I've seen him enough times lugging his hockey bag to the car to know he must be on one of the local teams.

"Hi! Is it always this cold in here, even in the stands?" I blow into my hands and rub them together to keep them warm as I stand on the stairs near her row.

"Sure is, gotta dress warm, or carry a hot drink." I take her advice and grab a coffee from the snack stand before returning to the second row, feet propped up on the bench in front of me, a few sections down from the team benches.

Looking out, I spot the reason I'm here. Towering over the mini players, Ian looks casual and comfortable on the ice in just gray sweats, a hoodie, and a backwards hat as he gives directions to a group of kids.

Sigh. How can a man look that delicious in clothing like that?

The kids seem to split up into different drill areas, and Ian skates in lazy figure eights around the various stations. His movements are so fluid, so controlled, and yet it looks like he is barely moving his feet to make them happen. I giggle at the thought that he would make an excellent figure skater instead of a hockey player.

Tights would look good on him, too.

Blushing, I realize my mind has gone way off track and others might notice the drool if I keep staring at him. I take a sip of my coffee and glance back over just in time to make eye contact with Ian as he turns around and gazes up to where I'm sitting in the stands.

A smile grows across his face until he is positively beaming, and he takes off immediately over towards where I am sitting. Putting my coffee down, I step over the bench to meet him at the glass perimeter around the rink.

Coming to a fancy stop on his skates, he leans against the boards and grins. "Hey there, beautiful. Didn't realize an angel was going to be watching practice today." I blush at his words and laugh a little at the sound of his muffled flirtation.

"Thought I'd watch what you've been up to before we go to Evie's later."

"Perfect, though now I don't know how I'm going to get through practice with such a gorgeous distraction sitting in the stands." He gives me a wink and then skates back over to his players, taking a long look over his shoulder at me on the way.

I mentally recover and then glance quickly around, and realize those around us definitely noticed that interaction, and are now whispering to each other and non-discreetly pointing at Ian and me.

We've gotten a fair amount of attention around town (because he is so good looking) but here, given his career status, he is probably more like a god to the kids and their parents.

I try to ignore the stares and focus on the man on the ice. For the next half hour, I get lost watching him interact with the kids, having fun, being supportive and kind to those struggling, and making sure even the littlest ones have opportunities for success.

He is going to make such a great dad. The thought crosses my mind, and it settles as if it is a foregone conclusion. He is a natural, and he is going to be the best dad. He'll be a supportive and loving father, always there for his kids.

God, that is sexy.

And because no one is there to stop me, I let myself fall into that dream for just a minute. Imagining what it would look like if he was out there coaching one of *our* kids, and I was here on the bench being a regular hockey mom.

Smiling to myself, I can't help but like that idea just a little.

...

IAN

"Is that your girl, Coach?"

Brandon and Brody, two of the little kids I'm coaching today, have been hounding me ever since I skated back from saying hi to Aria. They point in Aria's direction with goofy looks on their faces.

"What's it to you?" I bump their shoulders, playing it cool.

"C'mon man, you can tell us, she's pretty!" I nod, agreeing with that statement.

Seeing her here at the rink, it feels like a puzzle piece sliding into place. Like she is meant to be there in the stands watching. Like she belongs. It feels good having her here to watch, and hell, I wasn't even playing.

All I know is that I got a very similar feeling to finding her in the stands that I do when I find my mom in the stands.

She is starting to feel like home. And I'm starting to feel more complete every time she comes around. Like I don't want to let her go at the end of the summer. And that is fucking scary because if I let that happen, then everything has the potential to fall apart all over again.

"Thanks for waiting around—sometimes it takes a little while for all the kids to get their gear off and picked up." I swing my hockey bag over my shoulder as I walk towards where Aria is waiting for me outside of the locker room.

"Happy to, I had fun watching." Her smile is bright as she tilts her head a little and shifts the weight on her feet.

"Oh yah?" I drop the bag as I approach and draw her into my arms. "What did you like watching the most?" She brings her arms around my neck and looks up at me, a coy grin on her face.

"Well, the goalie was pretty good." She can barely get the lie out without laughing.

"Yeah, we are working on Jackson's reflexes. He has a way to go." I join her in laughing and then bring my lips to hers. As soon as they connect it is like a peace comes over my body, one that feels like it is where it belongs.

Her forest green eyes turn soft. "You know, you're really great with them, all of them. Teaching seemed natural for you out there. You'll make a great dad one day."

My heart gives a tug. The words mean so much, considering I've spent the past two decades questioning if I'll end up like my dad instead.

"That means a lot to me, thank you." Knowing this is a chance to act on vulnerability like my mom suggested, I test the waters, playing with her hair as I let her in a little more.

"My dad was pretty involved growing up, but then when I was a teen he started focusing less on hockey and spent more time at work, which ended up being a cover for an affair." Lines appear on her forehead and her eyes fill with concern."

I give her a squeeze and reach down to pick up my bag, looping it over one shoulder while using my other to tuck her into my side. "After that I didn't want anything to do with him and his new family, so sometimes I worry if I'll end up like him instead."

Aria stops suddenly, causing my arm to lag and force me to turn.

"You are not him, and whatever he chooses to do does not mean you will follow his path." She pats her hand over my chest. "You have a good heart, and will be a great dad."

I inhale deeply, her confidence in me bringing to life a desire to see that through. I lean down and kiss her on her forehead.

"Ready to head to Evie's?"

"Yup! But are you sure that's ok with you? You don't mind just hanging out at her place?" She is genuinely concerned for my comfort level.

"Nowhere I'd rather be. They are important to you and I want to get to know them better." And I mean it. We've hung out a few times with Evie, but I want to know all of Aria's closest friends, and the niece she talks so much about.

I'm learning that the things I want to know more about are making it easier and easier to become attached to Aria. It felt great to see my mom and Aria get to know each other, and I want the same for the people who matter the most to her.

We head out to the parking lot, making our way to my car, and drive together, leaving Aria's here to be retrieved later.

•••

Giggles erupt as Aria blows raspberries into Gracie's neck, the little girl collapsing with excitement every time. It's been over an hour since we arrived at Evie's little apartment, which is one part of a two-family home, and it's clear as day how attached the two of them are to each other.

Gracie squealed with delight when she saw Aria. After a slight disappointment to no "Big Bear" being in attendance, Gracie has been soaking up Aria's attention, dragging her from toy to toy, showing her her baby dolls, and having a tea party with Aria sitting cross legged at the little table. Not once has Aria tried to stop her, and she has been engaged the entire time, getting into character and asking thoughtful questions to encourage Gracie to tell her more about each thing. All of which results in a mostly indistinguishable babble that Aria somehow understands.

What's most impressive is she has done all that while maintaining an adult conversation with Evie and I. Evie is relaxed on the couch with a glass of wine, content letting Aria take control for a while so she can have a rest. I'm on the opposite couch holding a beer.

"She'll make a great mom." I look over at hearing her speak to see Evie smiling softly at Aria.

"She will." I nod in agreement and take a swig from the bottle.

"The biggest heart, willing to do anything for anyone, and always put others before herself. She'll be a natural." High praise, but looks like she is holding something else back.

I can easily agree with her statement, Aria is so kindhearted, and she always makes sure everyone is taken care of.

Gracie pulls Aria into the next room as Evie continues, "But what she is going to need is someone who looks after her. It is easy to lose yourself completely in parenthood, to give up all your dreams to make sure theirs come true. Aria will end up martyring herself before she even realizes it." She rearranges the blanket over her legs. "She needs someone to remind her that she is worthy of being loved and taken care of too."

Of course Aria is worthy of being loved. I pause before responding.

But to hear her best friend say that she needs a partner to be that constant reminder for her makes me wonder if I could ever be the right person for the job. I get busy during the seasons, and Amber always said I didn't make enough time for her. Would Aria feel unloved if we continued dating during the season and my attention and time were pulled away?

"Something to think about, that's all." Evie shoots me a smile, before redirecting the conversation to tell Gracie it was time for bed.

Gracie gives Aria kisses and hugs, and then toddles over to me, where she pats my leg with her chubby little hand. "Night, Night Eee-an." Her sleepy smile melts my heart a little. "Goodnight little one. Sweet dreams."

Later that night, we are both propped up in my bed, her reading on her tablet on a pillow, and me using Brady's enormous form as one of my own.

My right arm is draped over her thighs, my hand gently stroking her outer leg. There's a sportscast show on the tv, but my eyes barely see it as my brain works over time, reflecting on everything that day had brought.

Having her at hockey—and it felt so right—to tell her about my dad and how it only reinforced her belief in my ability to be better than he was as a father.

And of course, watching her with Gracie. It felt like the missing piece, seeing Aria tend to a baby, well, a toddler I guess, and seeing the joy it brings her.

Makes me want to experience it with her.

Makes me question whether or not my job and my lifestyle can be enough for her, or if she too will decide someone else fits the bill better, and tears down everything.

Some remote part of my heart is calling for me to put up walls and not let her in enough to see what will end up happening. But the call my soul feels towards her is too overpowering, too all-encompassing to oblige.

She is what I've been looking for, hell, even scared of finding. Because she is making me envision a future, and I'm falling for her more every single day.

26
IAN

Saturday, August 5th

After the heart to heart with my mom, she left a few days later to head back to San Jose. The house felt empty without her here, and I spent most of the day thinking over everything we had talked about, and everything that has happened over the summer so far.

I knew my time with Aria was different than anything I've felt before. She wasn't just a summer fling that I would be able to move away from when the season started. As much as it scared me, I knew she was slowly imprinting herself in my life and her absence would hurt more than I could handle.

I wasn't sure where that left me, but I thought over my moms words about trying to open up to Aria a little bit about what I've been through, and maybe that would help her open up too.

There's some sort of shadow in her past that lingers, despite her cheery disposition and desire to help everyone around her. I wanted her to trust me enough to share that with me, but I knew it went both ways.

If I wanted to be trusted, I needed to start giving some trust too.

Aria had to work a wedding, it being a Saturday in August which is apparently hot real estate for nuptials, so I sat down at the table and worked on a project for her.

Her Jeep has a collection of colorful rubber ducks that have been left on her door handle or windshield. She made a comment recently about how she loves to hand them out when she sees a cute Jeep but had run out of ducks to give.Which of course led to another great laugh and a new inside joke about not having any ducks to give.

The package had come in while my mom was here, so now is the perfect time to sit and assemble a line of ducks, each complete with their own themed costume.

I pulled out my phone and hit FaceTime to the group chat to see who would answer. To my surprise, all three of the boys did. Looks like we all have equally exciting offseason lives.

"Yo man, what's up!" Holden says, the screen showing him relaxing on his couch with his cat tucked under his chin.

"I see we have the King of Pussy here" Hughes says from the middle of a video game.

"Ah fuck off, probably have gotten more pussy than you this summer." Holden gives his cat some scratches, "and I don't mean from Miss Melanie here."

"That is the stupidest name for a cat," Whitty chimes in.

"Hey, I couldn't change it; she was already responding to it at the shelter, you know that."

"We know dude, he's just busting your chain." I say. It feels good having the guys back together even if it is just over the phone.

I use a glue dot to place sunglasses on a duck's face. "Um, whatcha working on there, buddy? Arts and Crafts?" Hughes asks as he leans in for a closer look.

I secure the pink cowboy hat to the duck's head and lift my hand to show it off. "Cute right? It's for Aria; it's like a Jeep owner thing."

"Oh, like where they leave them on other people's cars?" Whitty says, looking slightly confused.

"Yeah, exactly. Oh, look at this one..." I show them the best one out of the package, a gangster duck complete with gold chain, bandana, cowboy hat, and a miniature AK-47.

The phone cackles from the amount of laughter coming through the speaker.

"Wait, wait, wait, show us the rest of them." Holden says. I oblige, scanning the phone so they can see the witch, clown, and pool party duck, complete with a mini inflatable pool float.

"So let me get this straight. You, Ian Sanderson, NHL all-star and ladies man extraordinaire, are spending a Saturday night at home, alone by the looks of it, gluing costumes onto miniature ducks?" Hughes looks stunned and then bursts out laughing.

"I like it. It's a good look for you, man," Whitty nods in approval.

"What, the cowboy hat?" I say, gesturing to the duck in front of me.

"Naw man, looking happy," Whitty says. The other guys agree and we change the subject to sports and updates on other teammates, but I can't help thinking how it feels good to be happy, doing something special for someone that means a lot to me.

• • •

I pick up Aria the next day, and grin as I watch her reaction to the gift bag full of ducks in her seat. She oohs and ahh over each one, and gives me a big ole kiss as a thank you. She insisted on taking them with us to the restaurant where we met up with Evie and her brother for drinks.

"There's no way they do that." Aria's disbelief is almost palatable as I shut the passenger door after she exits the car.

"Dead serious—it's tradition." We somehow had started talking about wild things I'd seen during my time in hockey. She was in disbelief that fans would actually throw an octopus on the ice.

I grab her hand and pull her in close as we walk inside, kissing the top of her head as she shakes it and bursts into giggles, wrapping her arms around me. Her comfort level with being affectionate in public with me does things to me. We have fallen into a comfortable routine, spending more time with each other than not, but still ensuring we have our own time and space to do our own thing. Though I spend most of that time wanting, needing to be near her again.

As we approach the booth where Evie and Hunter are sitting with a few others standing nearby, I can tell something is wrong before we even get to the table.

Evie looks up and sees Aria, raises her eyebrows and takes a big breath like she is preparing herself. I slow my pace, and Aria finally notices everyone there with a forlorn look on their faces. She looks at me for some clarity, but I just squeeze her hand and shrug my shoulders, demonstrating that I don't know what it is about either.

"Is everything ok, what's wrong?" Aria slides in the booth, and pulls me down next to her.

Evie glances at the others and then reaches across to grab Aria's hands in hers. "We just heard something, and I don't want to tell you but I need to, because you will hear it soon anyways."

Well, that sounds ominous. I get the sudden urge to pull Aria back into my arms and shield her from whatever bad news Evie is about to deliver, but refrain, slinging my arm on the back of the booth instead.

"What is it?" Aria's voice is barely a whisper, as if she too is afraid of the dark territory this conversation is about to head into.

"A child from South Lake—he drowned—died, today, in a pool."

My brain processed what happened next but didn't fully understand it. Aria's eyes darkened and intensified with each word in the sentence. Upon the last one she let out a single cry so devastating, so heartbreaking, that it pierced my soul, leaving the jagged edge in ruins, and I watched as her eyes filled with tears and she pulled her hand free from Evie's to cover her mouth.

It's definitely terrible news, but I don't understand her reaction if I'm being honest. Evie had said a child, not naming one in particular, so it couldn't have been clear to Aria if she knew them or not. My brain pushed logic to the side and focused on caring for Aria, wanting to be her strength and help her through this pain.

Softly stroking her back with one hand, I place my hand on her thigh and rub my thumb slightly, hoping it brings her comfort.

She sits there, not speaking, for what must be at least a full minute, before clearing her voice. "I, um, need just a minute, please." Her eyes glance over without making eye contact, staring but not technically looking at anything as she motions for me to let her out of the booth.

"Of course baby, whatever you need." Rising out of the booth, she turned and walked down the hall to the restroom.

Evie wipes her eyes and pushes Hunter out of the booth to allow her to stand and begins to follow. I reached out and gently touched her arm. "What happened?" The look she gives me tells me Evie knew I meant more than just what happened here today.

"It's not my story to tell." She sighed. "But hearing that a child drowned is the worst case scenario for Aria. This is going to cause a lot of pain for her." She looked at me directly, waiting for me to give her what she is looking for.

"I've got her. I'll take care of her."

Evie nods, and follows Aria's path and a few minutes later, both emerge. Hunter and I standing around, waiting for their cue on what happens next.

"We're going to take a rain check on drinks." Evie says confidently, clearly putting an end to the evening.

"Do you want me to come over?" She asks Aria sincerely.

Aria lifts her gaze to mine, and finding the refuge she needs, shakes her head. "No, that's ok, Ian will be there."

There's something about her trusting me to be there when she needs someone—it gets to me in ways I don't fully understand.

There's something about her trusting me to be there when she needs someone—it gets to me in ways I don't fully understand. It messes with my head in the best kind of way. I grab her purse as both Evie and Hunter give her a hug goodbye, wrap my arms around her and lead her out the door to my car.

Once back at her place I got her settled on the couch. Brady reads the mood and rests his head on her lap like a weighted pillow. She grasps my hand tightly, as if she is afraid I'll disappear if she lets go.

Damn, if that doesn't do something to my chest.

"If you want to talk about it, I'm here." She gives me a loving smile while touching my cheek.

"Thank you. Just not yet."

We sit in silence for a long time, me running my fingers up and down her arm, through her hair, kissing the top of her head, as she stares quietly out the window, alternating between soft cries and solemn silence.

I get up to make a cup of tea to help her relax, and once she drinks it, try to think of the next way I can help her.

"Do you want to take a hot shower?"

Giving me a soft smile, the first one of the night, she shakes her head. "No, I just want to lie down." Following her as she walks into her room, Brady hot on her heels, I watch as she climbs into bed. Brady jumps on the bed and lies on her legs like a weighted blanket, providing comfort in the best way he can.

I turn out the light and kiss her forehead, and debate if she would prefer some space or me in bed next to her. Either way, there's not a chance of me leaving her alone, so I decide I'll sleep on the couch tonight to make sure I'm here for whatever she needs, and turn towards the door.

"Ian?" Her voice calls out, searching, yet sad.

"Yeah baby, I'm right here."

"Will you stay with me?" She moves the comforter aside for me.

"Of course. I'm not going anywhere." I take off my jeans and henley, and climb into bed, gathering her up in my arms.

"Promise?" She asks faintly.

"I promise."

It's hard to fall asleep, my mind trying to figure out what caused Aria to have that reaction. Being a lifeguard growing up and now wanting to train to be a water rescue K9 team, obviously Aria had water safety in the forefront. She must be affected due to her mission to want to help keep people safe in the water, and cares deeply for her community.

When I woke up the next morning, I let Brady out and started some coffee, and hoped the new day would bring some peace for Aria. I rubbed my chest at the memory of the pools of sadness in her eyes—seeing that brings out the viking in me, wanting to protect her from hurting.

I'm lost in my thoughts when a soft voice clears her throat behind me. "Hi."

I set my mug down and am around the island scooping her into my arms in less than a second. I breathe in her scent, "Hi sweetheart."

"Thanks for staying last night."

"You don't have to thank me. I wanted to stay, to be here with you."

"I suppose I should tell you why I reacted like that yesterday." She looks down at her feet.

"If you want to, and when you are ready, then I do want to know. But only because I want to share your pain, and support you. If it hurts too much to talk about, I'll understand that too."

Aria looked up at me with what I can only identify as love in her eyes. "Thank you," she whispered. I pour her a cup of coffee and we move to the couch. After a few minutes, our fingers intertwined, she breaks the silence, setting down her mug, and reaching over to hand me a framed photo of two little kids I hadn't noticed before. I can tell that one clearly is Aria, with blond wavy hair, and the other a little boy who looks just like her. I look up at her for clarification, and she reaches over and replaces the framed photo on the side table.

"When I was 12, my brother, Peter, was 4. There was a big age gap, but he was everything to me." This is a little surprising, as she hasn't mentioned having a brother. I take her hands in mine, silently trying to give her strength to continue.

"He used to follow me around and wanted to play whatever I was playing. It was summer, and I rode my bike to the library. When I got home, my mom asked me to go wake Peter up from his nap." Tears fall and she does nothing to stop them, doesn't try to brush them away. My heart clenches, and I use all my effort to not let it show. I want to wipe them away for her, but I'm frozen, anticipating, but not wanting to hear what comes next.

"He wasn't in his room. We couldn't find him, and then my mom checked outside, and that's, uh... that's when I heard the scream."

She hides her face in my chest as she continues, tears streaming down her face, soaking my shirt. "He had wandered out an unlocked backdoor and fell into the pool, and he drowned. We couldn't do anything to save him."

"Oh, baby..."

The finality of that statement hits me like a load of bricks. I wrap my arms even tighter around Aria, my own eyes watering for her brother and for her as a little girl finding him like that. My brain racing imagining what that must have been like, and having to grow up dealing with it her entire life.

Her body racks with sobs, and now her reaction to the child drowning makes sense as it reminds her of her own trauma. The commitment to water safety and rescue training also comes into focus. Aria puts everything she has into trying to keep people safe around water, to be the rescuer they need when they are in trouble.

She is trying to save the world from experiencing the pain she knows in the deepest depths of her soul. She has taken up that burden and it follows her everywhere.

I held her for a long time, trying to ease her pain yet knowing there was no way for me to possibly do so. The only thing I can do is to show her how much it meant that she made herself vulnerable enough to share her darkest moment with me.

"Thank you for telling me. For trusting me with that." And in that moment I knew, I would do everything in my power to help her carry that burden, until she is able to finally let it go.

We spend the rest of the day staying in, cuddling, as she tells me stories about her brother, some happy. She doesn't say much about the aftermath, or the years following her brother's death, but I don't force the conversation either, needing to be her safe space.

27

ARIA

Tuesday, August 8th

"No Brady, not right now." I pushed the slobber covered ball off the couch, where Brady had unceremoniously dropped it by my face in an effort to get me off the couch and take him out to play.

The ball bounces and rolls away, Brady retrieving it and bringing it back once again.

"I said no, leave me alone." Brady cocks his head in the way that usually makes me laugh, the type of silly dog move that makes it seem like he is a full part of the conversation. But today, nothing makes me laugh. Nothing makes me want to.

That's the thing about grief—it becomes so ingrained in the body, in the soul, that you function without thinking about how much it affects you until something pulls the ripcord, and it all falls out again. Then the rawness is revealed, and no matter how long it's been, it feels fresh, it feels real.

It's been two days since learning about the local pool accident and I'm aware enough to know I'm not handling it well. It's too similar, and it hurts too bad. I don't feel like functioning, so instead, I'm rotting away on my couch, ignoring Brady's attempts to cheer me up. His movements have become restless, mirroring the turbulence in my own heart.

He lays his big snout on my arm, and stares at me with those deep, all-knowing eyes.

"I miss him, Bear."

My phone dings, signaling a text, and I lift it from the coffee table to see another text from Ian.

"Good morning sweetheart, I hope work goes well today. Thinking of you, would love to see you after :)"

My heart clenches.

I feel guilty lying to him, but it's easier to carry the burden myself rather than explaining everything.

Knowing he has hockey practice with the youth team I respond, "Thanks, have fun on the ice."

He's been nothing short of amazing after learning about my brother, offering to stay over, take me places, or do whatever I need. But the thing I need isn't something he can give. He can't bring Peter back, he can't change what happened after.

And the deeper my thoughts take me, the more I start feeling that maybe I shouldn't be depending on him to make me feel better anyways. If there is one thing I have learned about the aftermath of tragedies, it is that you can't count on those that supposedly love you the most.

Brady's head pops up a little while later and then comes the sound of tires on the gravel, and a knock a few moments later.

The sun is piercing as I open the door, and I have to block it to see the man standing before me. His jaw firmly set, mouth in a line, a caramel iced latte from Snowy's Cafe in hand.

"Oh, um, Ian, hi." I shift my weight, unable to look him in the eye, closing the door behind me to keep Brady inside.

"Hi. I got this for you." He holds out the coffee, gesturing for me to take it.

"Thank you, how sweet."

"It probably would've tasted better if I could have given it to you right after it was made, but the weirdest thing happened." He pauses, taking off his sunglasses, and waits until he catches my eyes, holding them firmly in place.

"I went to drop it off to you at work as a way to cheer you up a little, but when I got there, I ran into Evie. Do you know what she told me?"

I shake my head, diverting my eyes.

"She said you weren't on the schedule for today."

"I'm not." A long silence follows, and I finally look up.

His eyes flash pain, his brow scrunched trying to make sense of it.

"If you didn't want to see me today, you can just tell me Aria. I'm mature enough to handle it if you don't feel like hanging out. I just wanted to make sure you were ok." He reaches out and grabs my free hand, his thumb rubbing the back of my hand softly.

My eyes become blurry, the tears filling them despite my best attempt to keep it inside.

"I'm sorry, I'm just.. feeling a little overwhelmed and I didn't want you to know because I just want to keep what we have for as long as I can."

Head cocked, Ian studies me trying to decipher the meaning of my words. "I don't know what that means, but I want to understand. Help me understand?" His gaze is soft, patient. My chest sags under the weight of the promise in his eyes that he means it.

"Just come in... I'll try." I open the door behind me. Ian brushes past me, heading straight to the couch and making himself at home, Brady instantly at his side. Like he belongs there. Like they both do.

I take a sip of my drink, the sweet caramel instantly healing a part of my soul in a way that only favorite treats can, and hang near the doorway until Ian gives me an expectant look and beckons me over with a tilt of his head.

Settling next to him on the couch, I take a deep breath, trying to figure out where to start, recounting

Evie's words that being vulnerable can make a relationship stronger.

Or make him run faster. I shake off that thought and start.

"Sometimes when I think about my brother, I can kind of spiral into this annoying depressive state after, and being alone is easier than letting others in. Or at least that's what my therapist says." Ian puts his arm around my shoulder, grazing his fingers across the bare skin next to my tank top.

Ian is solemn as he takes my words in, not pushing for more, but steady in his calming presence, even without the back story is clearly in the dark. But being the perfect boyfriend, he is comforting me even though he doesn't understand the depth of the story.

"After the accid—after Peter, my mom never really figured out how to move on. She pretty much kept to herself, and slowly stopped, well, everything." His eyes grow sad, deep grooves appearing on his forehead.

"She stopped caring for herself, and for me. It was as if nothing else mattered. She basically stopped paying attention to what was going on in my life, my needs." My fingers curl with the hem of his shirt, nails slightly grazing against his bare skin.

"Which, at first I understood and tried my best to just do things for myself for a few years since I couldn't really rely on her, but then she—uh—," Ian squeezed my shoulders in support. "Eventually, she stopped coming home." His hands suddenly stopped moving.

"It was a few days at first, but then one day there was a note, saying she couldn't be a mom without her son, and that she wasn't coming back." I coughed out a gasp at remembering seeing those words on the paper, a neatly folded note on the kitchen table that I had picked up, anticipating anything but those words. The feel of the paper is a phantom pain on my fingertips.

Ian's arms tighten around me as I give myself five seconds to feel the pain. I then count backwards from ten like my therapist taught me, to reground my body and my thoughts in order to continue, exhaling and opening my eyes when done.

Ian shifts to face me, his hands sliding up my arms to my neck and pulls our foreheads together. I ground myself in the feeling of his fingers playing with the strands at the base of my hair.

"What did you do after that?" His voice is gruff, like he is restraining himself, full of rage and sadness for me.

"I went to live with Evie, whose grandma insisted that I move in as soon as she heard." I smile thinking about Evie, who became my sister at that moment. "I stayed there for 2 years until I graduated."

I pull back a little, fixing my eyes on my hands atop his thigh. There is a loose string on the hem of the gym shorts I try distracting myself with as I share the part I don't often voice.

"I guess part of me always hoped she would one day regret leaving me, and maybe I'd be enough for her to want to come back. But I haven't spoken to her since."

Ian exhales loudly, grips both my cheeks in his hands forcing my tear stained eyes to his, shift from cloudy to fierce in an instant.

"No Ari, you are more than enough. She doesn't deserve you, and I can't fathom how she would EVER walk away from you but I know for a fact that nothing you did warranted that. You are worth more than all the stars in the sky. You are not nothing. You. Are. Everything."

It's a more poetic version of the same truth I've spent years in therapy trying to learn, at first, and then remind myself of—that I didn't deserve it, that it doesn't have to define me as a person. But it's a hard trauma to overcome, and doubt sinks in regularly.

He thinks I'm everything.

His eyes flash are genuine and the love I feel but can't express is so overflowing that I can help but reach out through my tears and pull his mouth to mine, soaking in and wanting to drown in his arms and never resurface.

On the couch, we made what I can only describe as love, not just sex, for the first time in my life. I empty my cup of emotions and he takes every last drop, his hands gently caress my skin as our eyes meet. And though we say nothing, I feel a million unspoken words between us. Each lost in our own thoughts, we stay on the couch for a while after, both quiet. A big part of me feels relieved to have finally told Ian the truth about my mom. Like I'm not having to hide the darkest part of me.

A small part, however, can help but fixate on what happens when, despite what he says, I am no longer enough for Ian too.

28

IAN

Friday, August 11th

"It's just there, on the right."

I pull in where Aria is pointing, and park in the gravel lot before rounding the car to help her out.

We are further outside of Sierra Springs than we normally stay, but Aria is excited about this little "hidden gem" as she calls it, right on the Truckee River. It's famous for apparently having chairs in the river, as opposed to just on the deck above it. Not sure about how all that works honestly, but her voice got all high and happy when she described it and I wanted nothing more than to see her eyes light up like that again, so here we are.

It's been a rough few days for her, and this was the first thing she was genuinely excited about. When both she and Evie ended up with the same Friday night off, they made the plans. It could be a hole in the wall and I would take her there every day, just to see her smile like this again.

I've spent the past couple of days fighting the urge to hunt down her mom and demand that she make amends for what she has done. Not that it would make up for the shitty things her mom did, but at least demand some sort of remittance. How anyone, much less a mother, could EVER leave—no, abandon her—is something I can't even begin to comprehend.

That girl is everything, and life without her doesn't make sense.

I've been feeling it for sometime, playing around with the idea in my mind, but when I heard what Aria's mother did, it was instantaneous.

The certainty that I would never walk away from her settled in me just like the feel of ice under my skates—familiar, steady, undeniable.

The reason I could never understand someone doing that is because I could never, because I am falling in love with Aria. I would rather cut out my heart than hurt hers. I would rather protect hers than allow anyone else the opportunity to hurt her like that again.

She is the calm I feel regardless of whether she is there, knowing she will return. And I am going to make sure she knows I'm not going anywhere, even though I don't think I'm at the place where I can say it yet.

I grab the faux log door handle and swing the door open, ushering her in front of me. We take in the rustic mountain decor paired with what can only be described as truck stop vibes in this definitely unique watering hole.

Reba's is a mishmash of different things, but somehow it all works. Aria waves her long tan arm above her head as we spot Evie out on the back patio, waiting in line at the bar there.

I feel a slender hand grab mine, and realize Aria has reached back from where she is standing to tether herself to me before she steps to lead us over to her— *our*—friends.

I give her hand a squeeze, running my thumb along her smooth skin. She turns her head back and smiles before leading the way through the patrons, only releasing it to wrap Evie in a hug.

"I'm so glad you guys finally got here! These guys won't shut up about which one is right, and I needed a buffer." Evie rolls her eyes in dramatic fashion before pulling me into a hug as well.

Aria must know something about how Hunter and the others interact because she laughs knowingly and gives a head shake.

"Ari, tell them that skiing is a million times more fun, but harder, than snowboarding," Hunter nods towards two guys in hoodies standing drinking a beer a piece next to him.

"You're just jealous because we only need one board to do what you need two for." A guy with black hair peeking out of his beanie responds, making everyone laugh.

"You just worry about not crossing tips with any other guys out there." The other says. I laugh at the rib—it sounds a lot like hockey banter to me.

Hunter's gaze fixated on someone across the deck when he absentmindedly says "Yah not worried about that, never been one to go after dicks." I follow his gaze to see a blonde sitting alone at a circular table, reading a book like we are in Mother Nature's library rather than a bar. He makes a move to head that direction before pausing and deciding better of it. I furrowed my eyebrows at him, not expecting him to be one to avoid approaching a pretty girl, and he just waved me off and followed the girls to the front of the line.

After ordering our beers, we follow a little pebble path down to a grouping of Adirondack chairs that—just like she described—were plopped down in a little curve of the river. We toe off our shoes and I roll up my jeans before wading into the water.

"It's a little cold," Aria's hand grasps onto my forearm as she wobbles slightly from the chilly water before lowering herself into a chair and pulling my arm so I land into the one next to her. A grin takes over my face as I sip and watch over the rim as she swings her feet back and forth in the water like a child on a swing, her face so expressive with joy that my chest tightens a little at the sight.

I link my fingers with her and pull her hand to my mouth, pressing a kiss to her palm. "So fucking cute, sweetheart."

...

A few hours later, after some food and shuffleboard, we are in the parking lot getting ready to part ways with Evie, waiting for Hunter to come out as they rode together. Aria leans her head back and tilts it to the side, and looks up at me from where I stand behind her, my arms wrapped around her torso.

"You guys are so cute together. I can't wait to go shopping and to see the pictures!" Evie claps her hands at her chest in excitement.

"Shopping for what? What pictures?" Aria's confusion makes sense, since I haven't actually told her about the little road trip I want her to accompany me on, despite having told Evie all about it while Aria was kicking some butt at shuffleboard against the others.

I spin Aria in my arms so she is facing me and lean my forehead on hers. "I want you to come to San Jose with me, and attend a charity gala as my date."

Her eyes go wide and her pouty little mouth falls open. "A Gala? When?"

"Next weekend." I run my hand up her shoulder, and tighten the string on the hoodie I insisted she wear once the temperature dropped.

"I don't know if I can, I don't have my schedule yet." She wavers between forlorn and happy, unsure which emotion will play out.

"Sorry it's late notice, I sort of forgot about it to be honest. If you can, would you like to be my date?" I stare into her green eyes, knowing this is more than just a work conflict decision for her. It would mean appearing publicly together outside the confines of the lake community. It would be publicized, potentially talked about on podcasts and social media.

It would be a major step in our relationship. And now I'm standing here waiting to see if she feels the same as I do about wanting to explore that next step.

Aria glances over at Evie, who gives her a reassuring smile and nods, before throwing her arms around my shoulders and hugging me close, "I'd love to, Ian, thank you!"

I grab her chin, dominating the area with my palm as I pull her in quickly, kissing her in relief and excited about what next weekend could mean to us.

29
ARIA

Friday, August 18th

As it turns out, getting time off didn't end up being a problem. Despite being scheduled for two weddings, Evie made it her mission to ensure that ALL of my coworkers knew why I wanted the weekend off. She convinced two separate people that this was my ticket to happiness and they were more than willing to each pick up a shift for me. Especially when Evie offered for me to cover the weekly ladies golf luncheon, the crew's least favorite, for one of them.

Evie also made it her mission to dress me for the occasion. This resulted in a full girls day boutique hopping until we found the perfect dress—a slinky champagne colored gown with thin straps that crossed over an otherwise completely exposed back, a drooping neckline, high slit, and silky fabric that flowed over my hips, giving me the appearance of curves.

She squealed when I came out of the dressing room and the sales attendant gave me a thumbs up and I'll even admit, I felt hot—sexy even—wearing it. Knowing I needed as much confidence as I could garner for the gala, I agreed it was the right choice as well.

The drive down went quickly, as did all my time with Ian. I've never had someone where the conversation has flowed so easily, so naturally, before (apart from Evie of course). I love how touchy he is when we are in a car together, how he is always linking hands or even just a pinky, has his hand on my leg or makes some reason to touch me so frequently. It makes me feel cherished, I guess.

We pulled up to his building, a sleek and modern one that gave off a converted industrial appearance, and into the parking garage beneath. Refusing my help and grabbing both of our rolling bags plus my dress bag, Ian led the way to the lobby entrance door.

"Hey Ian, good to see you." A short older gentleman with kind eyes waved at him from the security desk.

"Frank, my man, looking good! How have you been?" Ian made short but polite and unhurried conversation with the security officer, asking about his family.

"This is my girlfriend, Aria." He gestured for me to join them at the desk. Hearing the designation made my stomach flutter—there hasn't been much reason to say it out loud but it still makes me feel special that he would introduce me as that.

I reach my hand out to shake Frank's hand, and he gives me a kind smile before kissing the back of my hand. "A beautiful name for a beautiful girl," making me laugh.

"Hitting on my girl, Frank?" Ian covers his chest with his broad hand, pretending to be offended.

"Hi Frank, it's nice to meet you."

"Likewise, you just let me know when you are done with this boy and you and I will go on a nice date together instead, ok?" He gives me a wink and laughs along with the two of us.

"Ok smooth talker, we are going to head up, just here for the weekend. We'll see you around." Ian places his hand on the small of my back and directs me towards the elevator, before grabbing all our bags once again.

We ride the elevator to the 13th floor, and enter his penthouse apartment through a hallway that opens up to his living room and open concept kitchen to the right. But it is the view that caught my eye, as it overlooked the bustling Silicon Valley and surrounded by the Santa Cruz Mountains. While it wasn't a view like at home, it is still pretty, in a city dwelling sort of way.

I take in his comfortable yet fairly modern style, a couch that looks cozy for curling up on and a bar set up for entertaining. The kitchen is spacious and sleek with a refrigerator much larger than mine and a huge marble island.

Warm, strong hands snake around my belly, and Ian drops his chin to my shoulder. "What do you think?"

"It's perfect Ian, it is fancy but still cozy, kind of like you" I groan as he nips at my ear, making me bite my lip.

"You think I'm fancy but still cozy?" He kisses my neck and I open for him, giving him space to explore as his hands start to dip below the hem of my shirt and into the yoga pants I wore for the drive.

"Mmm-hmm. Yup. Fancy pants athlete. Good cuddler. Makes sense." I sink into him and press further into his steadily growing cock as his fingers find their way into my thong and begin stroking.

He turns my head forcibly by my chin and plunders my mouth with his tongue. Releasing me, he growls " The only thing that makes sense right now is getting you naked and in my bed." My hand wraps up and around the back of his head. "But I want the full tour."

He smacks my ass, and points behind us, "that's the guest bedroom, bathroom. Tour over. Time for bed." And with that he picks me up, wrapping my legs around his waist, and carries me into his room. The only thing I notice is the way the king size bed swallows me up when he tosses me onto it like I am an empty duffle.

A few hours later, exhausted from multiple rounds and orgasms, my head is on his bare chest as I trace the lines of his ab muscles with my finger. Worry begins to creep back in, leading me to ask the question that has been brewing since the invite.

"Are you sure you want me to go with you tomorrow? I don't mind staying here while you go."

His hand covers mine, forcing me to stop moving it over his carved body. "Of course I want you to go. Why wouldn't I?"

"I just don't want you to think you have to take me just because we are together. It's ok if you'd rather not put it out publicly and all." I go to turn in the bed but his grip prevents me from moving and he shifts to bring our faces closer together.

"Have I given any indication that I don't want to be with you publicly?"

"No, but I don't want to cause any issues for you or press distractions before the season starts back up..." Figuring out how to put into words what I want to ask is a struggle, but I owe it to myself to not retreat this time.

"Why would it be an issue?" Ian is patient, waiting for a response.

The dusting of hair on his chest is soft against the pads of my fingertips as they dance across his skin.

"Do you think I'm not serious about us?" His mouth turns down, his jaw tightening.

"Well, I mean...maybe? I don't know," I cast my eyes down, but then become resolute, and lift them back up. "I just didn't know if you would still want to date once the season starts and you are back here." My shoulders droop, defeated by the idea of not being with him. "I think I just need to know where we stand, like if this is a summer thing, or more."

I take a breath, building the confidence to clearly articulate my needs. "I'm not trying to rush anything, but I have struggled with feeling like a temporary option in the past, and I need to understand if this has an expiration date."

Sitting up and pulling the comforter across my naked chest, I feel both anxious and proud that I expressed my needs like that.

Ian sits up, and positions himself so I am sitting facing him, and grabs my hands in his.

"I don't know what the season is going to bring, and I know it will be tough, but I don't want this to have an expiration date just because we will be a few hours apart." He combs his fingertips through the layers of hair framing my face. "I didn't expect to meet someone this summer who lives in a different place, but now that we have, I'm getting a little obsessed with you in case you haven't noticed. I'm sorry that I wasn't clear about this being more than just a summer romance." He grins and I laugh, and then fall forward as he pulls me into his arms.

"Aria, I'm in this. Are you in this with me?"

My heart soars, my smile widening. *This man.* He wants me, and for more than just the summer. "Of course I am."

"Then I want everyone there tomorrow to know that you are mine; nothing will make me happier than having you on my arm."

My heart stumbles in my chest, tears flooding my eyes, and a foreign, overwhelming feeling consumes my soul. It feels like what I feel love is supposed to feel like. And while that may not be what this is, I settle into the feeling and keep it close, begging it to stay for just a little while longer.

• • •

The next morning, we headed into the Grizzlies' arena for what Ian called "Family Skate" dressed in pants and carrying jackets, despite it being 85 degrees outside. I guess since many of the players had returned home to attend the gala, the team was hosting a family day for everyone to hang out and see each other. Ian assured me that I was fine to attend since Family also included girlfriends, or the "WAGS and their kids", as he put it, but it wasn't until we were well into the event that my nerves started to calm down , my body relaxing enough to begin to enjoy it.

I don't know what I thought would happen that made me so nervous, but seeing big hulking hockey players skating around with little kids, some even tiny babies, and goofing off with each other while the wives and girlfriends visited and skated with their families put me at ease.

The family aspect seemed bigger than just the individual families, it was as if the team and all their related parts were one enormous family. Kids approach Ian as if they had known him their entire lives and he acts as if he is their uncle, lifting them up and skating around with them, or pretending to let them get around him in some sort of poor display of defense. It is all incredibly adorable and reminds me of the thoughts I had the first day at the ice rink.

Taking a break against the boards while Ian and a few players started up a small sided game, I laughed as they threw insults back and forth.

"It's Aria, right?" I turn to see a gorgeous girl about my age, wearing a cute letterman style jacket in team colors that looks both comfy and trendy at the same time.

"Yes, hi!" While people greeted me as a group, this is the first non player to approach me one on one.

"I'm Jill, my husband is the team's assistant captain, Brooks. It is so nice to meet you!" Her smile is wide and genuine, putting me at ease. "I had to come meet you when I heard that Ian brought someone. It's been so long since anyone but his mom has attended these events!" My head cocks to the side slightly, taking in that information. I assumed he had a line of girls waiting to go anywhere with him.

"Oh really? Well, that's nice of him to include me then." She turns back towards the ice, leaning against the boards with me as we watch the guys pass the puck back and forth with style.

"Yeah, ever since the whole Amber thing, he just has been completely closed off with girls, that was tough for him to get over." She gives a sad smile.

Ian and I haven't talked too much about past relationships—I know his last one ended over a year ago—so this is new information to me. Wanting to know more, but also not wanting to pry into his history before he is ready to tell me himself, I am cautious when choosing my response.

"Hmm, that makes me feel even more happy to be invited I guess."

She fluffs her perfectly styled chestnut brown hair a little. "It was just so hard for him, you know, like they were together for so long and it was such a surprise to him and all of us when it ended, we all thought they'd be endgame. And then for it to end like it did, it crushed him."

A knot forms in my chest, and I find it a little hard to focus. He dated someone for long enough that his hockey family thought they would get married, and then it just ended? Did she leave him? I can't imagine ever making a conscious choice to choose not to be with him, he is like the sun shining on a cloudy day.

My nails press into my palm, anxiety rushing through my veins, trying to make sense of this new information. Is he over her? Does he still want to be with her? What is this rage I'm feeling inside...jealousy? Over someone I have never met? Suddenly, I want to know everything and nothing all at once.

Jill must take my silence as a cue to change topics, because she moves on to talk about the charity gala that night. She explains how most everyone here will be attending as it is an annual event that all the Bay Area athletic teams support, and how much fun it is every year. She seems genuinely happy when I tell her that I am attending with Ian, and gives me a hug before skating off with a promise to meet up at the event to see each other's dresses.

Ian finishes up his game and comes over, wrapping me in a hug and placing a soft kiss on my lips. "Having fun?" He spins me around on our skates before pulling me to skate with him.

"I am. I met Jill and we talked for a little bit, and it was cute watching you play with the kids."

"I'm glad you met her, she was excited when I told Brooks you were coming. She wants to pull you into the depths of the WAGs." He winks, causing me to laugh.

Being here, surrounded by his normal environment and team, makes me crave to be a part of it all, to continue to learn this side of him. But if he is still recovering, or even missing his ex, is that something that is possible? We leave the event and grab coffee before he takes me on a brief tour of some of his favorite spots in the city, and then head back to his apartment to get ready for the evening.

30

IAN

Saturday, August 19th

I catch myself tapping my foot as I anxiously wait for Aria to come out of my bathroom to see her dress for the gala.

From the blush she gave me when she and Evie came back from shopping I knew she must have found something that looked incredible on her—though a potato sack probably would. She is beautiful no matter what she wears. If she is standing on top of a boulder in a Patagonia or in a bikini (especially in a bikini) or dressed for work I always think she looks great. But something about the anticipation of seeing her truly dressed up for the first time, ready to go out and spend the evening in my world, with my friends and teammates, makes me eager for her to exit the room.

The door swings open and I hop up from the bed, lifting my eyes to take her in fully and when I do, all the breath I had in my lungs disappeared and I'm frozen in place. I was expecting her to look remarkable, but there aren't enough words to describe how stunning she looks.

She is a goddess draped in a light rosy gold dress that hugs her body perfectly, showing off her toned and yet feminine body. A curved neckline that dips just low enough for her sweet breasts to be giving just a hint of cleavage draws my eyes first, and a slit that has them traveling from her ankle to the top of her thigh where it ends follows. My imagination continues, willing I could tear away the few inches of fabric between her and the pussy I'd love to be all over right now.

I groan, my cock stirring. "You. Are. Stunning." I wave my fingers in a little circle, begging her to turn for me and as she does I get a view of a low back, skin exposed and begging for my fingers to caress, which I eagerly do after I quickly move across the room. "That dress looks like it was made for you. Beautiful, just like you."

Aria beams and tucks her neatly curled hair behind her ears, which has me lifting my hand to release it from its constraint. She looks phenomenal, and I want her to radiate the confidence she should feel.

"You think so?" She asks, eyes searching mine for the truth.

I kiss her softly. "Absolutely. I have half a mind just to stay here and spend all night worshipping you in this." Her hands find my chest and she pulls me in closer.

"Thank you. Last chance, sure you don't want to go alone?" She grabs her clutch from the nightstand and fiddles with the latch.

"Not a chance. I have to show my girl off to the world, and then fight off all the punks who think they are getting within a 10 foot radius of you in this dress." I grab her hand and kiss it, and lead her out, turning the lights out on the way.

She might think I'm joking, but if any of the guys let their eyes linger too long on her in this, we'll be having words.

•••

The gala is at a ballroom downtown, an upscale venue with towering columns and dramatic lighting. Ornate chandeliers and live palm trees fill the space with colorful uplighting and there are tables set for 250 along with a dance floor in front of the main stage.

I've been here a few times before for similar events, but this is Aria's first time. Seeing it through her eyes is what it must be like to be with someone the first time they see snow or the Grand Canyon. Her eyes are alight with wonder, the light reflecting on the depths of green, as she looks around with a contented sigh and squeezes my bicep where she took my arm when I offered it upon entering. We are instantly surrounded by teammates, who along with their dates greet me and Aria alike like old friends, their wives and girlfriends enveloping her into their fold like she has always been a part.

It's effortless, and my soul feels like something has slid into place as I watch.

Like she is the missing piece.

And I realize then that that is the feeling I have felt but haven't been able to identify these past few weeks. Where we have existed in and around each other, where spending time and conversation is natural, not rushed or forced, almost like our souls recognize each other and say

"There you are," and are able to relax in knowing they found their person.

I snap out of it as I feel a hand on my shoulder as I watch our assistant captain's wife fawn over Aria's dress. I look back to see Holden with a dumb grin on his face.

"What, asshole?" I'm glad to see him, summer is always rough being away from my best friends for so long.

"Just taking in the look of a man who is so far gone for a woman. Just memorizing this for your wedding someday." He throws his head back and laughs and I punch him in the shoulder before pulling him in for a bro hug.

"I didn't say anything about a wedding."

"You didn't have to. I can see it written all over your pathetic puppy dog face. You have it bad for that girl." He nods over to Aria, who makes eye contact with me and smiles broadly, making my own mouth match hers.

"Yah, that I do man. She's something else."

"I'm happy for you, man. I truly am. But I'm still going to steal her for a dance just to piss you off." I push him away with a huff and smile, go and grab my girl for a dance before him or any of the others have a chance.

31
ARIA

The past few hours have flown by and have been much more easy going than I was expecting for such a formal event. I was touched to see the guys all bid on auction items to support the children's charity that the gala benefited. Jack, Marcus, and a few others each insisted on getting a dance in, much to the dismay of Ian whom I'm pretty sure muttered "should have made you wear a paper bag" under his breath during one such attempt.

Wrapped up in his arms, my head laying against his chest while we swayed to the music was heavenly, and I've gone from slightly dreading this evening and trying to fit in, to truly enjoying myself and feeling totally welcomed by our entire table and his friends.

Ian has been the perfect date all night, ensuring I'm looked after, well fed, and is always there with a drink, a touch, or a joke to diffuse conversation if I seem the slightest bit uncomfortable in meeting the various attendees.

I grab my clutch and lean over to whisper in Ian's ear. "I'll be right back." He squeezes my hand and gives me a kiss on the cheek, and I head to the restroom.

I push the ornate door open and move into the plush room. In the dim yet chic lighting, three women standing near the mirrors reapplying lipstick and touching up their hair, each uniquely beautiful and dressed to the nines, just like all the women here tonight. I glance away, not wanting to look like I'm staring and move down into one of the stalls, without making eye contact.

"God that dress is to die for Amber, no wonder the men can't take their eyes off you tonight." I hear one of them compliment the other. Love when girls support other girls.

"Especially Ian." I pause, trying to stay quiet at the sound of his name by one of the other girls. "Poor guy was practically drooling over you while dancing with whoever that chick was he brought tonight." All my senses point towards the conversation and I'm frozen in place.

Is that Amber, his ex? She's here? And Ian was drooling over her? Tears spring to my eyes but I fight them back.

"It's so sad," the third girl chimes in, "he was so desperate when he called me and asked me to come with him tonight like old times, he was so eager to get back together. But I had to tell I was already going with Lucas, so he must have just found someone else to take in my place since he waited so long."

This girl has to be Amber, and my heart plummets as it takes in the meaning of what she just said. Ian had asked her to go with him to the gala? He wanted to get back together? That must mean he only asked me after she turned him down, which means I wasn't his first choice at all, and still am not.

He'd rather be here with her. Toilet paper crumbles under my clenched fist, a visual representation of how my heart feels, tattered and bruised.

My eyes water and I take a deep breath, not willing to break down in front of them, despite the stall door being between us.

"She's awfully plain if you ask me, and she doesn't fit in with the other WAGs. Maybe Ian's just doing her a favor or something taking her to something fancy since he couldn't get the date he wanted."

My freshly manicured nails dig deep into my palm, willing this pain shooting through my chest to stop before I cry out. I knew no matter how fancy of a dress I got or how meticulous I did my makeup that I would still not fit in—it's why I told Ian he could go without me.

The girls exit the bathroom, leaving me alone with my heart in pieces, and I finally release the sob that I had forcefully held in. The realization that everything that has been developing between Ian and I, everything that I felt like was pure and poetic and making me wonder if this is what falling in love is like, is nothing more than just a second place stand-in for a boy who still has his heart set on the girl that got away.

I let myself fall apart for a few minutes, and then took a deep breath and forced myself to pull it together. This night is important for Ian, and even if I wasn't his first choice, I needed to put on a brave face and support him. Once I get back to the safety of Brady and my couch, I can let the feelings flow and figure out where to go from there.

Luckily, I had brought my clutch with me and am able to make a few necessary touch ups to my makeup to cover up the blotchy spots that remained from my heartbreak. I make sure my mascara is no longer running and rejoin the group at the table. Ian gives me a smile and my returning one must not be convincing enough because he cocks his head. "Is everything ok?" I stare into his eyes, which seem dark with worry.

"Everything is great. Just getting tired." It's only a partial lie; I am tired, but mostly from feeling.

"We can get going. The fun is mostly over anyway." He stands and offers his hands, and I place mine in his, wishing I could hold onto him for just a little longer, but feeling like he is slowly falling out of my grip.

It is hard to make it through the rest of the night, and eventually Ian falls asleep next to me as I run the past two months through my head.

How foolish it was of me to be falling in love with a man who is only settling for me because I was conveniently there at a time when he couldn't have what he really wanted.

Falling in love. Throwing a hand over my mouth I try to muffle the cries that come from the thought, playing it off as a cough. Knowing that even if I am not his first choice he is mine, my chest gasping at the idea that it isn't enough. That no matter how strong my feelings are for him, how much I try to be everything he needs, I'm not enough for him because I'm not what he wants.

I'm not Amber.

32

IAN

Sunday, August 20th

Something is off, I think for the hundredth time since I got up.

Last night when we got back from the gala Aria seemed withdrawn, almost sad, but when I tried to figure out what was wrong she just claimed she was tired so we went to bed. Even with her wrapped in my arms, it felt like she was a million miles away, similar to how it feels right now even though she is sitting in the passenger seat as we drive.

I took one of the scenic routes home, since any time spent with her is enjoyable, and figured we could stop around Murphys or Calaveras Big Trees to extend our day a bit, have lunch at a winery, or just walk around together. But the past few hours have been mostly quiet, with Aria choosing to read a book and me not knowing how to ask what's bothering her in a way different from the others I've tried, the ones she has already shut down.

We had a great weekend, I thought. Last night was a blast with everyone at the party, and she sparkled under lights and the adoration of my teammates and their families.

It couldn't have been more perfect, or at least until I saw Amber there. Should have known she would have begged her way back into one of the big social events of the summer by coming with someone from another team, anything to boost her social channels and keep people talking about her.

The way she ramped up her gestures and voice the few times she was nearby made it clear she was trying to get my attention.

Luckily, she didn't approach us or anything, but I will admit it felt like a bit of a sock to the stomach when I saw her there. I don't know that I'll ever be able to forgive her for what she did. Certainly didn't want to have to try last night so I avoided her and didn't even mention her being there to Aria, which makes sense as I haven't told her the entire story anyway.

"Want to grab lunch at the winery?" I motion towards the sign welcoming us to Murphys and some of the local attractions.

"I'm not all that hungry." Aria responds without looking up from her book.

Defeated from being shut out once again, I slouch against the seat and run my hand through my hair in frustration. I can understand not wanting to talk all the time, but I know something is bothering her, and she is not telling me, and it's starting to really piss me off. I don't like it when people keep things from me. It brings up all the raw feelings of betrayal and hidden agendas from my past.

20 minutes later, I've had enough and pull into the entrance for Calaveras Big Trees State Park, paying the

entrance fee to the park ranger and park. Only when the engine dies does Aria look up, glancing around and taking in the surroundings.

"Let's go for a walk." I open my door before she can resist, and then sigh when she opens her own door rather than waiting for me to do it for her. Turning towards the path, I put my hands in my pockets and pray that she follows me.

Walking silently amongst the massive Sequoias, I feel my frustrations diminish as their towering presence makes me feel small and inconsequential. These trees are ancients, having lived hundreds of years, remaining strongly rooted while humanity struggles on.

Nature is a perspective shift, one that reminds us that while we make our problems as big as the world, we are all just small specks in the timeline and map of greatness all around us.

When we get to a massive stump that has steps to climb it like a stage, I gesture for her to go first and then follow her across the large flat surface and sit down, legs dangling off the side at least 8 feet up off the ground. She sits next to me, without touching. My hands yearn to reach out for connection, but I don't want to push her too far.

"I know you've said nothing is wrong, but I have to say, I'm really not believing you babe." I lean back on my hands and look at her, waiting until she makes eye contact.

She takes a big breath, and tears flood her eyes. My heart aches at the sight and in an instant I'm pulling her into my chest and stroking her head, not saying anything but hoping she will let me in.

"Are you still in love with Amber?" Out of all the things I thought she might say, that came out of left field and I am not prepared.

Time stops, the wave of unpleasant memories accosts me and I freeze, which apparently is the wrong thing to do because Aria continued, "It's ok if you are, I understand." Her shoulders sag and she tears her face from my chest, trying to pull away.

"Why would you ask me that?" I genuinely want to know, because I definitely have not said or done anything to bring her up in any conversations, and made sure she didn't approach Aria last night at the gala.

She shifts and pulls herself out of my arms, and drops her gaze to her hands that fidget in her lap.

"I just need to know. I'm, ah, I'm starting to really care for you and just need to know if you are hoping to get back with her."

I stare at her, incredulous at the idea that I would ever go back to Amber.

Her voice is almost a whisper.

"I don't think I could take it if I let myself keep falling deeper for you for you to just leave me for her."

My mind processes what she is saying in two parts: 1. She is falling for me. And 2. She thinks I'm going to leave her for Amber. I feel the ultimate high at the first, and the lowest low at the second. And I can't stand to let her think that for a moment longer.

I jump to stand, and pull her up, and take her face into both hands. I need all of her attention like I need air to breathe. She needs to see into my mind, my heart, my soul when I tell her this. Her green eyes are without the vibrancy, the light that usually dances in them. The tears are muddling the colors, making them a mossy green that looks like the shadowed areas in the forest around us.

"Aria I need you to listen to me when I say this. I am not in love with Amber, and I have not been in a very long time. I would NEVER go back to her, not if my life depended on it." I plead with her to believe me as I watch her reaction, uncertain and hoping lingering delicately together.

"Then why did you invite her to the gala?" She grabs my hand in hers, not removing it from her cheek.

My brow scrunches in confusion. "I have no idea what you are talking about. I didn't and I wouldn't have."

She pushes my arms away and crosses her arms protectively. "Don't lie to me. I heard her tell her friends at the gala that you did, and that you want to get back together with her."

She hangs her head in defeat while I try to work through what I just heard. Amber told people I invited her? That's ridiculous, she burned any bridges we had long ago. Why would she say that, and how did Aria hear it?

Grabbing her elbow to keep her near, I plead.

"Baby, please, help me understand. When did she say that? I have no idea why she said it but I promise you I haven't had any contact with her in over a year."

Aria looks at me tentatively, wanting to believe me but unable to trust. "She said it in the bathroom, when I left after dinner. I overheard her talking to some other girls after I walked in."

My jaw tics, teeth grinding, the plot holes slowly filling in.

"Did she see you go in?" Suddenly it is starting to make sense.

"I don't think so, I don't know I tried not to stare at them when I walked by and I didn't know what she looked like so I didn't know it was her." Aria shrugs.

"I think she probably did, and I think she said that intentionally for you to overhear." Aria pauses and looks up at me, confusion spreading across her face.

"Why would she do that?"

Raising both hands to my head I sigh and pace around up top the giant stump. "Because she is a manipulative person, because she builds herself up by cutting others down," the silence of the forest is a stark contrast to the pitch of my voice that is slowly losing control. "Most likely because she was jealous of you and wanted you to think you didn't matter to me."

"Well, it kinda worked." The hurt in her voice cuts deep.

Instantly I'm at her side, grabbing onto her arm and forcing her to look me in the eyes.

"Aria I'm going to tell you what happened with Amber—the whole story—so you know everything. But first, I need you to know something." Aria bites her lip, but not in the sexy anticipation way I love—this time it's like an anxious tic. I pull her lip out and kiss it softly.

"You matter so much to me. You matter more than anything to me. This summer with you feels like it has brought me back to life, and that's because of you. You are funny and caring, and so adventurous and considerate. You are always there for others and you don't even see how much you mean to me or to your friends. And every day I am falling deeper and deeper for you, and I don't want to stop."

"Really?" Her voice is barely a whisper.

"Yes, really." I pull her in and crash my mouth to hers. She responds instantly, her hands finding the back of my head and pulling, tugging the hairs to bring me closer. My arms wrap around her back and up, pressing between her shoulder blades to try to crush all the air separating us to make that happen.

We pull apart, our foreheads resting on each other's. "You matter to me too Ian." Aria's voice is lighter, loving and full of meaning. She sends me a promise full of words unspoken in just a short phrase.

I grasp her hand in mind and pull her towards the stairs, which we descend and then start walking further into the grove of trees. The air between us is quiet, heavy with anticipation of needed conversation, but at the same time calm, like the security of being near each other has been restored. I try to figure out where to begin.

"Amber and I were together for 3 years. Everything seemed fine and normal, and I did love her. Some people thought we would get married, we had talked about it a little but weren't at that step quite yet, but still we were solid, or so I thought."

I keep walking, finding it easier to speak the truth of the past while moving. "The season was wrapping up, we didn't make it to the cup that year but we had a pretty good run." I feel a set of squeezes in my hand, a prompt to keep going, letting me know she was there. I squeeze back.

"We were having an end of the year party at one of the guys' houses, and ..." I pause, not sure how much detail I want to go into. Not that I don't trust her with it, I do, but it just makes me sick to think about.

"I couldn't find Amber at one point and went looking for her." Aria slows us down, pulling my arm so I'm facing her, as if she knows the blow that is coming.

"I found her, along with one of my teammates, well, former teammate. They were in the middle of it in a back room." A small gasp is the only sound in the silence of the trees around us. Her nails dig into my arm, like she is holding back her disgust while letting me finish.

"Turns out they had been hooking up behind my...behind everyone's back, for a few months. Never even knew." I shake my head, still mad at myself for not realizing something was up long before that point.

"Oh God, Ian, that's awful." Her eyes search mine as she strokes her fingers across my neck, as if seeking out the hurt and trying to saddle up beside it. Her comforting touches make it easier to continue.

"Yah it sucked." I huff. "It completely fucked with my mind. I obviously broke up with her, and then instead of just her moving on for some reason she decided to try to make me out to be the bad guy in the relationship to save face for her audience on socials." Kicking at a rock in the path, I laugh to myself as I tell her the rest.

"She started spewing ridiculous stories about me treating her poorly, controlling her, and I swear to God I didn't but she said some pretty hurtful shit and made people assume I was that kind of guy."

"She said WHAT?" Aria's pupils blow wide and she tenses, ready to pounce. "How dare she do that, when she was the one fucking around behind your back and treating you so badly! I could kill her!"

Seeing her riled up like a tiger ready for attack, all at the defense of my reputation makes a smile breakthrough on my face, thinking how fucking adorable this hidden spitfire appearance is and glad she is mine. And feeling so...loved, I guess. She was willing to go to battle for me, and hadn't needed to hear any evidence to know I wouldn't do the awful things Amber claimed.

"I kind of like seeing you like this, like you are ready to avenge my name." I wrap my arm around her waist and pull her close.

"I am ready, I'm ready to kill that terrible bitch right now." She squirms as her people pleasing body tries to come to terms with the need for violence. "Give me a freaking baseball bat, or a bow and arrow, or hell, even a paperclip and I'll figure out some way to make her suffer" she mutters as I press her into my chest.

Laughter breaks out of me, bringing down the intensity of the moment. I kiss the top of Aria's head and hug her tightly.

"Thank you my little warrior." She gives me a playful push away. I grab her hand and we continue walking.

"So that's why I think she knew you were in there, and was trying to make you feel bad. I'm sorry you had to go through that though, but I wish you had said something right away. I would have handled it and made sure she knew I will never let her treat you that way. I'll never stand by and let anyone make you feel less than you are."

We wander into a massive cutout at the base of a tree that lets the path cut straight through the trunk. I lean against the velvet bark and tug her by the waist into me. "I need you to talk to me when something happens that makes you upset or gets you thinking crazy things about us. I don't want you stressing over something not true and if it is a problem, then we need to handle it together. Please, trust me with what's going through your mind, and let me in."

"I'll try. I just didn't see any reason to think she was lying because I didn't know."

"And that's on me. I should have told you about our history before going. If I had known or even thought she would be there I would have. I'm sorry for withholding it from you."

She kisses the tip of my nose, and I do the same back.

"All is forgiven. Now, how about some lunch?"

33
ARIA

Friday, August 25th

Only four more hours to get through. You can do this, Aria.

It's another Friday night wedding, and if something could go wrong during this wedding, it has. And of course, I'm not only serving but pulling double duty as Bridal Attendant tonight.

Aka, the bride's bitch.

In addition to my normal responsibilities, I've herded the bridesmaids around, running up and down stairs trying to find the stragglers. I've lugged a massive bin of drinks and champagne down to the beach for photos.

Anything she or her wedding party needs, I take care of it. No request is too big. Or too stinky apparently.

Another first tonight, as I literally changed a baby's diaper on the beach bar because too many groomsmen were failing at that attempt. At least all that time with Gracie has paid off.

And then of course, burned my hand on the hot box (again).

But at least when this is all over I can relax and crash into Ian's arms. I'm getting used to spending the night with him, or having him sleep in my bed.

Even if I'm way too tired after a shift to physically move, having his strong arms wrap about me is such a soothing way to fall asleep. I'm definitely getting used to it.

Possibly addicted.

We've spent every night together since coming home from the gala last weekend, and despite still having some lingering uncertainty after the whole ex situation, physically it just keeps getting better and better.

And the thought of his arms around me, snaking down the front of my belly, hands down my shorts is what has me so out of sorts that I completely miss the puddle of water forming in front of the ice machine.

The puddle sitting right at the corner that I'm taking to drop this heavy tray full of chowder cup remnants to the dish line.

It happens in slow motion. My left foot slips, the full soup cup stacked precariously on the two below it right above my right shoulder, wedged onto the tray with the other dirty dishes like it's the last lifeboat on the Titanic, starts wobbling, and there is no amount of righting the tray that will keep it balanced.

I keep myself on two feet at least, but my celebration is quickly demolished as the cup of chowder tumbles the exact wrong way off the tray, turning over directly on to my neck before crashing to the floor, breaking into pieces.

The slimy, sticky liquid fills my senses and forces me to close my eyes, coming to accept that I now have cold clam chowder all down my back, inside my polo.

And, ew, it is a bowl I cleared, meaning someone's germs... Ok don't think about that.

I hear a gasp and turn to see everyone nearby giving me looks ranging from sympathetic to horrified, and generally disgusted.

"Well, that was fun." I try to diffuse my embarrassment of the situation. I am totally grossed out and yet I still have 30 lbs of dish and drinkware on my shoulder. I drop the tray on the line and give a grateful smile as another server offers to take care of it for me.

After sweeping up the broken soup bowl, I frantically try to wipe out the literal gunk that is sticking to my body, while trying to push back my gag reflex.

Thank god we have a room full of uniform pieces for new hires. I trudge up to the office to get a new shirt, and try to savor whatever is left of my dignity with a quick clean up in the bathroom.

Only 3 and 1/2 hours to go, Aria. You might hate this, but you can handle it.

· · ·

"Fair warning—I smell like low tide." Ian gives me a strange look and cocks his head before shaking it a little.

"Ok, I wasn't expecting that, but, thanks for the warning." Before I can step across the threshold he is picking me up with his arms around my waist, spinning me in a circle and kissing my forehead, Brady running over to greet me, tail wagging. He spent the day with Ian while I was at work.

"I missed you today. And I don't care what you smell like." He nuzzles into my neck and takes a whiff, clearly immediately regretting that decision.

"But yes, whoa, you weren't kidding. Is there a reason you smell quite...fishy?" Brady's nose is working overtime too as he circles around us, trying to find the source of the smell.

"Long story. Even longer day."

"Tell it to me in the bath." He takes my bag out of my hand, and scoops me up in his arms bridal style, before carrying up the stairs to the primary suite bathroom, shutting the door to keep Brady from following us.

I gasp as I take in the candles surrounding the soaking tub, which is half way full currently being filled and bubbles floating on the top.

"What's all this?" I turn to face him.

"It's for you. I know how tired and sore you are after a wedding shift, and I wanted to take care of you." He smoothes a hand down the side of my face and neck, and I step into his arms.

"Thank you Ian. You are the most thoughtful man I have ever met." I tilt my head up and reach up to kiss him, wanting to show him the words I haven't said but have been feeling growing stronger every day.

"Cmon, let's get in." He turns off the hot water and strips his t-shirt and sweatpants off.

"Mmm commando. I like that." I throw my unflattering uniform in a heap on the floor and grab his hand as he steps into the tub, settling on the back and lifting his arm to guide me in between his legs.

The water is biting hot, but as soon as I am fully in I collapse against his chest and close my eyes.

"Heaven. This is heaven." I rub my hands over high thighs, and lean forward as he pushes his hands up my back and starts to slowly massage my shoulders.

"Careful, I might not let you go if you do that."

"That's the idea." Ian's voice is sensual and deep, and I let it lull me into a state of half-consciousness.

He drags the loofah over my body, washing away the memory of the chowder as I recap the night for him, in the way I always wanted to do but never had the person to do it with.

He always acts so interested in what goes on at events, and he is probably just humoring me but it seems like he actually cares, and cares how it affects me most of all.

I know it's just a boring job, *and one I am starting to get fed up with*, but it makes me feel safe being able to talk about how things went, and have someone to vent to when it's been a shitty day.

It makes me feel a little less alone in all of it.

His thick hands glide over my chest, slowly circling my nipples, before tugging on each one. I arch my back, pressing into him, and lift my hands up behind me to grab at his dark hair.

My head falls to the side and he's there, kissing my temple, my cheek, my jaw, before working his way back up.

His right hand slides over my stomach, while his left caresses my breast, alternating between squeezing and kneading. His fingers are feather light as they find my lips, doing slow strokes to start before spreading them and teasing them partially inside.

My hands lift in a dream-like state, my entire body drowsy and yet pinpricks of energy bursting to the surface. I try to reach back for his thick cock, and he huffs a little laugh.

"Not tonight princess. Tonight's about me, taking care of my girl. It's all about you right now."

"That doesn't seem fair," I protest half-heartedly, enjoying the feeling of his hands working my pussy, moaning when he finds my clit.

"It's all I want, and it's what you deserve, baby. This and so much more." His fingers move in a figure eight, slowly building up causing my breath to shorten, my muscles to clench.

He inserts two fingers, turning his fingers up to graze the spot that I crave, which his other hand pays steady attention to driving my clit insane.

My body is arching, the tension building making my toes curl, and then he is whispering "Let go sweetheart, come for me," and biting my earlobe, and I shatter.

The dream-like state I felt earlier is no match for my orgasm. I can barely lift my eyes as I come back down.

"Perfect. Just perfect, baby. Let's get you to bed." I'm not sure how I function but know he does most of the work to get me out of the bath, wrapping a fluffy white robe around me, and carrying me to his bed, where I fall asleep as soon as I feel him curl up behind me.

34
ARIA

Sunday, August 27th

"Missing the big city options?" I glance up from the meat selection to see Evie pushing a cart with little Gracie riding in it.

"Hey! Maybe when it comes to grilling, but not really for any other reason." I laugh and toss the package of steaks into my cart. The options and amenities tend to be a little less up here. But the funny thing is I don't find myself missing the endless options and larger footprint of the stores at home.

Leaning over the handle to get eye level with Gracie, I grin at her smiling face. "Hello there little lady, out shopping with your mom?"

Gracie gives me an even bigger smile. "Cookies!" Evie and I both laugh.

"Yup those are on my list too." I give her a little fist bump. Her little fingers are so small they make the world's tiniest fist.

"She is basically obsessed with snacks right now, " Evie explains. "I promise I feed her more than that." She shakes her head with a loving smile.

"I'm not here to judge your parenting choices. With that little face I'd give her all the cookies she asked for." I shrug.

"Remind me not to ask you to babysit during dinner then."

"Speaking of dinner, what are you ladies doing this week? Some of the guys are coming out to stay for a few days. We plan on grilling, going out on the boat, just hanging out. We'd love to have you."

"Aria told me, that sounds fun, you sure this one won't be the way?" She tickles Gracie who squeals.

"Of course not. Plus the guys want you there. Remember them from the bar?" She smirks.

"How could I forget, a bunch of beefed up hockey players take over the local place, not something one easily forgets."

"It's settled then. I'll see you both later on then!" With a wave and a tousle of Gracie's hair I push the cart out to the checkout, which is basically just two lines, only one of which I've ever seen open. There's something charming about a small town grocery, it's quaint and homey, and always the same.

Like Doris, the little old lady who is running the checkout and who without fail, checks me out unashamedly every time. She gives me a wink after handing me my recipe, and sends me on my way after telling me to come back tomorrow to see her again.

•••

Tuesday, August 29th

"The Boys are heeeere!" A loud sound occurs two days later as Holden and Jones push through the doorway and toss their duffles on the floor. "The fun has arrived!"

I throw down the kitchen towel I was drying my hands with and move out to the hall to greet them, giving a big slap on the back to each.

"Welcome to my little oasis," gesturing to the expansive space. "Make yourselves at home douchebag" I say as Holden opens the fridge and grabs a beer. These guys know where they stand with me, my home is always open to them and vice versa, so he waves off the remark and turns his hat backwards before taking a sip.

"How was the drive?" Holden had flown in earlier this week and caught a ride with Jones who had stuck around San Jose after the gala. Hughes is coming up later tonight and Whitty flies into Reno tomorrow, and they are all crashing here.

"Fucking uneventful. Half that drive is a one horse town." I laugh even though it's completely true. The towns that people have to drive through on the way to Tahoe are basically all just one Main Street strip that flies by in a "blink and you miss it" kind of way.

Jones strolls over to the back wall of windows overlooking the lake. "This place is nice. Are you going to try to keep it after the summer?"

"I've thought about it, I love that it's right on the water and it would be fun to have an escape from the city. My mom loved it." I smile looking out the window at the fire pit, thinking back to sitting out there with my mom and having our little heart to heart.

"How's Mama doing?" Holden throws himself on the couch, stretching out his arms and getting comfy. Mom treats him like another son, saying she has to give him a little extra love since his mom doesn't live nearby, and boy does he milk that shit.

"Good, really good. She loved meeting Aria too, and keeps asking me when she can see her next." I chuckle as I collapse on the far end of the couch.

"Heh, that sounds like her. Things are good with Aria too?"

I hesitate a moment too long. "What happened? Did you fuck it up?" I toss a pillow at him at the assumption.

"Thanks for the vote of confidence. No, I didn't do anything. It was fucking Amber."

Jones's head whirls from the back window. "What did the witch do this time?"

"She made Aria think I was still in love with her and that I asked her to the gala but that she turned me down. She got Ari questioning whether or not I wanted to be with her," I flipped the remote a little too hard, anger rising up recounting Aria's sad eyes and uncertainty.

The boys let out a collective whoosh of air, accompanied by a few barely audible *fucks*. Holden raises his eyebrows, "Then what?"

"Then I told her all about Amber being a master manipulator and that I'm in this with her. And I am." I toss the remote on the table, causing the batteries to spill out .

"I'm halfway in love with the girl," Jones's mouth drops open, "and I think she still doesn't believe that I want to be with her."

"Well then we better come up with a plan so she doesn't doubt it for a second." Holden leans forward, elbows on his knees with a pensive look.

"Yah... She could use something good, she had a rough week at work apart from the whole Amber thing too."

We settle in and turn on a baseball game before dinner, and after Hughes arrives we all crash out. The next morning I pick up Whitty at the airport, and we spend the drive back catching up, him telling me about the ranch and the new horse trainer that seems to be rubbing him the wrong way—*or maybe not rubbing him enough*—he seems to be awfully stuck on this chick.

I fill him in on my idea for Aria, giving her a chance to shine for more than just me. He already knew everything that happened with the gala, and being the loyal and protective guy he is, he wanted to help make things right however he could after I told him the story afterward.

We take the boat out when we get back, and spend the day fishing, drinking beers, and just enjoying summer like it is supposed to be. Aria and Evie are coming over this afternoon to join us, and the plan is to grill and have a fire pit under the stars. A perfect summer night with my girl.

35
ARIA

Evie pulls up to Ian's place, and lets out a breath, taking in the house and property around it, "Wow, this place is nice!" I am excited to have Evie and Gracie, and of course, Brady, along for the fun.

Seeing Ian in his element with his teammates at the family skate day was fun, and it will be nice to get to know his close friends more than just the night at the bar and then again at the gala, as not much real conversation could happen with all the commotion that night.

I love that they came out for a few days, one even flying out just for this. I think it says a lot about a person to see them have a close group of friends, and you can learn a lot about the type of person they are about who they choose to let into their inner circle. Ian's friends are a mix of personalities it seems, but they go together well.

And of course I want Evie to see the house, I know she has been dying to snoop as part of her BFF duties and though I have spent a ton of time here, for various reasons it just hasn't worked out to get her over here yet.

"Gracie see EE-an?" A tender little voice pipes up from where she is strapped into her carseat, Brady's head laying across the side of her lap as she gives him soft pets. Evie picked me up and we drove over together, knowing I'll probably stay the night and she is so used to Brady at this point I never have to ask if he can ride her car, it's just expected or else Gracie has a fit.

"Yup! Ian is in there, and so are some of his friends ok? So lots of new people but they are all so nice."

I open my door and Evie does the same, with her grabbing Gracie and her bag. I let Brady off the car tether, but keep him on a leash, not being sure how the other guys feel about dogs and knowing Brady can be a bit overwhelming the first time.

"Whoa, it does look like a bear!" A deep laugh cries out at the front door, and I turn to see the funny blonde guy—Hughes I mentally remind myself. The door opens wider behind him and I see Ian look over his shoulder and push him aside making his way down the front steps.

"EE-AN!" Gracie squeals and her grubby little fist opens and shuts repeatedly in a wave.

"Hi Gracie girl! I'm glad you came over to my house today." He reaches them first, ruffling Gracie's hair and gives Evie a side hug, and then moves to me, sweeping me in for a kiss that makes Hughes hoot and holler.

"Hi Baby." I blush like I do every time he calls me that.

"Hi. Ready for all of this?" I gesture to Brady and the girls. His head falls back with a laugh. "Oh this is easy compared to what's inside. You all just made the party a whole lot prettier. I'm sick of looking at their ugly asses—I mean, faces." He hikes up his shoulders in an *oops* motion after Evie scolds in his direction.

Ian grabs Brady's leash and then gestures for me to follow Evie inside, and then we all congregate in the kitchen area. I watch as Evie spots Jack, and she does a shy smile to herself like she is happy he is here, even though she swore she didn't care. He turns just as she looks away, his pensive gaze stuck on her and Gracie as she moves around the island and puts her bag down. Blake says something to him and he shakes his head like he is snapping out of a daze, and then they both move in to welcome us.

Hmm, interesting.

The guys take turns giving Brady pets once he is off the leash, and they make all the regular remarks about how he is such a big and good boy. Brady soaks it in and then starts chasing his tail in a circle, which sets Gracie off in giggles, making all of us laugh.

"And who do we have here?" Blake motions towards Gracie, wiggling his fingers to say hi.

"This is Gracie, my niece," I pipe in, "and you guys remember Evie from that night at the bar? Gracie is her little girl."

Evie puts Gracie on the floor to play with Brady and the guys move in to give her a hug, Holden taking a second longer to release her as he whispers something in her ear that makes her blush.

She makes eye contact with me after and I raise my eyebrows, and she shakes her head, dismissing me in fake annoyance.

The guys decide they want to go out on the boat again, so we all head to the dock to load up. I get settled in next to Evie and Gracie at the bow of the boat. Between having four hockey players, a giant dog, and the three of us this boat is at capacity. Hughes takes control of the music and pretty soon the boat is rocking, both musically and literally.

"Did you ever imagine our summer going this way?" I laugh as I watch the guys fight over who gets to drive.

Evie shakes her head. "No, definitely not. It's a good thing we went to the bar that night, huh?"

Brady settles down, curled up in the foot well. Evie and I both put our feet on top of him as a footrest. Gracie peers over the edge of the boat.

"Mama, fishy."

"Ohh do you see a fishy baby girl? That's so fun." Evie holds onto the strap on the back of her life vest to keep her from falling in and we both look over to try to see if we can spot a fish. There's not one, but because we're on the water if Gracie says there's a fish, we will always play along.

An hour later, we're back near the house and heading towards the dock when Ian hands over the steering wheel to Jack and makes his way over to where Brady and I are sitting on the backseat.

"Hey remember when you were telling me about the dogs that can pull people in on the boats?"

" Oh, like the rescue dogs, of course, why?" I ask, but then I take in the smirk on Ian's face and I get what he's trying to say.

"You want Brady to pull us in?"

" Do you think you can?" At that, Brady throws his head back and looks at Ian and I swear this dog is human because he gives him this look of like *Are you doubting me? Of course I can do it.* We both laugh and Ian pats Brady on the side with big hard thumps.

"I think that means he wants to."

"Sure ,we can try. He's never pulled in anything this big, especially with half a hockey team aboard, but I'm curious to see if he could."

Ian tells Jack to cut the engine causing the guys to exchange curious looks. "We're gonna try something."

I grab a tow line from under one of the seat cushions and tie a big knot on the end for Brady to grip, securing the other end to the cleat.

"Ready, bud?" Brady stands up on the seat, tail wagging ferociously back-and-forth as he looks towards the line and the water, just waiting for me to throw it. Pulling my arm back, I let it fly. "Go get it!" With that he launches himself over the edge of the boat and lands with a giant splash in the water.

" Yay, bay-dee bear" Gracie claps her hands cheerfully.

"What is he doing?" It's Blake that asks, but the guys all lean towards the edge to watch as Brady grabs the rope with his mouth and turns his body to look at me.

"To the shore." I only have to tell Brady once, and he maneuvers his body so it is facing the shoreline and begins to swim, rope tucked firmly between his jaws. It takes a minute for the line to go taught, and when it does, the boat does a little lurch and then slowly begins to glide through the water.

" He's doing it!" I beam up at Ian, who has placed his hands on my shoulders, both of us wearing dorky proud smiles as we watch Brady pull off his biggest rescue yet.

We spend the afternoon playing cornhole, drinking beers and seltzers, and the guys take turns tossing bumpers for Brady to retrieve from the lake, which turns into a competition of who can throw the farthest.

I'm watching Evie and Gracie run around in the grass, with the guys in the background at the shoreline, when Ian comes up next to me, and pulls me under his arm.

"This is perfection," I sigh.

"It is." He agrees, taking a sip from his bottle and offering me some which I shake my head at, lifting my own in refusal.

"I love having everyone here, being able to hang out with friends, right near the water. It's like a dream spot." I nod my agreement. It really is the perfect spot, with a big grassy yard that holds tons of people, a gorgeous view of the lake and mountains, and a shorefront that Brady takes advantage of all day long.

"I'm thinking about seeing if I can extend my rental agreement, or maybe look into getting my own place here," I swing my head in disbelief, my mouth opening in surprise. Happiness flows through me at the thought of having him near after the summer.

Ian stares out at the water, continuing "I wouldn't be able to spend much time during the season here obviously, but over the holidays and summers, I'm finding more and more reasons to want to be here rather than just in the city." He looks down at me, and smiles. My heart skips a beat.

"Oh yah? Any particular reason?" I joke, but silently beg for confirmation.

"Yah I'm committed to spotting Tahoe Tessie, figure I need a place lakeside for the best chance." I poke him in the ribs and we both laugh. I hug my arms under his, around his ribs, and gaze up at him, my laughter dying out.

"Are you seriously thinking about a place here?"

His gaze is soft, and I think, loving. "I am. What do you think about that?" My chest blooms with contentment and joy.

"I think I'd like that very much." And while I can't quite shake the little voice telling me it's the environment that is drawing him here, the hopeful part of my soul gives way to daydream about a future that involves both of us here, together.

A little while later, after the grilling is done and Gracie has gone down in the pack n play, we all don hoodies and blankets and sit out by the fire, with Jones pulling out an acoustic guitar he must have brought with him and starts strumming softly. The air is crisp but not too cold, the wind almost non-existent, the deep smoky smell of the fire pit, the smell of burnt marshmallows filling my nostrils as I snuggle up next to Ian on the couch.

It's the idyllic summer lakeside night.

Heaven.

Hughes is entertaining everyone by making obvious passes and terrible pickup lines at Evie, who laughs at each, and tells him he can't handle a girl like her, making everyone roar in agreement. He shakes it off by declaring himself too much for one girl anyway, but to let him know if she changes her mind. And all the while Holden sits silently watching, his fist opening and closing, like he is restraining himself. I catch his eye at one point and quirk my eyebrow in question, but he just smiles in response.

It's not until I'm in the kitchen getting a refill of the makings for s'mores when he approaches me.

"You're a good match with Sanderson." I smile, pushing down the tiny bubble of insecurity that at the beginning of the summer would have made me question if it's true, but instead, agreeing and thanking him for saying so.

"Thanks, I'm lucky he took a chance on me." I open a fresh bag of marshmallows and pour some out onto the tray, popping one in my mouth, just to check the softness level. Jack grins at the action and takes a handful in his massive hands, and does the same with all of them at once.

"Geez, I'll never get over how much you hockey players can eat."

He chuckles and then his gaze falls on Evie through the sliding glass door. I can't help but investigate, the bestie in me craving answers to something I've been picking up on all night.

"She's pretty great, isn't she?" Jack whirls his head around, almost sheepish that he got caught looking.

"Um, yah, she is. Gracie's dad is a lucky guy." He grabs the tray I finished filling and goes to turn to take it outside. I touch his elbow to stop him and look him straight in the eyes.

"Gracie's dad is not in the picture. There is no one. But anyone would be lucky to be with the two of them." Jack takes a deep inhale, processing the information I just gave him. He glances back over at her, and his eyes flit over to the wall where Gracie lays sleeping in a pack n play on the other side—I'm almost certain I see a brief pained look on his face before he does a small nod. He looks at me once more, smirks to lighten the mood, and then walks out the back door.

The rest of the night goes smoothly, and the topic of Brady's background and training comes up. The guys ask a bunch of questions, mostly about how he uses his skills, and what type of rescue experience he has around Tahoe.

I know they mean well, but the way the questions come out has me admitting that he hasn't actually done much, isn't a part of any search and rescue companies, and that he hasn't been out on official rescues. I'm kind of embarrassed, actually, seeing it through their eyes that I've been training him for 3 years with nothing to show for it.

Training with Brady has been something I've really loved doing, but it sounds sort of silly when I hear myself admit it's just a hobby. Even though they are only acting interested, I feel the need to defend myself internally, needing to prove that he has the potential to actually help people—and that my time with him hasn't been wasted.

I grow increasingly quiet as the night progresses, with Ian patting my leg in question at times but I just play it off as being tired.

Later in bed, after some incredible foreplay and two rounds of sex, I lay awake thinking about how I need to start making progress on my goals with Brady. Or else they are only going to stay lofty aspirations and I'll have to keep admitting that while I may enjoy training with Brady, I'm not actually making a difference

36
ARIA

Sunday, September 3rd

"Earth to Aria."

I glance up to see Betsy nodding towards my hands, and I look down to see the water pitcher I am filling overflowing at the faucet.

"Oh whoops," I rushed to turn the water off, thankful I was filling it over a sink and not just on one of the spigots without drainage under it.

"You ok, honey?" Betsy's calm gray eyes are concerned, and grandmotherly.

"Yah, of course, I'm fine, just got lost in thought there for a second."

It's the truth; I was lost in thought alright, brainstorming how I could get Brady volunteering quickly. The sooner I can, the sooner I can keep kids safe.

The logical part of my brain keeps telling me that once fall hits Lake Tahoe isn't exactly the place to be swimming and it's not like I'll be able to do anything large scale til next summer.

But the ever-grieving part of me feels urgency to take action and counteract the drowning from earlier this summer, and the guilt that the conversation around the fire last night brought up, proving I'm not making a difference at all right now.

I need to keep kids safe; I can't just sit here and do nothing. Maybe I can figure out a way to give swim lessons at an indoor pool over the winter, or teach kids in the classrooms about the dangers of pools.

Something, anything, to make his death matter to more people. To make this mountain on my chest slide off slightly, to let me breathe a little easier.

And if I'm being honest, to give me an outlet for when Ian leaves for the start of the season.

He said that he wants it all with us and that we can make it. And I want to believe that with my whole heart. But the trauma side of me echoes the worry I have been pushing down all summer—*if I wasn't enough to make my mom stay as a teen, I can't depend on anyone else, even Ian, to be the one who does.*

It's probably for the best to just keep myself busy, and avoid thinking about the what ifs.

The rest of the night passes slowly, it takes extra effort to put on a warm welcoming expression to the event attendees for whatever company they belong to—I didn't even care to ask today. I just want to be here, collect the paycheck, and curl back up in bed.

I'm officially in a funk. I make a mental note to schedule a digital check in with my therapist, knowing that I could use the help to recenter my thoughts after the extra doubts have been creeping in.

I'm pulling a rack of silverware out of the server dishwasher when Betsy rounds the corner and spotting me says "Hey, Lucy wants to talk to you, she's in her office." I frown a little, not having the energy to chat with the Director of Catering, but I thank her for passing the message along and head out to find my boss.

"Hey, Betsy said you wanted to see me?" I pop my head into Lucy's office and she motions for me to take a chair across from her at her desk.

"Yes, I do, I have some good news. We've seen an uptick in people interested in event bookings and need to keep with the demand. I'm ready to have you apply for the event manager position. I know you've been waiting so long for it to open." She leans back in her chair, smiling broadly like she just handed me the biggest news of my life, a golden ticket position that would bring a big bump in salary and fits well with my degree and projected career path.

If that's the case, why does my stomach drop at her words? My gut reaction isn't happiness, but something darker.

"Oh really? Wow, thank you for considering me." I feel the need to stall, to give myself breathing room before I accidentally pigeon-hole myself into a position that will change my day-to-day life for good. "I know what the other managers do, obviously, but can you tell me what the schedule and expectations would look like?"

As she jumps into a lengthy monologue detailing the role, I half listen as she describes the schedule. It's a set rotation that consists of both days and nights, as the job requires meeting potential couples for venue tours and wedding planning, and then attending actual events as day of coordinators. What is surprising is how little interest I have in the role. My brain wavers back and forth between knowing that a solid position in a role people expect me to want means certain financial stability for the future, and the growing part of me that doesn't want anything to do with catering ever again.

That half of my brain focuses on how much time I would lose time with the things that mean the most to me. Working with Brady in the summer would be severely diminished, and volunteering at all might be a struggle. The bigger issue that comes to the forefront is how this schedule would make being with Ian and attending his games almost impossible. I would have to hope that my schedule lines up with home games, and his game breaks, and there would be no guarantee that I would have days off back to back in order to get to San Jose and back.

A tiny voice stirs, telling me this isn't the life I want for myself, and that maybe, just maybe, my happiness is ok to put first. Only for another to reinforce the need to make a choice that others want for me, the desire to keep them happy, to be in a place where I can be financially independent, not having to rely, or be a burden, on anyone ever again.

I thank her for telling me about the role, and make a promise to think about it.

An hour later I'm sitting in my car, the passenger side holding my bag, my apron, and a vase of leftover flowers all buckled in and ready for a ride, but I can't bring myself to start the car. I see a text from Ian, wanting to know if I got home safe, but I'm not ready to respond yet.

My brain is tired from fighting itself over the survival instinct of a financially stable position that directly opposes building a relationship with him, so I decide to wait until I'm at home to respond.

A sharp shrill ring cuts through the dark car, but I don't recognize the number, so I send it to voicemail and finally put the car into reverse. It isn't until I'm at home that I check my voicemail, and when I do, the world that I've tried to escape and rebuild from, strikes another blow.

37
IAN

After the guys all left, with Whitty hitching a ride with Hughes back to San Jose, I brought my water to the couch and set it down on the coffee table. I flip through the folders my agent sent me, requests and opportunities from different outlets in our confidential bid to figure out my future post-hockey.

Everything seems like a practical and logical choice, but nothing sparks my interest. I throw the file down and lean back on the couch, my hands going behind my head against the soft back. I gaze out across the backyard, where the sun is slowly setting, and I think back to how full the yard was yesterday, the sounds of baby giggles and guys laughing, the splashes down at the beach and the crackling of the fire.

It felt like home. Like a peace I could rest and relax in. It's all I've ever wanted in a place, and unlike anything I've found before. I told Aria I was thinking about either keeping this house or finding a new one, and I meant it.

As I look out over the yard to the water beyond, I can suddenly envision Aria and I out there, with kids of our own running around, throwing a stick for Brady before roasting hot dogs for dinner over the fire pit.

This girl is everything I've ever wanted, and was always too afraid to let myself have. I've been scared to admit the level of feelings I have for her, but suddenly it is clear as day.

I love her. So much. I can see a life with her, mixed between here and the city, hockey and summer swims, finishing up my dreams while helping her to build hers.

I've spent the past year playing defense not only in games but in my life as well. Keeping anything that resembled long term commitment away, protecting myself just like I protect Holden in the crease. It's my job there to make sure nothing gets in the blue, because when the puck crosses into the crease he is all on his own to stop a goal.

In the same type of way, I focused for a long time on not letting anyone slip under my defenses, unable to control what happens when they do.

But there is a certain peace I get when I think about a future with Aria. A calm knowing that even though I can't control the outcome, I know it's suddenly all I ever want, and the future I see for myself in these contract files pales in comparison to the future I see with Aria.

She is my life going forward, and everything else is just a bonus. I know the next step I have to take, one that I should've dealt with a long time ago.

Pulling out my phone, I scroll to the number I worked hard to forget, and compose a text that leaves no room for interpretation. One that clearly articulates how much Aria means to me, how I will never accept the type of treatment she was given at the Gala, and as a final piece of closure, promise full media cooperation to exposing Amber if she does so much as spit one word in Aria's direction ever again.

I should have done this a year ago, but was more focused on trying to move on out of the media storm to stand up for myself. But standing up for Aria? Any day, any time.

I hit send on the text to Amber, confirm she read it, and block her number. Glancing at the time, I see it is getting late, and Aria should be getting home from work soon. Sending a message to make sure she does, I wish she could just come stay here instead but knowing she wanted to go home after staying last night.

A couple of emails later, I put the plan that I came up with the guys this week into motion. A chance for Aria to showcase her skills with Brady and to help her gain the confidence to do whatever she wants with that—with her the sky's the limit. She is incredibly talented and capable, and I just want to help her pursue whatever dream that may be. The guys were so impressed learning about everything Aria and Brady have done, and I know the community will be as well.

After Brady pulled the entire boat in and the guys asked more about what else he could learn to do, I showed them the video of the dogs jumping from the helicopter and a new idea came to fruition. Not sure if it's possible, but it's worth a little Instagram digging to find out.

Anything is worth it when it comes to Aria.

• • •

I let out a sigh of relief as I saw Aria's Jeep in her driveway. After not hearing back last night to see if she got home safely from work, I stayed up for a few hours debating coming over here before deciding she must have just passed out as soon as she got home from exhaustion.

She's working too hard. If it was just water training it would be ok, but she is covering extra shifts and working herself to the bone, I can tell, and I don't know how to support her without her feeling like I am trying to take away her independence.

I can easily give her a life of ease, where she doesn't have to work and she can do whatever she wants with Brady all day long. I just have to convince her to let me do it.

When I didn't get a response this morning and my calls went unanswered, I hopped in my car and drove over, needing to see that she was ok.

Brady's bark greets me as I knock. The door opens slowly. "Hey, I was—" My voice catches as I take in Aria, only it's not the same Aria that normally greets me with enthusiasm.

In her place is what can only be described as a shell of her. Slumped posture, body tired and dragging, her PJs wrinkled and mismatched. Her hair is pulled back into a messy bun that looks like it was made even more messy by constantly dragging fingers through it.

But it's the sullen look on her face, the shadows under her eyes, and the lifeless stare which is directed towards my chest and not my face.

A manic desire to rush in and rescue her, to save her from whatever has caused the life to be sucked out of her, rushes over me.

"Baby," I wrap my left arm around her waist and pull her to me, my right hand tucking behind her ear to lift her eyes to mine, and when I do, the sadness and defeat nearly knocks me off my feet. "What's the matter?"

Her eyes fill with tears, which she shakes away with as she pulls out of my arms and opens the door wider, gesturing for me to come inside.

I move inside, but as soon as I'm through the doorframe,I close the door and grab her hand as she tries to walk away.

"Hey." I wait until she makes eye contact. "C'mere." I pull her into my arms, and as I do, she breaks, her hands fisting in my shirt as her head falls onto my chest. I caress her head and tighten my grip around her shoulders as she does, and wish death on anyone or anything that made her feel this way.

38
ARIA

ME: I need you. Something big.
EVIE: On my way.

I had opened the door expecting Evie when instead I saw Ian, and subsequently broke down here in the hall. I'm finally starting to pull myself together when the door opens behind us.

"Ok, what's going on, I'm—oh Ian hi, guess she called in the calvary on this, wait hun are you crying? Who do I have to torture?" She pulls me from Ian's arms and wraps me in a hug. My whole body relaxes, having the two people I care for most in the world here by my side.

I wipe my face, not caring about how blotchy it must be at this point, and only then glance down to realize the entire state of my outfit.

"Don't worry about how you look. You are as sexy as ever, right Ian?" She shoots a look at Ian, who nods despite his furrowed brows and concerned demeanor.

We move into the living room, and Ian sits on the couch, pulling me on his lap, where I snuggle in and rest my head on the crook of his shoulder while Evie dumps her bag on the ground and plops into the chair.

"Ok, what's going on?" Evie asks what Ian has clearly been wanting to do for the past five minutes.

I trace a circle on his hand, which is lightly gripping my thigh.

"I got a call last night. A voicemail actually," they both sit silently, waiting for me to continue. "It was a county office, informing me that my mom died." I lifted my eyes to Evie on the last few words, and watched as her jaw ticked and her eyes flash between hatred and sympathy in a millisecond, and then commingling between the two.

Much like how I'm feeling right now. Rage and sadness mixed within me, not because I found out the news, but because it's final, a closing of a book I never wanted to read but was forced to carry daily, and one I always hoped would have an added epilogue showing a change of heart.

Ian's arms tighten around me. He murmurs into my hair while kissing my head, "I'm so sorry, baby, I'm so sorry." I can feel his love pouring over me, his heart is breaking for mine, feel it surrounds me like a blanket and I curl into it for strength.

Evie gets up from the chair, coming to sit next to us on the couch and grabs my hands. She gazes at me, steadfast. "Whatever you want to do, or say, or feel, is ok. Anything you are feeling right now is ok, you know that right?" Her eyes lock on mine, fiercely promising loyalty, a thousand unspoken words float between us. I nod.

Taking stock of my body, trying to pinpoint exactly what I am feeling, I tell them "I don't know what I'm feeling to be honest. I feel drained. I don't want to care, because I feel like I lost her long ago," Ian thumb softly grazing mine keeps me connected to the present while my mind swirls, settling on the ache that I try to ignore and don't often give voice to. "But it also hurts, knowing that part of me...kept hoping she'd have a change of heart," I quietly admitted.

I have told myself for years that I know she wasn't going to come back, that she made her choice clear, and that my life with Evie, Mimi, and Gracie eventually, and now Ian, was enough. But no matter how much I pretended to believe it, I could never outrun that fantasy that she would.

Truthfully, it wasn't even that I wanted her to be around. Part of me still hated her for abandoning me, while the other part just wanted to have a mother.

But the biggest part just wanted to be enough for her to want to come back. I've lived my life wanting to be enough for the people around me to not leave, to have a reason to stay.

"I hoped that one day she would regret everything and come back with an apology, and then I could decide what to do with that."

I slide off Ian's lap and sit between them, turning towards Ian while Evie hugs me from behind and rests her head on my shoulder. "Now it just feels like the choice was taken away from me, never mind the fact that she didn't regret it."

"So trying to process her, um, death is just a little weird, ya know?" Ian nods in agreement, silently lending me the strength to continue expressing myself. "I feel like I already grieved losing her, but this is just a little more final, and I guess," My throat is dry, trying to keep me from saying the hardest part but I push through, "I was still hoping, deep down, that I'd be enough for her to want to come back."

Ian moves suddenly and is in front of me, on his knees, demanding my full attention.

"No Ari, don't say that, you are more than just enough." He gently cups my cheek and kisses my forehead. "She is the one who missed out on how amazing you are, and I'm sorry you didn't get a chance to make the choice, but your worth is not in how she or anyone else chooses to treat you."

I barely register Evie giving us space as she gets up. Finally glancing over, I watch as she makes tea in the kitchen, smiling softly as she touches the photobooth strip we snuck in to take during last year's New Year's catering event.

When she returns, I tell them the last part as Ian covers up my legs with one of my cozy blankets from the basket.

"So there is something else, too. They said she had a bunch of outstanding debt, and that while most of it wasn't my responsibility, apparently she had a loan through a joint account that I held with her, and they told me I have to pay it." I wring my hands in my lap, my stomach trying to break down the boulder sitting there, crushing my insides and my dreams.

All that money saved for the advanced water rescue training.

Finally getting to the point of having enough after saving for the past few years. And now it's all going to be gone.

It will disappear, just like she did.

I can't tell what hurts the most, her exiting this world without looking back at me, or her doing so while taking everything I've worked hard to overcome and find a passion for after digging myself out of the hole she left me in.

I was never her priority, and then soon became not even a consideration. When my sweet brother was no longer there, I wasn't enough for her. And now she is taking the only thing I have done for myself that makes me feel strong and independent and proud.

What a fucking legacy.

"When did you set up an account with her?" Evie speaks and then she and Ian lock eyes, looking like a silent conversation is passing through them.

I pull the fluffy blanket up to my waist and then throw my arms down onto my thighs. "That's the thing! I don't remember ever having a joint account before she left, or setting one up, and I definitely didn't after she left seeing as I haven't talked to her in 12 years!" Ian runs his fingers through my hair.

"So that doesn't add up. Maybe she forged your signature and pretended to be you? Gah, I know she just died and I'm sorry, but I am so sick of that selfish woman treating you this way!" Evie stands up and stomps around the room, growing more upset with each word.

"Baby, don't do anything, don't pay anyone a cent. Something is obviously wrong here." Ian's jaw is tight, his tongue moving inside from cheek to cheek as he tries to hold in his own anger at the situation.

My shoulders fall, defeated, as my eyes grow watering for the zillionth time today. "What am I supposed to do, Ian?"

"We." He grabs both my hands with one of his, and using the thumb of his other, wipes the tears from under my eyes before kissing each eyelid.

"We, what?" Confused, I tilt my head, imploring him to tell me what to do.

"What are WE supposed to do? Ari, this isn't just your fight; you're mine, and together we'll figure this out. I will comb through every detail of what's happening because I won't let a penny of yours repay the debt of that woman who's been indebted to you her whole life."

39
ARIA

Friday, September 8th

Numb.

It's how I've felt the past few days, and it's followed me to work. My therapist says it's a common reaction, but has been pushing me to work through it.

Ian and Evie hardly left my side, the two of them arranging their days to make sure I was never alone unless I forced them to leave, which I couldn't do because as much as I hated to admit it, having them there for me helped anchor me. I hated that this cloud has been cast over some of Ian's last few days, and slowly I'm working through it but not without struggle.

But work is always there, especially this time of year, and so I'm standing here setting tables for yet another wedding, my fingers working automatically to lift, and hook glass after glass until I have 5 champagne glasses hanging from the fingers of my left hand, my right grabbing a few more. I set them down, slightly above and to the right of the water glass, creating a perfect triangle with that and the wineglass.

And then I repeat, 8 place settings per table, for 17 more tables.

It's mindless, numbing, and repetitive work. Boring, but welcome, giving my mind a chance to bounce back and forth between hope and heartache.

Ian's been making lots of calls lately, he said he has amazing lawyers who will absolutely take care of this for me, and while I am so appreciative of him and his willingness to do so, I can't help but feel guilty for using his resources.

The rest of the team makes small conversation as they set up the room, someone from the band chimes in and makes a comment I don't hear and have no desire to.

Even if the lawyers can prove I didn't have an account with my mom, paying them is going to drain my savings anyway.

It's probably for the best. I would have likely spent all that time and money doing the advanced level training and then it would have gone to waste since there isn't the infrastructure to do anything with it here.

Probably better to let someone else have that spot. Someone with a dog and job counting on them, someone who can actually make a difference and save lives.

I mull over the event manager job offer, and try to psyche myself up about it. It's the logical step I've been working towards, and they don't open often, so I'd be a fool to not accept. My stomach turns sour at the idea of it though—the entire industry has lost its appeal after schlepping trays of meals for the past 6 years. Do I really want to spend 40+ hours a week talking about minor details for weddings and trying to convince brides to spend an extreme amount of money just to get married at The Alpine Club?

No, not in the least.

Why don't people just get married somewhere on the mountain, with the view and just the people close to them? That's what I would do.

I do an internal tally. While I'd be giving up a lot of my daily activities and training time with Brady since the job has more day shifts, the bump in pay means I could realistically save up for the registration fee in just under another year and then I could do the training at that point.

I've already taken this long; what's another year, I guess.

The thought has my chest tightening, my eyes tracing over everything around me that instead of feeling so familial, it's so uninspiring. Another year of doing what I have to do, not what I want to do.

It would also mean a lot less flexibility to watch Ian play during the season, something I've been eagerly looking forward to supporting him in. I want to be by his side whenever possible, cheering him on like his mom does when he wins games, being there for him when he loses. And he wants me there too.

For now.

I try to fight off the teeny voice that is building inside of me, the one that has resurfaced in the aftermath of my mom's death.

The voice that tells me that people only want you until they don't anymore. I'm scared to death of that voice, the one that has followed me from my teen years to college, whenever the few boys I dated decided it was time to move on.

The one that is trying to pry into my mind and pull apart this dream future I have concocted with Ian—where I imagine us one day getting married, having lakeside fire pits with Brady and a few kids running around, Gracie having a built-in bestie with a daughter of my own. Growing old together in our own little alpine paradise.

I know it's just my fear talking, but it is hard to overcome. Because if I'm being honest with myself, this has all been a reminder that one day Ian might decide that I'm not enough for him anymore.

And that would break me worse of all.

• • •

I let the door to the storeroom—home to a mix of random storage items just off the grand ballroom—close softly before letting out a violent, yet silent scream.

"It's one of those nights, huh?" I glanced over to see Evie had come in the opposite direction, through the door that connects the bar to the same room. It's a shortcut we use to avoid going through the ballroom during the evening.

"Ugh. It sucks." I huff and lean up against a cart holding empty food chafers. "I hate the entitled ones. They just look straight through you and then assume you are stupid and wrong for every little thing." I pull my hair tie out and vigorously put my hair back in a bun, trying to tame the flyaways. "Like no, lady, I did not steal your ugly ass sequined purse just because I'm the lowly and poor server."

Evie sets down the rack of glasses and comes to lean on the cart next to me, putting her head on my shoulder.

"I'm sorry, people suck. Of course you didn't; it's always the same story. A family member picked it up for them, thinking they forgot it."

"Yup." I pick at my flaking nail polish, thinking back through the night and how everything seemed worse than ever before.

Suddenly it's like I'm watching a movie reel of what it will be like if I accept the job offer and I have to continue down this path forever.

"I can't do it."

"Do what?"

"Be an event manager. I can't do it. No, that's not right... I can do it, but I really, really don't want to." Evie raises her eyebrows, not saying a word. Her silence gives me room to process and space for an alternate future to develop, one where rather than doing what's expected or what makes everyone else's lives easier, I consider my own needs for once. The instant the decision comes to my mind, I feel light—I feel free.

"I think I'm done here."

"Already? I think I have another 15 minutes to clean up at least." Evie looked impressed, but she didn't get my meaning.

"No, like I'm done here, working here." Evie raises her eyebrows. "I'm tired of this, it's not fun anymore, and I'm tired of being treated like I'm beneath the people who can afford to attend events here."

Evie opens her mouth, maybe to tell me it's just a bad night, or maybe to remind me that I'm not, in fact, beneath her, but I'm finally seeing that and can say it myself, so I cut her off, continuing my rampage. "And I'm not! I am just as good of a person as they are, whether I have the money to do fancy things or take advanced training. But I'm tired of being exhausted and I'm burnout. And I HATE the idea of missing out on Ian's games and building a life with him if I were to stay here and move up."

I feel a fire in my soul, urging me to take a risk, to jump off the deep end—to choose myself for once. "So if I'm saving up for something in the future, why not find something that gives me the flexibility I want in the meantime? Like, I don't know, I'd rather work at Hunter's place than be here, or figure out a way to work around the hockey schedule up on the mountain." Evie goes from open mouth surprised to her mouth set in a line, a smirk fighting to come out.

Turning fully to her, I say, "Ok fine, let me have it. Tell me it's stupid and I should just let it go." Her smirk turns into a wide smile. Her blue eyes are sparkling with happiness and pride.

"I'm actually not going to tell you that, at all. I'm just wondering where this version of my best friend has been hiding and why it's taken her so long to figure out the thing I've always known about her."

She grabs my biceps. "That you are worth everything and deserve nothing but the best. So no, I'm not going to tell you to stay in this shithole—hell, I might even quit with you." I give her a knowing look, and she laughs. "Ok, you're right, so I'm not quitting just yet, but if I didn't have Gracie I would just out of solidarity." I chuff out a laugh, and retie my apron strings into a bow at the front.

"So you think I should do it?" I know in my heart this is the right move, but something deep still needs her approval. She is not only my best friend, but my heart sister. Her approval means the world to me.

"I think you should do what makes you happy. Even if that thing is a person, and not just another job path." Evie winks, and then picks up the glass rack. Pausing at the door I came in from, she turns around. "I support you whatever, or wherever you go, you know that, right?"

I look up at her, acknowledging what she is saying about Ian but she sees through me straight to the uncertainty that is blooming in my chest.

"We'll always be family, no matter what. Now get your ass back to work; don't get fired before you can quit in a really dramatic fashion."

I laugh, and take thirty more seconds to regain my composure, but my mind is made up.

It's time I choose myself and my happiness.

And Evie is right; there is another person in that equation as well.

After my shift ends I show up on Ian's door without warning, and knock. He answers in just a pair of gray sweatpants, slung low on his hips, the lines of his lower abs stealing my attention, unable to pull my eyes from the sight. I hear his throat clear, and when I look up he is smiling knowingly.

"What a pleasant surprise. I don't think I ordered delivery, but I'll take this one any night of the week." Laughing, I head inside as he swings the door open for me. I toe off my black sneakers and drop my phone and keys on his console table. Ian comes up behind me, wrapping his arms around my waist and peppering my neck with kisses. "How was work?"

I spin in his arms and place my hands on his chest. I'm feeling a little nervous about my idea, but also excited. I just need to talk it through with him and gauge his reaction.

"It, well, it sucked, to be honest." His mouth turns down and he grabs my hand and goes to pull me down the hallway. "C'mon, let's draw you a bath then help you relax." His care for me ignites my soul, and I just love this man. Full stop. It's time to stop pretending I don't know that.

But I don't say it.

I have things I want to say tonight, and I'm not sure if he is ready to hear it yet, and I'm not ready to learn if he isn't in the same place.

"Actually, there's something I wanted to talk to you about. Can we just sit for a bit? Thank you though, that's sweet of you." I rise on my toes to kiss him, and he grabs the back of my head pressing me deeper into the kiss.

"Of course baby, everything ok?" He pulls me to the couch instead.

"It will be; I've been doing some thinking and kind of wanted to talk it over with you." His knee bounces a little, perhaps nervousness, or simply curiosity making it hard to sit still, not knowing where the conversation is going.

He spreads out his thick corded arms and wraps them around me, pulling me so my right shoulder is pressed into the left side of his body, his arm encompassing my entire torso. "I love that you want to talk to me about whatever is going on. It means a lot to me that you know you can. I always want to be that person in your corner, babe." I cock my head to the side, and just smile at him, my heart overflowing with love and admiration for this selfless, generous man.

"I think I'm going to look for a different job." He remains quiet, letting me continue without reaction. "I started thinking about the manager position, and how much that would take away from my goals with Brady, but more importantly, time with you, and decided I didn't want that." Ian grins, and squeezes my arms.

"And then I started thinking, that although it is pretty good money, I'm not really happy anymore at work. I don't feel passionate or excited about anything, and the stuff that used to seem cool or exciting, like weddings and events with famous hockey players," I wink and he tickles my sides making me laugh, "they just aren't inspiring anymore. Actually, I feel kind of depressed going there, and I don't want to feel that anymore. I'd rather work someplace I enjoy and save up to figure out a plan for working with Brady professionally someday."

Ian shifts on the couch and pulls one leg up under him while he faces me, giving me his full attention, his calm expression and soft smile not giving me a ton of insight into what he is thinking.

"Do you think I could do something like that, create a role for him in the community in a bigger capacity than just volunteering?" I bit my lip, the fundamental question I need backing on to know I'm not just fooling myself with this dream of mine.

Ian's eyes gleam with pride. "Yeah, baby, I really do. I know you can do it, and I know you are going to be incredible at it." He pulls me in for an all-consuming hug, and then kisses my forehead. "I am so proud of you for coming to this conclusion, for thinking about what makes you happy."

"I love you." I blurt out, not being able to hold it in any longer. His eyes sparkle and he opens his mouth to speak, but I put my finger over his lips in a need to get it all out. "I love you so much, and not just for agreeing with me—" he laughs as I pull my finger away—"but because you are the kindest, most generous, and caring person ever."

"I'm not sure about all that," he pauses only briefly, kissing my fingers that are now tangled with his, " but I've never been more sure that I love you, Aria. I know you've been taught to believe people leave. But I'm not going anywhere, Aria. I love you. I'm here, and I'm staying. No matter how hard it gets."

Warmth spreads like sunlight filling my chest. Hearing him say those words back. "I want to be there for you, cheer you on at your games, and spend as much time with you as I can. I want to learn about hockey so I can support you."

Ian plays with my fingers as he gives my forehead a soft kiss.

"I would love that. I want you around as much as possible. I know you said you were going to look for another job, but what if you didn't?"

I scrunch my eyebrows, trying to understand and curl into him resting my head on his shoulder.

"I mean if you want to you can, and then I'll come visit whenever I can and will fly you out whenever you want to go to a game." He plays with my hair, softly stroking down the lengths before returning to the top. It's a soothing caress that feels like home.

"But if we're being honest, I make more than enough for both of us, and I'd be lying if I said I didn't want you around all the time. Maybe it's selfish, but if you don't want to get another job just to get one, I would happily cover all the expenses if it means we can have more time together."

My mind races at this new possibility. Earlier this evening I was thinking about how to make things work once Ian went back into the world of hockey and now he is talking about letting me choose to not work just to be closer to him.

It's a lot to deal with in a day—the I love yous, job changes, the offer—so I need to take some time to think about everything and not rush into a decision.

"I don't even know what to say, Ian. That's incredibly generous of you."

He pulls me up and wraps me in a hug, kissing just below my earlobe.

"Just think about it baby, that's all."

And for the next few days, it is just about the only thing I do think about.

• • •

I've never felt like such a weight slide off my shoulders than when I give my notice that I'll be working at The Alpine Club only through the start of the hockey season. This gives me both the flexibility to attend Ian's games and some time to mull over my options of looking for a new job that can support my lifestyle choices, rather than constrict them, or going all in with Ian.

It is freeing to know that my future is now open to new possibilities, and despite the sadness and attempts to get me to stay by my manager, I held strong on my end date.

I now look at my remaining shifts with a renewed season of purpose, one that comes from outside the walls of the club, and from finding my passion and putting the work into making it come true. I still don't have a clear path to make it work, and especially dealing with having to save up again while job hopping or even scarier, relying on Ian for everything, but I know I can do it. I can feel it in my soul. I want to succeed, and finally believe in myself enough to know that I can.

As the days wind down before Ian leaves for training camp, I alternate between soaking in every last minute with him, and shaping my ideas for getting Brady attached to a local rescue unit. I research talking points on how it can benefit the various county departments, so that once I have narrowed down my ideas and when I can get meetings, I'll come across as knowledgeable and prepared.

I let myself daydream, weighing spending my days on the water with Brady, using a boat to patrol and keep people safe on the waters of Big Blue, or creating safety awareness programs and being active in the community.

Maybe it's just the act of walking away from something that freed up more space in my mind, but I think it's also a mindset shift. Rather than trying to fit my ideas for Brady around my work life, for the first time ever, between being in love with Ian and having the flexibility to have a choice, I have the chance to sit quietly and see what spark my soul on fire, visualize what my dream life looks like, and how I want to show up for it.

Never did I think being in a place financially where I didn't have to work if I didn't want to was a possibility. Being able to think about what life could be like if I pursue my passions, and not just pennies it is as if a thousand pound boulder has been lifted off my back.

Once my mom began checking out mentally after Peter died, my life became a logistical checklist to make sure things were taken care of. Our roles reversed, I reminded her of bills that were due, and I made sure we had food to eat.

And though it's not an excuse, it's honestly probably one of the reasons she felt like she could just up and leave. I had become parentified—a term my therapist used to describe the process when a child is forced to grow up and assume responsibilities too quickly, taking on the role of caregiver and putting my own childlike needs aside.

After I moved in with Mimi and Evie, I felt guilty for taking up space and resources, and did everything I could to not be a burden. I worked during my junior and senior years as many hours as I could at the coffee shop to save money, and spent my free time studying to get a scholarship for college.

Evie had desperately wanted me to stay and go to the local university with her and had filled my head with visions of being life long roommates and spending our college years together, but I was committed to going anywhere I could get a full scholarship, which led me to

Colorado. It's why I moved into my own place when I came back here, too.

My life has been spent trying to be the least burdensome I can on those around me. And now Ian is not only asking me to depend on him, but is encouraging me to do so.

It feels so weird, but at the same time, feels so right.

The more I sit with it, the more I realize what I want in life is to just be with the people I love, and to help others do the same.

And maybe it's ok to depend on people.

Maybe not everyone will leave.

And while I'm not at the place to forgive my mom for walking away and not looking back, my heart doesn't clench at the idea of opening it up for someone else to do the rest of my life with.

Instead, it really, really, likes that idea.

40

IAN

Between trying to figure out the shitstorm from Aria's mom (who I'd like to bring back from the dead just so I can kill her myself), the high of finally hearing Aria tell me she loves me and getting to say it back, my emotions are all over the place.

Looking back there is no way I could have predicted that by the end of summer—the one that was supposed to be a solitary escape—that I would be laying it all on the line for the woman I am in love with, and using all restraint possible to not beg her to let provide for her for the rest of her life. That's all I want to do. I want to be and give her everything she could ever need. And in return, have her by my side, a constant source of love and comfort I can fall back into when I get home from being on the road.

As much as I crave to know what her answer is, I have to give her time, though it eats me alive waiting.

Instead I spend the last few days of the off-season getting in extra workouts to prepare for camp, packing, and finishing up the top secret project I've been working on since the week with the boys, and that means I've been making and fielding calls all week long.

But that last call made me pump my fist. Not only did my lawyers easily establish fraud in Aria's mom's case, but they were able to ensure that any assets she had were redirected to Aria. There wasn't a chance on earth I'd let Aria walk away with anything less.

She deserves the world, and you better fucking believe I am going to to give it to her.

My phone buzzes and I see a notification for an Instagram direct message in a thread where I had outlined my idea for one more way to bring a smile to Aria's face. Opening the app, I see a profile picture of a black and white Newfoundland wearing a rescue vest like the one Brady uses. We've been communicating for the past week, and I'm waiting for good news.

A quick read later, and now I've got yet another surprise for Aria—one that is going to make her giddy with excitement, I hope. I know I'm freaking stoked about finally getting the go ahead to tell her all about it.

And it couldn't have come on a better day.

Excitement courses through my veins, even more than I feel stepping on the ice for the first game of the season.

Today is the big day, the day I've been working to arrange for the past few weeks, and Aria has no idea.

She has no idea that all her hard work is finally going to be noticed and appreciated by those around her.

Today is the day she gets to take the next step to make her dreams a reality. And I'd be lying if I didn't admit that part of me is hoping that it will also prove to her that I truly do want her to achieve everything she desires, and that I'll support her fully in every way.

While that may not have been my initial goal, I've never wanted to provide for someone so badly in my life. Even if she decides to work here and visit during the season, I'm going to keep finding ways to make her life easier so she never feels alone again.

It took me quite a while to figure out what to do and how to pull it off. I hated hearing how she felt her dreams were unattainable and kept getting pushed off.

I am so impressed at how seamlessly Brady and her work together, and I knew the community would be as well. They just needed a chance to see her in action and to learn all about it.

The boys and I talked over my initial idea of having the community see Brady in action, and they did some more digging by asking questions about the local agencies she'd like to work with when we were all around the fireplace so that she wouldn't grow suspicious if I asked all of them myself.

That gave me the info I needed to use my fame and clout (I'm not above it if it means getting my girl what she wants and deserves) to get calls with the Sheriff and department heads of the agencies in question and tell them about the little unofficial showcase of Aria and Brady's abilities.

And in just 45 minutes, Aria finally gets to experience it all.

41
ARIA

Ian asked for one more hike and beach day before he has to report to preseason camp, which I find so endearing. I love how much he enjoys the same activities we do, and so a few days before he leaves, I'm ready, wearing both my swimsuit and my hiking clothes. I've added a few extra layers since the weather is definitely changing, the quaking aspen trees beginning to transition to vibrant yellow now that we are midway through September.

Brady hears Ian's car before I do, and he bounds to the door, wiggling his butt while I grab his leash, and my hiking pack. I open the door just as Ian has his arm up to knock, and his smile lights up the room, where the morning sunlight is still soft and casts a serene glow.

"Hey baby, ready for our adventure?"

"So ready." I stretch up for a kiss, and yelp in surprise when he sweeps me up bridal style and carries me to my Jeep before setting me down the passenger side, opening the door and giving a lavish bow.

"My Lady" Giggling over what in the world has gotten into him, I give him a little curtsey and climb in. The entire drive over his hand doesn't stop moving, whether he's tapping his thumb on the steering wheel, or reaching over to grab my thigh and give it a squeeze.

He's full of energy today. *Must be the start of the season that has him so pumped.*

"Why are there so many cars here?" I scrunch my forehead in confusion as we pull in, seeing the Hidden Cove trail parking lot packed full with cars, some parked in the lines for every spot, and others pulled haphazardly into any free space available. "It's a Thursday in September; it should be empty."

"A hiking club maybe?" Ian looks unsure as well, shrugs his shoulders and then pulls my jeep into the only open space available.

"Do you want to go somewhere else? Someplace quieter?" I mentally go over the map for the next best trail to go to today given the weather and time of year.

"No way, this is our place, I don't mind others being here, but I want to go here one more time." He jumps out of the Jeep and opens the door for Brady, who he unlatches and then moves out of the way for Brady to join him.

"Ok, just put him on the leash though, I'm sure the trail is busy." Ian nods and hooks Brady up and we start down the trail, which is surprisingly empty. It isn't until we get closer to Hidden Cove itself that I hear signs of people.

We break through the clearing in the trees and what I see stops me in my tracks. I freeze, my mind unable to process the surrounding sight.

On every open surface, there are people. Sitting on boulders, lining the beach with chairs, some just plopped right down in the sand. There are people standing behind the chairs, people lining the dock. I start picking familiar faces from the crowd.

I see Hunter, who waves, and Doris, the checkout lady at the grocery. Destiny and Marcus, the owners of Treat & Trout, are there, alone with the town librarian, the police chief and it's at that point I realize the beach is full of members of the community, adults and kids alike. Even Old Man Stan is sitting in a camping chair. It's like the entire town came out, but I'm not sure why.

I find Evie standing close to the water line, holding Gracie, with the biggest smile. She beams when I make eye contact and laughs at my confused look. She uncurls a poster board that she and Gracie hold up. Written in large blue and green letters, it says "GO BRADY & AUNTIE ARIA!"

"What the—" I turn to look at Ian, and stop when I see his wide, knowing smile on me. "What is all this?"

He grips the back of my neck with a firm hand and stares lovingly into my eyes. "This is your community, coming to see all the great work you've done with Brady, so they can support all the goals you have with him."

"They are? What do you mean? Did you do this? How—" I stop as a member of the Tahoe Water Rescue unit approaches me in his uniform.

I recognize him immediately as Jim Blackstone, captain of the county's unit. I've spoken with him once before, and it had been that conversation that jump started saving for the advanced water training certification. He is in charge of the unit I had been hoping to volunteer with once finished.

He reaches out a hand, which I shake, despite my confusion at why he is here. "I hear we are going to get to see some pretty great rescue efforts today." My mouth drops open wide.

"You are? I'm sorry I just didn't even know this was happening today..." He laughs and puts a hand up to stop me.

"It's ok, Ian here told us this was a surprise. We would love to see what you guys have been working on. I brought a small craft out," he points to a small boat moored at the dock, "feel free to use that as well. I'm excited to see all the great things you are going to hopefully add to our unit soon." With that he gives a wave and walks to join a group of men and women from his team.

I spin to Ian. "How did you do all of this?" I look around, seeing everyone together on the beach, overwhelmed that he planned an event where I can show off Brady's expertise, where I can make connections to the community and the agencies. He didn't have to do any of this, but he did, and he surprised me with it.

"Why did you do this?" My vision is blurry, as I take in the meaning of everything around me.

"Isn't it obvious Ari? Because you deserve to have everyone see how amazing you are, and you deserve to have your dreams come true, whatever you decide they are." He uses his fingers to delicately put an errant chunk of hair back behind my ear.

"I love you so much Ian. Thank you."

"I love you too baby."

And with that, he kisses me, and I kiss him back, pouring all of my feelings out to him with my mouth. A cheer goes up all around us.

A throat clears and we separate, suddenly remembering we are in front of a large crowd who are now staring with smiles on their faces. Evie grins. "You ready to do this?"

"Hell yes I am. But you are going to tell me EVERYTHING later on." I hug her and Gracie and then walk to the water and meet other officials from local agencies and introduce them to Brady.

The event is more than I ever dreamed of. Ian figured out all of the gear I'd need and arranged for it to be here at the beach, laid out and ready for a variety of maneuvers and rescue demonstrations, including wetsuits and life vests.

A few brave souls stepped up to be volunteers, and Brady got to show off his power by pulling 8 of them, linked like a human chain, to the shore. We showcased rescues from land, from the dock, and jumping from a boat, showing how Brady can support a lifeguard by providing the power needed to reach the shore, freeing them to focus on keeping hold of the victim.

It was pure entertainment for the spectators on the beach who cheered him on, passed around snacks, and took bets on whether any of them were stronger than Brady.

And as a grand finale, Brady pulled the boat—once again full of people—all the way to shore all on his own. His jowls were full of smiles all day, a happy boy living his best life soaking in all the love and attention from his crowd of fans, and my smile was just as big.

Ian's body was bursting with pride as he constantly pointed out cool things Brady did, shared all he had learned about water rescue capabilities, and he made sure to always phrase things in a way that showed my role in Brady's success. He talked non stop about how hard I worked with him, rather than just focusing on Brady's achievements.

I learned what a true high is, having the man I love demonstrate his pride in who I am, and getting to put my passions on display.

The crowd watched eagerly before finally dispersing. I spoke with the various agencies and shared some of the initial ideas I had that went beyond just volunteering, and made promises to schedule appointments with them to talk about next steps.

Evie, Gracie and Hunter helped clean up all of the training gear and after they pulled out of the parking lot (after Gracie smothered Brady's fluffy head in kisses for being such a good boy), I leaned against the Jeep, a little exhausted and slightly overwhelmed, in a good way. Ian loaded Brady in the backseat and shut the door, before coming to cover my body with his, enveloping me in his arms, the smell of the lake lingering on his skin.

"I am so proud of you." He dips his head and kisses me, and rests his forehead on mine. "You were amazing out there."

"Me amazing? You were amazing! I still can't believe you planned this whole thing for me." I looped my arms around his neck. "Thank you," I whisper.

"Ari, I would—will—do anything for you. But I also know you don't need me to do things for you. That you can do them yourself." He brushes his fingers across my temple. "I hope I didn't overstep here, but I knew I could use my name to get the attention of the higher-ups and get them in one place for you to show them what you and

Brady can do together." He looks a little unsure, hopeful that he didn't cross any boundaries.

"Ian, I know how much you don't like your fame to be a selling point. But the fact that you used it to help make my dreams come true, and did it in a way that let me take the lead, is incredible."

It's like he knows me on a cellular level, knew that I needed to prove to myself that people would be interested. "I can't thank you enough."

I kiss him slowly, my tongue sneaking in and chasing his. I pull away and whisper. "I love you Ian. With everything I have." His lips turn up and then the most genuine smile breaks out.

"I love you Aria. You're mine. Always." He nuzzles my neck. "I do have two other pieces of information for you. Well, one information, and one surprise."

"You do?"

"Yup. Do you want to go home first... " My look cuts him off. "Ok, now it is. First thing is, the lawyer finally called," I freeze up a little, but he rubs my arms and presses through, "and everything is taken care of. It was all bullshit—they saw through it and proved it without issue." Another invisible weight is lifted from my shoulders. "You don't owe anything related to your Mom."

My body lets out a huge breath of relief. Paying anything related to my mom was a tremendous burden on my soul, not being on the hook for something she did felt like I could breathe again. I pull him in for what must be the thousandth hug today.

"Oh my god, thank you, tell him thank you! Oh, I need to pay him, how do I get that to him?" Ian laughs and shakes his head. "It's taken care of baby, I told you, I will never let someone treat you that way, it's done."

"No I'm serious, I have the money saved up, it's ok."

"Aria, there isn't a world where I would let you pay for this. In fact there isn't a world where I want you to pay for anything, ever, unless it is something that makes you happy."

I open my mouth, but nothing comes out. I'm speechless. The money I thought was gone is suddenly back and available for use for training.

His generosity is unbelievable, and my kiss, though backed with everything I feel, is a small show of gratitude. "Thank you."

He pushes us apart, "And for the surprise—"

"That wasn't the surprise? That's a good surprise!" I interject.

"Nope. This one is going to be even more fun." He rubs his hands together in excitement. "I know you were saving up to do the training with the Italians on the East Coast, and so I reached out to the guy in charge—"

"Like the guy all over their Instagram page?"

"That's the one. DMs are a great thing." He grins as he takes one of his fingers and uses it to close my jaw.

"Anyways, I was telling him all about how beautiful the lake is here, how it might even be better than back home," I laugh alongside him, still wondering why he would reach out to the person that heads up the advance training, "and we got to talking that it makes sense to host a training out here on the West Coast as well, to open up more spots for other dogs in the area to get their certification like you've talked about." He pauses. "If you would want that, of course. It's your choice."

"WHAT?" I squeal and jump up and down before launching myself into his arms and wrapping my legs around his waist. "Are you for real, they are willing to do that?"

Ian spins me around before setting me on the sand. "Yup, so you can still do the fall training if you'd like, but if you'd rather have it happen here, then we can make it happen, as soon as the spring. I've already told him I would cover the necessary costs and expenses."

Happy tears slide down my cheeks as I just shake my head and kiss him, hoping it makes up for the loss of words I'm experiencing. Brady barks and sticks his head out of the open window to join in the celebration.

The warm air of Ian's breath teases my ear. "I even found us a helicopter," he murmurs, "so we can make Brady all badass and jump from the bird. I might even try to jump with him."

I can't hold back my laughter.

This guy, man. What would I do without him?

42
ARIA

November

"These are our seats? No way!" Evie does a little shimmy as we scoot into the front row, right behind the glass.

It's Evie's first pro hockey game, and I knew she would love being up close. I got these seats for the game in a section just down the ice from where the WAGs-Wives and girlfriends- that I've gotten to know, sit with the rest of their families.

We set our beers down in the seat cup holders and press our hands against the glass, watching in awe as the lights and crowd go crazy when the team skates onto the ice for warmups. Cheering loudly for Ian and banging on the glass, I look over to see Evie mimicking my actions and shouting just as loud.

"This is so cool, it is just like a boy aquarium. C'mere little fishy...." Evie taps her red gel manicure on the glass with a seductive smile.

Laughing out loud, I can't help but agree. "I know, I—." A giant body slams into the glass right in front of us, cutting my response short and causing us both to jump back in surprise.

Jack pushes off the glass, a grin emerging as he flips up his goalie mask. "Hi girls." He gives a wink and then calls out to Ian across the ice, whose face breaks into a wide smile when we make eye contact. He skates over, smooth as butter, spraying Jack with ice as he stops quickly.

"Asshole." Jack gives him a nudge before turning his attention back to us. Their on ice banter is something I have loved getting to watch. The entire team dynamic has been so fascinating and being able to see Ian in his element has made me understand him so much more deeply than just learning to love him in the off-season.

"Hey baby." Ian puts his glove on the glass and I mirror it with my own as he nods to my outfit. "The new jersey looks good."

I've been having fun shopping for and wearing different team merch, but I love having his name and number on me the most. The other girls told me to live it up while I still do, because eventually I'll grow tired of it and want to look cute after attending so many games. I don't see that happening, but I also love the idea of spending so much time watching Ian play that I'll get to that point.

"Thanks, I tried getting Evie to wear one but she said she felt weird wearing my boyfriend's number." I nudge Evie in the ribs.

"It is weird," she says as she shrugs and brushes it off.

"So wear mine then." Jack"s eyes linger over her body long enough for us all to notice.

"And why would I do that?" Evie stares up at him, playing coy.

Before he can respond, a whistle blows and the guys push off the glass. "Good luck babe! Kick some ass!" Ian laughs and blows me a kiss while Jack tosses Evie a wink. She lets out a breath and we both settle into our chairs waiting for the game to start.

"He's got it bad for you." I take a drink out of my plastic cup. "He's always asking when you are coming to a game. You probably made his night by being here and now he is going to try to show off for you."

Chuckling into her beer, she slings a hand across her mouth to catch the drops and laughs. "I doubt that. But I wouldn't mind a little post game celebration..."

"Even if they don't win?" I watch her as she tracks Jack on the ice.

"Yeah, even then." She looks back at me, laughing at the excited expression on my face. "Let's just wait and see how tonight plays out."

We spend the rest of the night banging on the glass and screaming with excitement when Ian steals a puck, Blake scores a goal, or when Jack makes a great save, and then celebrate after the final buzzer ends in a win.

• • •

The first few months of the hockey season were a whirlwind, and quite the adjustment. But it was exciting and wonderful and I loved getting to experience it all with Ian.

After Brady's demo day, and fully understanding the extent Ian is willing to go to for me, I admitted I wanted to be together as much as we could during the season.

After the first week of living in San Jose together, I knew I was there to stay. My home was no longer tied to a place, but to a person. I wanted to be where he was, even if that meant he'd be gone for games. I wanted to be there for him to come home to.

He was able to get the owners of his rental to agree to let him lease it for the full year, so I gave up my rental (since his place has more space for his mom and others to visit) knowing we have a place to stay anytime we can get back there. I still drive out during his longer stretches on the road to spend time with Evie and Gracie and get some nature time, but have surprisingly enjoyed city life too.

Brady is also adjusting to city life. He is obsessed with the attention he gets everywhere we go and the dog treats Frank has started keeping for him at his desk. The team even had a dog night at the arena and Ian took Brady out on the ice where he slipped and slid his way into the rest of the team's and crowd's hearts.

The announcer commented that he should be the new mascot which of course the real Grizzly mascot made a big deal of out on the ice with them, making for some great photos that instantly went viral on the team's social media. That led to me making him his own page to share brief insights into his life with Ian and I, and photos and videos from our training sessions as well.

At 2.2 million followers, it's safe to say he is quite popular there as well.

My meetings with the various agencies have gone so well, and once we complete our training in May we are officially going to be joining the Water Rescue unit during the summers thanks to a grant that the chief was able to apply for using my research as his base.

The plan is for Brady and I to work a few shifts a week alternating between patrolling boats and jet skiers from watercraft, being out on the beaches with the lifeguards, and serving as a way to spread water safety awareness during the summer in the community.

While I am excited about that, while planning Sierra Springs' Advance Water Rescue Training week, I have found another area I enjoy too. I have loved reaching out to Newfoundland and other water dog breed training groups on the West Coast of the United States and in Canada to invite them to the advanced training if they qualify, and Ian and I have been discussing ways to get as many trained K9 lifeguards as possible, to make the biggest impact.

My favorite of which is the Peter Foster Memorial Scholarship, which covers the cost of the K9 training for teams that need financial support. It was Ian's idea, and that was the moment I knew this was the man I'd be spending the rest of my life with. The way he saw me, and knew I needed something to keep Peter's memory alive, spoke volumes.

I carve out as much time as I can when back in town with Evie and Gracie, and while I know Evie misses the amount of time we used to have together, she is so happy for Ian and I. I've stopped telling her how often Jack asks about her, but I know she watches the games more frequently now and I don't think it's all because of Ian.

The other unexpected benefit of living in San Jose is that I have become close with Ian's mom. Even before I finally broke down and told her about my own mother, she took me under her wing and now helps fill my time when Ian is away. We do day trips to San Francisco, wine tasting in Napa, and for her birthday we got her VIP tickets to see Jade Taylor in concert which we all rocked out at together.

She, like her son, is slowly healing a wound that had nothing to do with her, and showing me what a mother's love is truly capable of versus what my experience has been.

There is also no filter when it comes to her wanting grandchildren one day.

Not that I mind—I'd love to one day be Ian's wife and mother to little hockey playing kids.

43
IAN

Sunday, June 16th

As the clock wound down on the final game in the Stanley Cup, I looked to see Aria sitting in the glass seats, cheering her heart out and crying happy tears for me and the guys. As good as clinching the title for the second year in a row feels, it is nothing compared to the life changing experience of living through this season with Aria at my side.

I never knew what I was missing. Having pure love and support being a constant from a partner, someone who was there for the highs and the lows, bad games, hard practices, injuries, and all the behind the scenes stress that comes with traveling during the season. Being with Aria this year is night and day different from being with Amber, and not just because of how that relationship ended. I've learned what a true soulmate and partner feels like, and the positive impact it has had on me, creating the desire to work hard to be the man I want and know I can be for both her and my mom, but also for myself, is something I will always be grateful for.

From the moment I heard her say that she loved me, I went full steam and didn't look back. We still had a lot of growing to do as a couple, but there was never any reason or desire to look back. There was no second guessing. It was as natural as breathing, loving her.

My life before Aria and my life after meeting her are two different beasts, and I know it would never be complete without her in it. She is the endgame, the final buzzer on the last game of the finals. She is the celebration and the legacy that follows. She is everything.

Getting to have her sitting next to me at the table at this year's Stanley Cup Tahoe Party, held once again at the Alpine Club the Saturday following our win, was the icing on the cake. It was full circle, but rather than having her serving us, watching her dress up and be a part of the team family showed that she was exactly where she was meant to be.

Her old coworkers greeted her like a long lost friend, which I guess she is at this point, seeing as she hasn't been back since the fall. I told her I wanted to take care of her, cover the rent at both places to give her freedom to explore her passions and let her design her life working with Brady however she wanted, and after the first week of trying out living together she agreed that was all she wanted too.

That benefited me too of course, as I wanted her to get to jump in fully for the season to experience it all alongside me and the boys.

I have more than enough to provide for both of us, and our future family, which I can't wait to start building with her, and she doesn't have to ever work a day in her life again.

But I know her, and I know how passionate she is about her dreams and goals, and I fucking love that about her and will support her in every way to make them come true. If that means spending my summers on the beach watching her patrol the lake with Brady in tow, then I will do it gladly, cheering her on from the sidelines.

I actually have her to thank for giving me direction at this point of my life as well. The struggles I've faced trying to decide my future after my impending retirement have slowly dissolved, my future becoming clear to me by supporting her goals. I've discovered I actually have a pretty good knack for speaking with people about topics that are important, and connecting with people on more than just hockey. When I brought up working alongside Aria on some initiatives we dreamed up, rather than going into broadcasting or coaching on a pro level, I was initially nervous, thinking she might not want me jumping in on her dreams, afraid it would take the attention off of her.

But I should have known how her heart is solid gold—she was ecstatic at the idea, both for how much quicker and better we could make things by working together, but also at the idea of getting to work closely on something together. It has brought a new level of intimacy getting to see each other in a project dimension.

I love watching her facial expressions as she thinks through obstacles, and how her brain can identify potential roadblocks and come up with solutions to help navigate them. She is incredible. She is my heart, my soul, my one and only.

I've known she was the one for me since before training camp; having her in my life solidified that everything I wanted out of life was no longer tied to what I can accomplish or the choices I make, it all boils down to her. She fills my life, the gaping hole, perfectly. She is what makes me excited for the years to come. As I watched her over the season, it just further cemented her place in my life.

And now I finally get to do something about that, and make sure she knows that. I thought long and hard about the best way to propose, and can't wait to give her the ring I've hidden in a specially made bumper I packed for our beach day today. By the end of the day, I'll be able to call her not only the love of my life, but my future wife as well.

• • •

ARIA

The sun is shining bright over the sparkling sapphire blue of the lake, the trees a vibrant green, the birds singing like this is a movie set. I look around our group of friends here at the beach from my beach chair, which I've parked right next to Evie's, smiling to myself how much has changed since this time last year.

Our closest friends are laughing and playing together on the beach, Blake, Jack, and Hunter are throwing a football, while Ian and Hughes are splashing at the water line while Gracie and Brady swim freely in the water. It's cozy and happiness and peace all rolled up together, and it's a perfect image of what the past year has felt like.

I had no idea what to expect jumping into the world of professional hockey, and at times it has been surprising and overwhelming and loud, so loud. But every minute with Ian—no matter the craziness of the fans or the driving or flying back and forth or the packed schedules—has felt like a wave of calm that sweeps through my body, sending everything that doesn't belong out to sea, before settling in my soul. No matter where we go, it feels like home. He feels like home.

I don't know what I thought finding the one would feel like. I guess I supposed it would be life-altering in a way that took focus off everything else and narrowed my vision down to just the one I was meant for. But in reality, being with Ian has brought greater focus into my life in all areas. He has helped me redefine my desires and passions, building up my confidence to dream bigger than ever before, expanding my world and my focus rather than narrowing it.

My soul, to its very depths, feels at peace, and I know without a doubt that he is the man I will share my life with, that I will one day build a family with.

Getting to attend the Stanley Cup party last night was such a thrill. Being a guest, and not the server, it felt foreign. Sitting in the gold Chivari chairs I used to set up, eating at the tables I would have rolled out in the past, holding the silverware I spent hours of my life sorting and polishing (to which Jack made quite the pretend scene as if I was going to throw a knife at him, again). Eating the food at mealtime, and not propped up on a counter afterwards or sneaking it from the hotbox was a special kind of treat.

Leaving without cleaning up made me feel a little guilty, however.

I giggled a few times throughout the evening, first when my old coworkers swarmed me, oohing and awing over my outfit, then when Ian ordered from Evie at the bar and the team gave Evie all the attention she could ever want, plus the tips.

The crowning moment of the night was when I pulled all of my old coworkers into the Photo Booth for one last film strip.

Ian's eyes were on me each time, giving me the sweetest look like it filled him with happiness to hear me laugh at my new place at the literal table.

And today we all met up at Hidden Cove, my favorite place in the world that I have now gotten to share with Ian and subsequently his teammates. They have all carved out a place for themselves here in Sierra Springs, whether it is at the mansion they rented for the next few weeks, or through their insistence on plenty of guest rooms for the house Ian and I will be building.

Yup, a house.

When Ian told me this spring he decided it was time to retire after one more season (the upcoming one), he asked me if he could join me in officially building a program for K9 water rescue here in Tahoe and on the West Coast. I was surprised he asked—not that I didn't think that he was interested, but that he felt he needed to ask. Nothing makes me happier than getting to support him in his dreams in the league and knowing that we will get to work on new dreams together.

I was thrilled at the thought of building our life together here in Sierra Springs, and we decided together on a new house to start that part of our lives together. And while it took some convincing for me to let him handle all the financial aspects of it, Ian has included me in every step so it is truly "ours".

Instead of buying the perfect house, we found a cute cottage with a gorgeous piece of land available next to it, and are in the process of buying both. We are going to build our dream home on the empty land while staying at the cottage and then renovate it over the winter to be the perfect guest house for his mom. We would love for it to be her permanent home, but she hasn't decided what she wants to do after next season just yet.

It's a life I never thought to dream of, never imagining something like this could be possible. I've accomplished more in the past year than my entire life, after learning that it was ok to trust the love of others—and allowing myself to believe that I was worthy of their love, just the way I am.

"Does something seem a little off with him today?" I follow the directions of Evie's gaze to where it lands on Jack, who is now staring out at the water, gaze locked on nothing of significance, arms crossed with his chin lifted, as if the water was offending him.

The two of them have grown so close and she is buzzing with excitement about him being in Sierra Springs a lot this summer. We've talked at length about what it will be like for them to finally be in the same place and have a chance at something real.

"Yeah, maybe, or he might just be in a postseason crash like Ian talks about. He says it's like going from 100 miles per hour to a dead stop, and it's hard to find your groove after the season ends."

"I guess so." She adjusts in her chair, giving him a final look before bringing her attention back to Gracie and Hunter further down the beach.

I'm about to suggest that she go talk to him when a tan, thick hand breaks the sunlight in front of me, held out with an open palm.

"Take a walk with me." Ian's handsome face smiles down at me.

"Ok." I grab his hand, giving Evie a smile, and he pulls me up, his hand lightly resting on the top of my ass as I adjust my bikini top. He reaches into his bag, and pulls out a shiny red bumper—a new one, definitely not one of our training ones—whistling for Brady to join us.

We walk hand in hand down the little beach, laughing as we go around boulders as Brady jumps excitedly seeing the bumper dangling from Ian's grip.

We stopped at a place just down the beach from our friends, a private area surrounded by larger boulders framing the mountains across the lake, with sounds of the beachgoers diminished to a murmur. The soft sound of the water lapping on the shore, my favorite sound, surrounds me as I close my eyes and listen, feeling the sun beat on my face. I feel a tug on my hand and open my eyes.

Ian turns me towards him, and kisses me with pure love and adoration in his touch. I sink into him as he holds my gaze, brushing the hair out of my eyes.

"Thank you for showing me this place a year ago." His deep blue eyes piercing mine, likely reliving that day when we first ventured here as strangers just as I am doing the same. Remember how he asked if Brady could swim, seeing his reaction to the freezing lake waters the first time we jumped in. The first in water kiss, which has been replicated many, many times in the months since.

"I love that we can share it together." I stare at his perfect face, his strong jaw, kissing the smooth skin of cheek before he smiles, turns and throws the bumper far out into the water, calling for Brady to retrieve it.

He turns back and pulls me into his arms. He looks down with absolute love and devotion. "I have loved sharing everything with you this past year. Your favorite places, the season, our dreams." I smile, overwhelmed in the best way with how safe it feels to live this life with him. "You have opened my eyes to what true love and commitment is like, and you have made me want to be a better man for you everyday."

He takes a deep breath, like he needs to steady the pounding of his heart, mirroring how my heart is racing and slowing all at the same time. "I love everything about you, from the way your feet get cold to the ducks in your jeep, but mostly the generous way you give your love to those around you."

Brady comes dripping out of the water looking like Tahoe Tessie, the mystical local lake legend with the bumper in his mouth, and he trots over, interrupting our intimate moment.

Ian releases my body and crouches to take the bumper from Brady. I glance away and wipe the tear from my eye that snuck in, surprised at the depths of Ian's words. When I look back, Ian is there, on one knee, the bumper discarded on the sand next to him with one end opened like a package. And in his hands, a small box.

I gasp, my hands flying up to cover my mouth, my heart racing and my body wanting to fly in his arms but unable to move a muscle. Ian breaks into a beaming smile.

"Aria, I came here last year as a man who won a game but who was lost in life. You filled a hole inside of me that I never could have identified, because it was made specifically for you." His eyes get glossy and I smile through the tears, mine doing the same. "Brady tried to rescue me the first time we went swimming," I laugh, and Brady flops onto the sound and rolls around at the sound of his name. "But you were the one who truly rescued me. And I want nothing more than to spend my life thanking you for that, and building a life with you here, full of dogs and kids, with you as my wife." He opens the box to reveal a slim gold band with a sparkling emerald cut diamond, light reflecting off the stone like late afternoon on the water. My hand covers my mouth at the sight, unable to keep the tears at bay.

"Will you marry me?" He asks, eyes pleading with me to give him this gift, to spend the rest of my life with him at my side.

"Yes! Oh my god, nothing would make me happier." Springing to his feet just in time to catch me as I jump into his arms, Ian hugs me tightly, swinging me around in a circle, causing Brady to jump up and bark and try to climb up as well. We are laughing and crying and then he is kissing me, his body covering mine and tipping me back, but I don't fear falling, never with him. He's got me.

He slides the ring on my finger, a perfect fit. "It's an Emerald cut because it made me think of our sunrises over Emerald Bay." He admits a little shyly, wanting to see if he made a good choice.

I admire it and bring one hand to the base of his neck and the other to his temple. "It's perfect, you're perfect. I love it and I love you so much."

He kisses me again, and then suddenly our friends surround us with cheers and laughter in celebration as they join us from where they were apparently watching from the beach.

This place, this man. Everything I've ever loved and wanted. It's all mine, forever.

• • •

"Excuse me, I just need to scoot in and kiss my *fiancée*." I giggle as Ian bypasses Evie at the kitchen island and wraps his arms around my waist, kissing me softly on my neck. "Man, I love getting to say that."

My hand reaches behind to run my fingers through his hair as he nuzzles in tighter. "And I love hearing you call me that."

It's just past 8:00pm of what has been truly the most joyful day of my life. What started as a day of celebration for the team merged into a different, even more magical celebration after Ian proposed. When we finished up on the beach we all came back to the house, where we spent the day lounging, and laughing. The guys made jokes about Brady being a ring "bear", Evie and I jumping into wedding brainstorming mode, and as the sun began to set, a calm lull brought cuddles on the outdoor sofa in front of the fire pit, watching as the sky darken, bringing and ending to this milestone day. Once the mosquitoes showed up in full force we relocated inside. Well, all except for Jack, who stayed outside on call.

The sliding door to the deck opens, and his towering frame fills the doorway, spine ramrod straight. He takes a few steps in before standing unmoving, phone gripped in his hand at his side. The room goes eerily quiet as he gives a small nod, almost indistinguishable from across the room. Ian squeezes my stomach and kisses my cheek. "I'll be right back."

I watch as the guys all file back out to the deck, shutting the door behind them. Glancing over, I see Evie watching the same scene, head tilted slightly trying to uncover meaning.

Maybe it's just team stuff.

An alert make's Evie's phone vibrate on the counter. She tears her eyes from the shadowy figures on the deck as she picks it up, swiping to unlock it. A second later her breath catches, mouth left slightly ajar, frozen in place. Her fingers grip the edge of the counter, and she looks up at me, gutted.

"Jack's been traded."

The End

45
BONUS EPILOGUE

Want to know how Evie feels after being blindsided by Jack being traded, suddenly stripped from her chances of a happy ever after like her bestie?

Scan the QR code to download the bonus epilogue and get a sneak peak into Evie's POV before Book 2 comes out!

ABOUT THE AUTHOR

Ava Blair writes swoony contemporary romances filled with heart, heat, and the kind of longing that keeps you turning pages late into the night. When she's not dreaming up love stories, she's exploring hidden gems, chasing sunsets, or forcing her friends to listen to her latest book idea over coffee (or cocktails). *In the Blue* is her debut novel.

Follow Ava (@authoravablair) on Instagram, TikTok, Threads, and at AuthorAvaBlair.com for book updates, behind-the-scenes sneak peeks, and excessive dog photos.

Author's Note

Dear Reader,

Thank you for taking a chance on a debut, indie author and giving Ian and Aria a chance. I'm so grateful that you spent time with these characters and I hope you loved reading them as much as I did creating them.

If you enjoyed this story, I'd be so honored if you left a review—even a few words are a huge help for authors like me. Evie's story is coming soon, and I can't wait for you to meet the man who would do anything for her and Gracie. Be sure to sign up for my newsletter to stay up to date for release information and a first glimpse at her book.

Writing this book was therapeutic for me; an exercise in focusing on a goal of my own and pushing through when times were tough on a personal level. I sat with the idea for far too long, and as ideas for book after book started to fill the space in my notes app, I knew I needed to just do the damn thing and bring it to life. I fell in love with the process, found joy in its creation I hadn't expected, and can't wait to bring you more of those stories.

While these characters are fictional, the idea for the K9 Lifeguard plotline was inspired by the real life K9 Lifeguards from The American Academy of Canine Water Rescue and the Italian School of Water Rescue Dogs in Milan, Italy. While Aria and Brady's actions are not representative of the training and actions of those organizations, the dogs and humans of these organizations are true heroes—their life saving tactics, dedication to water safety, and rescue efforts are simply amazing. I highly recommend you follow them on social media (@AcademyWaterRescue & @ferrucciopilenga) to support the incredible work that they do *(and to see videos of real Newfies that jump from helicopters)*.

A special thank you to my PAs: Joy, Fozi, Daph, and Tancy—thank you for your willingness to join me on this very first journey, and I can't wait to see what the future brings. Similarly, to my BETA readers, I greatly appreciate your feedback and support. Thank you for helping me to understand my characters from a reader's perspective. And to my ARC readers who have already taken the plunge and left reviews, thank you.

To the best mom friends ever—Alexis, Samantha, Amanda—thank you for your friendship the past nine years and for being pillars of support the past few years especially. I am forever grateful for your encouragement.

Wishing you, reader, all the confidence that you are more than enough, just the way you are.

Plus, all the swoons and real life book boyfriends, too.

–Ava